W9-BRC-753

Tori felt Sam's gaze on her.
She turned to look at him.

Regarding her with a strange intensity, Sam grasped her chin with a gentle hand and tipped her face up. "There's a bruise right at your hairline." His fingers slid into her hair and moved over her scalp. "And you have a bump there."

"When he broke in he hit me," she said, "with the gun."

Sam's chin jerked back and he sucked air through his teeth, making a hiss. "I hate what he did to you," he said in a fierce whisper.

Tori bit her lip. She was not going to cry.

Sam studied her face for several moments, then lowered his hand. "You're the bravest woman I've ever met."

Books by Brenda Coulter

Love Inspired

Finding Hope #216
A Family Forever #342
A Season of Forgiveness #417

BRENDA COULTER

RITA® Award finalist Brenda Coulter started writing an inspirational romance novel the same afternoon she finished reading one for the first time. Hopelessly addicted from that first hour, she had a complete manuscript and an interested publisher less than a year later. Although that first book went on to win both a Holt Medallion and a *Romantic Times BOOKreviews* Reviewers' Choice Award, it took three rejected manuscripts before Brenda figured out what she had done right the first time and did it again, resulting in a second sale to Steeple Hill Books. *A Season of Forgiveness* is her third novel.

Married for more than thirty years, Brenda and her husband, a mild-mannered architect, have two otherwise charming sons who torment their parents by interspersing requests for college money with harrowing tales of their latest daring adventures.

A Season of
Forgiveness

Brenda Coulter

Steeple Hill®

Published by Steeple Hill Books™

If you purchased this book without a cover you should be aware
that this book is stolen property. It was reported as "unsold and
destroyed" to the publisher, and neither the author nor the
publisher has received any payment for this "stripped book."

STEEPLE HILL BOOKS

Steeple
Hill®

ISBN-13: 978-0-373-87453-8
ISBN-10:   0-373-87453-7

A SEASON OF FORGIVENESS

Copyright © 2007 by Brenda Coulter

All rights reserved. Except for use in any review, the reproduction
or utilization of this work in whole or in part in any form by any
electronic, mechanical or other means, now known or hereafter
invented, including xerography, photocopying and recording, or in
any information storage or retrieval system, is forbidden without
the written permission of the editorial office, Steeple Hill Books,
233 Broadway, New York, NY 10279 U.S.A.

This is a work of fiction. Names, characters, places and incidents are
either the product of the author's imagination or are used fictitiously, and
any resemblance to actual persons, living or dead, business establishments,
events or locales is entirely coincidental.

This edition published by arrangement with Steeple Hill Books.

® and TM are trademarks of Steeple Hill Books, used under license.
Trademarks indicated with ® are registered in the United States Patent
and Trademark Office, the Canadian Trade Marks Office and in other
countries.

www.SteepleHill.com

Printed in U.S.A.

Who of you by worrying can add a single hour to his life?

—*Matthew* 6:27

In loving memory of my Gram, who probably coined the phrase, "Call me when you get home so I'll know you're not lying dead in a ditch." She made us crazy with her constant worrying, but we loved her and we miss her terribly.

Chapter One

From the corner of one eye, Victoria Talcott glimpsed a flash of blue steel as Bill Kincaid pressed the cold barrel of his gun harder against her temple, forcing her head toward her right shoulder. He had already struck her with the weapon, slamming it so hard against the side of her head that Tori had seen stars and tasted bile. The blow had knocked her to her knees, but Bill had hauled her up again and shoved her against the wall, extinguishing Tori's last hope that she might somehow survive her brother-in-law's murderous rage.

"You think she's worth dying for?" Bill sneered.

I'd save you, Rinny.

Tori wondered why she wasn't seeing her whole life flash before her eyes; why her swirling thoughts were instead coalescing on a single incident from her childhood. As the memory flooded even the most remote corners of her awareness, she felt hot sunshine prick the bare skin of her shoulders, heard the gentle lapping of lake water against a pea-gravel beach, saw brilliant shards of light glint off distant waves.

I'd die before I'd ever let anything bad happen to you.

On that summer afternoon at their grandparents' place on a lake in Indiana, Tori and Corinne, ages thirteen and eleven, had stood hip-deep in the water, cool mud squishing between their toes. Although forbidden to venture further without adult supervision, they'd launched themselves in twin belly flops. With skinny arms windmilling, they splashed toward the rickety diving platform at the outer limit of the swimming area. When they sat on the weather-roughened wood and Corinne, her arms prickly with goose bumps, asked what would happen if she got a cramp on the way back to shore, Tori had answered that as long as she drew breath, she would keep her sister safe.

The words might have been uttered with childish bravado, but right now Tori was proving them true.

Lord, just let it be over quickly.

After he finished with her, Bill would tear her apartment to pieces looking for a scrap of paper with an address and phone number on it. He'd never find one, because Tori had committed that information to memory rather than write it down. But she wanted him to look. The longer he spent searching, the better the chance he'd be caught. Then he'd be locked up for good and Corinne and the babies would be safe.

Was the door still open? Unable to move her head, Tori couldn't be sure. She'd certainly had no opportunity to close it after Bill had shoved his way into her apartment. Had *he* closed it? And if he had, would anyone outside hear the gunshot?

The daughter of a cop, Tori ought to have known the answer to that last question. But she'd never seen a gun up close. Regina Talcott had carefully shielded her daughters from the harsh realities of their father's dangerous job. Even now, three years after the event that precipitated her father's early retirement, Tori and her sister were as squeamish as their mother when it came to using words like *shot* and *bullet wound* to describe his leg injury.

In the movies, handguns made a lot of noise. Tori just hoped reality lived up to that promise because her garden apartment complex had been designed for maximum privacy. The sidewalk leading from the residents' parking area to Tori's front door curved past two large mounds of earth planted with evergreen shrubs that not only blocked the view of busy Chicago streets but also buffered their noise. Tori's apartment was even more secluded than the others; it was an end unit, abutting a ravine, and the place on the other side was currently vacant. Would anyone hear the shot?

"I'll ask you one last time." Bill's left hand tightened its grip on the front of Tori's cotton sweater as he leaned closer, his bulging gray eyes just inches from hers, his stale breath fanning her face as he spoke slowly and distinctly. "Where is my wife?"

Tori pressed her lips tightly together, terrified that if she said anything at all, she might inadvertently give him a clue.

"Drop the gun." A man's voice, deep and authoritative, rolled in like thunder from the direction of the front door.

Tori was immediately released. As she slid to the floor, Bill swung around and fired at the intruder.

It was loud. Even louder than the scream that ripped from Tori's throat.

The man in the doorway hesitated for an instant, staring in stunned disbelief as the gun was again leveled at him. Then he uttered a feral cry and flung himself at Bill.

Their bodies collided with a thud and both men went down hard, overturning a rocking chair. As they struggled on the bare wood floor, Tori scrambled to her feet and backed away until she felt herself flattened against a bookcase.

The gun went off again and a window exploded. This time Tori's scream and the echoing shot were accompanied by the sound of glass clattering like hailstones on the wood floor.

As the men continued to wrestle, the gun was knocked out of Bill's hand. It skated across polished maple and collided with Tori's right foot. Horrified, she edged away from it.

There had to be some way she could help. She glanced wildly around the room, searching for a heavy object to hit Bill with. She didn't have a fireplace, so there was no iron poker; and she didn't have any big ceramic vases like people in the movies always used. All she had were books.

Her eyes lit on a large volume of *Anna Karenina*, ancient and clothbound, seriously heavy. She snatched it off her coffee table, gripping one narrow end with both hands. She raised it high, then took three running steps and swung with all her might at the back of Bill's head.

At the last instant she lost her nerve and shut her eyes, but she felt the book connect with her target. Hearing an outraged "Ow!" she opened her eyes to see if her blow had knocked Bill out. It hadn't, but he was now on his stomach, groaning as the other guy dug a knee into the middle of his back and captured his flailing arms.

Not knowing how else to help, Tori replaced the book on the table and waited. She was amazed that Bill, a big man who had played college football, was losing the wrestling match to a wiry guy who probably wasn't even six feet tall. Less than ten years ago, Bill the Bull had been a fullback to be reckoned with. But now this lean stranger was defeating him with a series of quick, fluid, strangely beautiful moves that looked like they'd been choreographed for a scene in an action film.

"Sam?"

At the sound of the shocked male voice, Tori's gaze whipped to the doorway, where a second stranger now stood.

"Get the gun!" Tori's rescuer yelled as he twisted one of Bill's arms and neatly folded it behind the big man's back. It was, Tori realized with an odd detachment, exactly like watching her mother tuck in the loose wings of a Thanksgiving turkey before roasting it. "Then check me for bullet holes," the hero added with grim humor. "This jerk was shooting at me." He fired an accusing look at Tori. "And keep your eye on *her*. She packs a wallop."

Tori opened her mouth, but was too shocked to produce any audible words.

The newcomer spotted the gun and bent to retrieve it. Straightening, he swept Tori with a look of impersonal but not unkind appraisal. "You okay?"

She nodded, but she wasn't anywhere near okay. She felt dizzy, so she shut her eyes and concentrated on breathing deeply. When she opened her eyes a few seconds later, the man who now held the gun was pressing a cell phone to his ear. In a remarkably calm voice, he gave his name, Reid McGarry, and Tori's address.

Bill jerked in a desperate bid to free himself. The man on top of him simply leaned forward on his knee, bringing more of his weight to bear in the center of Bill's back. Bill groaned and went still again.

The conqueror met Tori's shocked gaze. "I'm Sam McGarry," he said, breathing hard. He jerked his chin in the direction of the other man, who was still speaking into the phone, but he kept his eyes on Tori. "That's my brother, Reid. Want to tell us what's going on here?"

"H-he was going to k-kill me." Tori blinked in surprise as a high, squeaky voice came out of her mouth.

"Yeah, I got that part." Sam McGarry's thin lips quirked in a humorless smile as he pinned Tori with a cool emerald-green stare. "The question is, why?"

"My s-sister," Tori managed through chattering teeth. "He's…her husband. He was t-trying to make me t-tell him where she is."

"You didn't tell." The green gaze softened into one of frank admiration. "Brave lady."

No, he was the brave one, running straight at a man who had been shooting at him. His white T-shirt was spattered with blood, but he didn't appear to be wounded. Tori looked at Bill, whose head was turned toward her, one cheek flattened against the floor. The sight of his bloodied nose sent a frisson of pity through her, but she carefully avoided his stormy gray eyes.

Reid McGarry dropped his phone into the chest pocket of his denim shirt. "Your sister is somewhere safe, I take it?"

Tori nodded, then looked at Sam again. The men couldn't be more than a year or two apart in age, both of them hovering somewhere close to thirty. Reid had serious hazel eyes and light brown hair in a short cut that emphasized his angular jaw. He looked sober and trustworthy, so Tori pegged him as the elder brother.

Sam had the same lean, rugged jaw, but his too-long,

wavy hair was lighter, streaky and sun-bleached. He was
deeply tanned and had the attractive squint of a man who
spent his days outdoors. His eyes sparked with suppressed
excitement as he shifted his knee and bounced lightly on
top of his vanquished opponent. After rushing at Bill with
the grace and speed of a jaguar attacking its prey, Sam now
appeared almost to be enjoying himself.

"You saved my life," Tori murmured, dazed and dizzy.

"We could use some duct tape," Reid observed when Bill
put up another halfhearted struggle and was quickly
subdued.

Tori's mind was spinning, so her response was a little
delayed, but Reid's last two words finally registered.

Duct tape. She had that. Her father was always giving
her rolls of the stuff and every time Tori asked what it was
good for, exactly, he would reply, "Oh, it's good for everything. Keep a roll in your car, too, for emergencies."
Tori had never found a use for it, but neither could she
throw it out, since it apparently had something to do with
safety. Tori was big on safety.

She ran to the kitchen and yanked open a drawer so hard
it came off its tracks and crashed to the floor, sending five
leaden doughnuts of duct tape bouncing and rolling across
the immaculate white tile. She snagged two of them and
raced back to the living room.

"Thanks," Sam said, throwing an amused look at his
brother as he plucked a single roll from Tori's outstretched
hands. "But there's just the one guy here."

He passed the tape around Bill's wrists a couple of
times, then tore and secured it. He jerked more tape off the
roll to wrap around Bill's ankles, the screech of the adhe-

sive providing a welcome distraction from the profanities and death threats Bill had begun yelling.

Sam tore off a short strip of tape and pressed it over Bill's mouth, then nodded approvingly. "Good old duct tape." He pushed up to his feet and handed the roll back to Tori.

Reid lowered the gun to his side. It looked like a little silver-blue toy in his large hand, but the bottom half of one of Tori's double-hung windows was now gone, so the weapon was plenty real.

Bill had meant to kill her. Tori's mind was simply unable to process that as she looked down at the man she had once loved like a brother. When he flayed her with an accusing stare, she turned her head sharply, only to be trapped by Sam McGarry's inquisitive gaze. For a man who had his mouth closed, Sam was asking an awful lot of questions.

Well, Tori had some questions, too. "What made you c-come in here?" she asked, her voice still shaking right along with the rest of her.

"I'm helping Reid move in next door." Sam pointed to the wall that separated Tori's apartment from the neighboring unit. "Your door was open, so I walked in by mistake."

"God sent you," Tori said, certain of that.

The brothers exchanged a look. "So it appears," Reid said quietly.

Sam bowed his head and stared hard at the floor. Tori guessed he was praying and she wondered what words he was finding to express his relief and gratitude. *She* couldn't pray at all. The preternatural calm that had washed over her when Bill pressed the gun against her temple had already ebbed; her anxiety was increasing every instant. And those crimson splotches on Sam McGarry's T-shirt weren't helping.

"Y-you don't have any…bullet holes?" she asked when he looked up.

He flashed a dazzling smile that would have been toothpaste-commercial quality if a sizeable chip hadn't been missing from one of his front teeth. "No holes," he assured her, spreading his arms and looking as solid as an oak tree.

"We pretend not to notice that big one in his head," Reid confided. He slid his free hand into the pocket of his jeans and propped one shoulder against the wall, his expression oddly wary as he watched his brother.

"Just out of curiosity." Sam hiked up his sleeve and inspected his right bicep. Its tanned, bulgy perfection was marred by a darkening bruise surrounding a red checkmark of broken skin. "What on earth did you hit me with?"

"What?" Suddenly afraid he might be as unstable as Bill, Tori backed away from him. "I didn't hit—"

"You did," he said shortly.

"Oh." Well, she *had* closed her eyes. Realizing that a corner of the massive book's cover might indeed have gouged his arm that way, Tori dropped the duct tape onto a chair and pointed guiltily to her weapon. "I'm very sorry."

Sam glanced at the big book on the coffee table and recoiled in apparent horror. "You hit me with a Bible?"

"Of course not," Tori replied, shocked by the very idea. "I hit you with *Anna Karenina.*" Ignoring Reid's startled guffaw, she glared at Sam, who didn't seem to have grasped the fact that she'd hit him by accident. "And I *said* I was sorry."

As their gazes tangled, Tori became aware of an insistent pounding on the left side of her head where Bill had struck her with the gun. At the same moment, the terror she'd managed to hold at bay for the last few minutes began to swirl around her like thick black smoke. She fought against breathing it in, but it seeped through her pores, making her light-headed.

"No, don't do that," Sam said, looking alarmed as he moved toward her.

The room was spinning now and, just like in the old cartoons, Tori's field of vision narrowed to a small circle surrounded by black. Then the circle was extinguished and she slumped forward into the nothingness.

Under normal circumstances, Sam McGarry didn't put his arms around a woman without knowing her name and a whole lot of other things about her. So now as he clutched the unconscious female to his chest, he looked at his elder brother for a hint on what he should do with her.

"The sofa," Reid said, glancing toward the open door as the wail of an approaching siren rode in on a chilly blast of late-October air.

Sam caught a pleasant whiff of a light floral scent as he braced the limp woman's shoulders with one arm and bent sideways to slide his other arm behind her knees. Her slender limbs dangled as he carried her a few steps and carefully deposited her on the sofa.

Relieved that her breathing seemed normal, he smoothed back the hank of chestnut hair that had flopped over her face. Just moments before she'd checked out, Sam had been admiring the graceful way her hair fell from its side part to her shoulders, where its blunt ends curved subtly.

She looked deceptively harmless in her delicate pink sweater and long black skirt, but those pretty brown eyes of hers had just stared down a guy who'd had murder on his mind. And then instead of running away when Sam drew the man's fire, she and *Anna Karenina* had stayed to fight. Her blow had practically dislocated Sam's shoulder, but he was a forgiving man and, besides, it was the thought that counted.

He turned and found his brother sweeping the room with a covetous gaze. "Wow," Reid breathed. "Look at all these books."

Sam was trying not to. Books made his brain itch. But it was hard to miss the three tall bookcases that snuggled against two of the living room walls. They were so loaded with hardcover books that some of the shelves bowed under the weight. Clearly, this woman—or her husband—had a problem.

Yes, she was some guy's partner in domestic bliss, no question. Something about this tidy living room and the modest way she was dressed told Sam she was all about home and family. She probably knew exactly who she was and where she was headed in life.

Unlike Sam.

He shook off that thought and looked at his duct-taped prisoner. The man's eyes were closed and he wasn't moving. "Is he getting enough air through that bloody nose?" Sam wondered aloud.

Reid, a former firefighter with a solid working knowledge of first aid, was already bending down to check. "He's fine."

The captive's eyes opened. As he fixed a malevolent glare on Sam, the sirens outside faded into the distance, responding to someone else's emergency.

"You sure you're all right?" Reid asked.

"Yeah." Careful not to scratch the glossy hardwood floor by grinding broken glass under his work boots, Sam gingerly made his way to the window and pushed aside a fluttering lace curtain. "What's taking them so long?"

"It's just been a couple of minutes," Reid answered, unruffled as ever.

Another puff of autumn air blew into the room. Idly poking his finger through the bullet hole in the window screen, Sam shivered and wished he hadn't left his leather jacket in his truck.

That he had nearly been killed didn't rattle him all that much. This was hardly the first time he'd looked death in the eye. But he'd never known anything like the horror that had gripped him when he'd believed he was about to see a woman murdered. Shivering again, he turned away from the window.

His restless gaze landed on a patchwork quilt neatly folded over the back of a chair. He pulled it off and gave it a gentle shake to ascertain that no glass fragments had rained on it, then he draped it over Reid's pretty neighbor.

Her left arm slipped off the sofa and as Sam tucked it back against her side, he noticed that although there were two gold rings on her hand, neither circled the finger that mattered. He sent up a silent cheer and started making plans.

"Forget it, Sam."

At the sound of his brother's mildly disgusted voice, Sam jerked guiltily. "Forget what?"

"You just saved her life," the ever-practical Reid explained with his usual maddening patience. "She's going to think she owes you, and it's not fair to take advantage of that. You can't ask her out."

That was his brother, Mr. Straight Arrow. Reid was nearly always right, but habit goaded Sam into trying an end run around his annoying certainty. "Yeah? Well, what about that Chinese thing?"

Reid's eyes narrowed in suspicion. "What Chinese thing?"

"That Chinese thing that says if you save somebody's life, you're responsible for it from that day on." Sam shoved his hands into his pockets and tried for a nonchalant look. "It's a proverb or something."

"Sam." Reid directed a long-suffering look at the ceiling. "We're *Irish*."

"So? All I'm saying is—"

"Don't do it," his brother interrupted. "After you've saved their lives, they've too vulnerable."

Sam sucked his bottom lip into his mouth. How could he argue with somebody who had spent several years in the lifesaving business? Hearing the wail of another approaching siren, Sam took one last look at the courageous woman on the sofa, then made his way to the door, glass crunching under his boots.

"Where are you going?" Reid asked.

Sam stopped in the doorway. "Out to warn the cops that you're holding the bad guy at gunpoint," he grumbled. "So nobody ends up shooting at *you*."

Chapter Two

Tori awoke to the commotion of men shouting. It took a few moments for the fog in her brain to dissipate, but then she jackknifed to a sitting position and threw her legs over the edge of the sofa. Something tangled around her feet as she tried to stand, and when she looked down in confusion at her grandmother's lap quilt, the room took a wild spin.

Sam McGarry's quick reflexes prevented her from falling. "Easy," he said, holding her upright with one arm as he grasped the quilt and gently tugged it out of her way. "You don't want to pass out again."

Tori barely heard him. Her attention was on Bill, who was thrashing and screaming like a wild stallion between two uniformed police officers. Whether someone had removed the tape from his hands and mouth or he'd managed to free himself, she didn't know. But he was still a wild thing cornered and he was terrified.

"Don't hurt him!" Tori cried. Wobbling again, she instinctively clutched Sam's iron arms for stability.

Bill broke free and threw a punch at one of the cops.

He missed the man's jaw and, because his ankles were still bound, he lost his balance and fell against the wall. He shouldered himself away from it and came back swinging.

Reid started forward, but the other officer, a husky, tough-looking woman with a short blond ponytail, barked at him to stay back. Her partner captured one of Bill's hands and slapped a handcuff around his broad wrist.

Bill screamed his outrage as his other hand was yanked behind his back and secured. Tori wanted to go to him, calm him, but when she flattened her palms against Sam's rock-solid chest and tried to push away, his arms just tightened around her.

The male officer, bald and dark-skinned and nearly as large as Bill, turned a grim face to Tori. "What's this guy on?"

"It's not drugs," she insisted, still pushing ineffectually against Sam. "It's brain damage." Tears pricked her eyes as she watched Bill being alternately dragged and shoved toward the door, where two more cops waited. "Don't hurt him!"

Her plea was drowned out by Bill's snarled threats to kill Tori and everyone else in the room just as soon as he got free.

Only when Bill was safely out of the apartment did Sam relax his steely grip. Tori jerked away from him and collapsed on the sofa, stunned and heartbroken. When she buried her face in her hands, Sam sat down next to her and patted her back in the same awkward, tender way her father would have.

The first two police officers returned a minute later. The ponytailed blonde introduced herself and her partner, then produced a small notebook. After Sam gave a careful account of all that had happened since he'd walked into the apartment, Tori filled in a few details. Then she explained that Bill hadn't known what he was doing.

The accident hadn't been his fault. His car had been broadsided by a truck, leaving Bill with a severe traumatic brain injury. According to the doctors, the insult to his prefrontal cortex was irreversible.

"He was in a coma for three weeks," Tori continued. "And after he woke up he was…different. Not Bill anymore. Now he loses his temper and…" She shuddered.

The stony seen-it-all faces of the cops registered no pity for Bill. Reid pursed his lips and stared at the floor, his expression thoughtful. But Sam, who had pressed the flat of his hand between Tori's shoulder blades and was rubbing slow, comforting circles there, murmured that he was sorry.

Reid looked up. "Medication?"

"He's supposed to be on antipsychotics. But he has no faith in his doctors, so he doesn't—" Tori's voice broke as the horror of what had almost happened caused her brain to stall again. "I'm sorry," she squeaked.

Beside her, Sam rose abruptly. "That's enough for now."

Reid backed him up. "Ms. Talcott has just lived through a nightmare," he said to the officers. "If you have any more questions, save them for tomorrow."

The female cop's face remained impassive as she clicked her ballpoint pen and tucked it back into her shirt pocket. She slapped her little notebook shut, then lifted a pale eyebrow at her partner, who hadn't yet spoken.

He scratched his ear and squinted at Tori as though trying to recall something important. "There was a Blake

Talcott on my old beat," he said. "I heard his daughter got roughed up by her husband. That would be the sister you told us about?"

Tori's nod reminded her that her head was throbbing. "Blake's our father."

The man's face lit up with friendly interest. "How's he doing? It's been...what? Couple of years since he was shot?"

Tori winced. "It's been three years since he retired," she answered with a slight emphasis on that last word.

The big cop looked at his partner. "Talcott was a good man."

"He still is," Tori said sharply.

"Yes, ma'am." The officer looked abashed.

"I'm sorry." Tori put a hand to her aching head and wasn't surprised to feel a lump there. She'd forgotten to mention being struck with the gun, but there seemed no point in bringing it up now. "I just..."

Sam strode purposefully to the door and flung it wide, his jaw twitching as he directed a pointed look at each of the cops. They took the hint and left.

As Sam closed the door, Tori's lace curtains billowed and a gust of cold wind swept into the room. Staring at a bright smear of blood on the floor, Tori hugged herself and shivered.

Reid dropped to one knee beside an overturned ceramic pot that had held a clutch of English ivy. As he repositioned the plant, Tori surveyed her trashed living room.

"Tell us what we can do for you," Sam urged as he righted the chair that had been overturned in the struggle.

Tori was a stickler for order. If someone so much as left the soap on the wrong side of the sink in her guest bathroom, she had to set it right. But now as her gaze settled on the glass littering her normally immaculate floor, she cared about only one thing.

"I have to see my sister."

"Does she live nearby?" Sam asked.

"This side of Milwaukee," Tori replied absently. "Less than an hour away."

"I'm free for the evening," Sam said. "Let's go."

"N-no," Tori stammered, appalled that she had answered without thinking. Only she and her parents knew where Corinne lived. "Thank you, but I—"

"You shouldn't drive." Using the sides of his hands, Reid swept loose potting soil into a pile on the floor. "You've had a shock and you fainted. Let Sam take you."

Impossible. No intelligent woman jumped into a car with a strange man. Tori managed an apologetic smile. "I appreciate the offer, but—"

"The police just had a good look at us," Reid reminded her, his lips twitching as he tamped soil around the ivy. "So I'd be real surprised if Sam grabbed your purse and shoved you out of his truck in the middle of the interstate."

"Thanks for that vote of confidence," Sam said dryly.

Tori supposed it was ridiculous to worry that a man who had just saved her life might have nefarious designs on her person. And she *was* too unsteady to drive.

"You're sure you wouldn't mind?" she asked Sam.

"Positive." He caught his brother's eye, then glanced meaningfully at the window.

"I'm on it," Reid said, rising. He set the plant on a nearby table and looked at Tori. "You won't be able to get the window replaced on a Sunday evening, but I'll put up some plywood. That'll hold you for a day or two."

"Get someone to bring you the wood," Sam suggested to his brother. "That way, you won't have to leave the apartment unsecured."

Obviously, they were thinking more clearly than Tori was, so she acquiesced to their plan. She excused herself long enough to pop two aspirin tablets, then she grabbed her handbag and a light jacket and told Sam she was ready to go.

A short while later, he glanced over at Tori as he guided his pickup truck onto the ramp of northbound I-94. "Are you sure your sister will be home?"

"She'll be there." Tori wished her sister could get out more, but not only did Corinne have the babies to look after, she needed to stay hidden. Bill had a wide circle of friends, and even those who knew about his personality change didn't realize its extent until they'd witnessed one of his terrifying outbursts. Tori had lived in fear that a casual acquaintance would spot Corinne in Chicago and innocently mention it to Bill, who believed she had taken the babies to California, where a favorite aunt lived.

Worry lodged in Tori's throat like a hot stone. She longed to feel her father's strong arms around her and hear the reassuring rumble of his deep voice, but she would have to do without that comfort tonight. This was her parents' thirtieth wedding anniversary and she wasn't going to ruin their celebration; especially not when she knew her mother was about to be surprised with a gorgeous diamond ring.

"If you want to talk, I'll listen," Sam said, keeping his eyes on the road. "But if you just need to collect your thoughts, that's okay."

Tori had no idea what she needed. She was nothing like the heroines in novels who, when thrust into danger, were suddenly transformed into brave, capable women. *She* was a jittery mess.

An impulse pushed Sam's name out of her mouth. When he looked at her, Tori smoothed her black wool skirt over her knees, stalling for time as she translated her jumbled thoughts into words. "I'm…so grateful. You saved me from Bill and you handled the cops and now you're taking me to Corinne's." Stress had nudged her voice to an embarrassingly high pitch, but she went on. "You've done so much and you've been so nice and I just don't know how I can ever—"

"Hey," he said gently, stanching the flow of her near-hysterical words. "Don't worry about it." He winked at her and drawled, "It's all in a day's work, ma'am."

A nervous giggle slipped past Tori's lips. "You sound like some kind of superhero." Making an effort to match his playful tone, she asked, "So, how many lives have you saved this week?"

Sam's amused look fled in an instant. "I can't say this is the first time I've saved a life," he said slowly. "But it's definitely the first time a pretty women and bullets were involved."

Tori opened her mouth to ask what other lives he had saved, then closed it when she realized he had just called her pretty. No man, not even Julian Knowles, who she'd been casually dating since high school, had ever called her pretty. Her eyes were set too close together and the little bump of a nose her father had found adorable when she was young was just plain ridiculous now. Her hair was good: thick, nut-brown and glossy. And she had good skin. But except for her father, no man had ever told her she was pretty.

Sam was probably just trying to cheer her up.

They drove in silence until Tori pointed out their exit. Ten minutes later they turned into an old, well-kept sub-division of starter houses built in the fifties.

Tori hadn't used her cell phone to call her sister because she'd thought this would be easier to explain in person. But when Corinne opened the door of her doll-size rental, Tori grabbed her and burst into tears.

Once again, Sam came to the rescue. "Victoria has had a bad scare," he said. "She's not hurt, but she needed to see you and she wasn't steady enough to drive. I'm Sam, by the way."

A shocked Corinne dragged them both into the house and pulled Tori down beside her on the sofa. Clutching both of her sister's hands, Tori drew a shuddery breath and described her encounter with Bill. Omitting the lurid details, she said only that he had threatened her with a gun and then fired at Sam.

Corinne's eyes, dark brown and almond-shaped like Tori's own, were soon as wet as her sister's. A nearby lamp highlighted the tear tracks on her cheeks as she gravely thanked Sam for taking care of Tori. Then she pulled Tori into a crushing embrace.

"Why did God let this happen?" Corinne wailed, her face hot and damp against Tori's neck. "Why didn't He just *take* Bill instead of letting him turn into this…this *monster*!"

Feeling her sister's desolation in every cell of her body, Tori raised her head and was startled to find Sam's compassion-darkened eyes on her. Anyone else would have looked away, politely ignored such a raw display of grief, but Sam McGarry intruded. Yet as his emerald gaze held Tori's, a comforting warmth began to spread through her.

"I need to see him," Corinne whimpered.

"No, Rinny. You know that man isn't Bill." Tori smoothed back a wisp of the honey-blond hair that had escaped from her sister's ponytail. "Not anymore."

"But he *is* Bill," Corinne protested, reaching for the box of tissues on the table beside her. "And I promised to love him for better or worse, in sickness and in health."

Leaning forward in his chair, Sam laid his forearms across his knees as he turned that deep, compassionate look on Corinne. "Honoring your marriage vows doesn't mean putting yourself in this kind of danger," he said gently. "If Bill were capable of understanding what he's doing, I'm sure he'd tell you to stay away from him. He'd want his family safe, no matter what."

Tori shot Sam a grateful look and squeezed her sister's denim-covered knee. "He'd say that, Rinny. You know he would."

Corinne sighed heavily. Tori looked at Sam for more help, but just as their eyes met, he flinched. When he tucked his chin against his chest and looked down, Tori followed his startled gaze and saw one of her baby nieces crawl out from behind the upholstered chair Sam sat in.

"Hi!" Little Mollie smacked Sam's knee with a pudgy hand and gazed adoringly up at him.

Sam had frozen, all except for his eyes, which widened comically and appealed to Tori for help.

Chuckling through her tears, Tori held out her arms.

"Hey, pumpkin." Mollie toddled over to her and Tori patted the baby's diaper-padded, flannel-covered behind. "What are you doing out of bed?"

Corinne sniffled. "They've learned how to climb out of their cribs." She gathered her daughter into her arms and stood up. "What am I supposed to do now?"

Tori gave her a commiserating smile, then blew a loud, smacky kiss to her niece. "Night-night, Molliekins."

With the baby in her arms, Corinne started toward the hallway. Just then, little Merrie came trotting around the corner and collided with her mother's shins. Without missing a beat, Corinne bent sideways and scooped her up. Then as Corinne entered the hall and turned in the direction of the girls' room, something small and blond streaked past her legs, heading in the opposite direction. Maggie.

"Look!" Sam cried, pointing. "There goes another one!"

"Yeah, it's a regular infestation." Corinne reappeared in the doorway, a wry smile lifting one side of her mouth as she clutched her girls like footballs, Mollie and Maggie wriggling under one arm and Merrie trying to escape from the other.

Sam looked thunderstruck. "She has three babies."

"They're triplets," Tori explained, just in case he hadn't caught on.

Corinne chuckled. "He looks as stunned as Bill did when the doctor told us we were going to have—" She stopped abruptly, her smile collapsing as she locked gazes with Tori.

Once again, they shared the horror. Fifteen months ago, Bill had been driving home from the hospital, the happiest man in the world. Corinne had just delivered his babies and she and the three tiny girls were perfectly healthy.

And then a half-asleep truck driver had run a red light.

Tori pushed some words into the awful silence. "Why don't I make us some coffee while you settle the girls?"

Corinne shifted Merrie into a more secure hold and managed a small, brave smile. "That would be good."

"She has three babies," Sam repeated when Corinne was gone.

"Yes." Tori let go of a long breath. "And I'm worried sick about her. She could move in with our parents, not just to save money but to have help with the girls, but she won't because she believes God will answer her prayers and make Bill better. But Sam, the doctors say he won't *get* better."

Sam sucked his bottom lip into his mouth and pushed his fingers through his shaggy hair and just looked at her. Tori wished he'd offer advice or clichés like everyone else did; anything but that naked, silent, unrelenting compassion that was pushing her back to the verge of tears.

She jumped up. "I'll go start the coffee."

By the time she reached the sanctuary of Corinne's tidy kitchen, Tori's heart was seizing so hard she had to clutch the edge of the porcelain sink for support. Then the old vinyl floor creaked and Tori sensed a presence behind her.

Sam said nothing, just cupped his hands around her shoulders and leaned his head against the top of hers. The contact implied an emotional connection that shouldn't have been possible between two people who'd been strangers just two hours earlier, but it felt oddly right. The slow, even tempo of Sam's breathing comforted Tori, as did his scent, which was nothing like the complicated designer fragrances Julian favored. Sam smelled of soap mingled with the faint odor of leather.

His jacket. It was quite warm in the house, but he hadn't removed his jacket when Tori had shrugged out of hers, and now a flash of insight told her why: because the T-shirt he wore beneath it was stained with Bill's blood. Sam hadn't wanted Corinne to see that.

"Let's start that coffee," he suggested, lifting his head. "And then maybe we could pray together."

By the time they left Corinne's house, a remarkable calm had settled over Tori. Staring out the passenger window of Sam's truck, barely noticing the lights and shapes that rolled past her, she wondered how she could feel so safe, so comfortable, with a man she'd known for only a few hours.

"Where do you go to church?" she asked idly. When Sam didn't immediately answer, she looked over at him.

He cleared his throat. "I'm not a regular churchgoer."

He wasn't? Studying his profile, Tori wondered about the simple yet beautiful prayers he had offered at Corinne's house. Sam had addressed the Lord with a confidence that suggested they were on intimate terms.

"I used to go," he said, answering the question Tori had been struggling to phrase. "My dad was a pastor. But since we lost him, I can't stand being around the people who knew how great he was. They talk about him constantly."

"I think most people need to talk out their grief," Tori ventured. "Don't they?"

Sam flashed her a wounded look. "Sometimes words aren't enough."

"That's true," she murmured.

"And if I have to listen to one more platitude…" Sam shook his head.

In the drafty darkness, Tori hugged herself for warmth. "How long has it been?"

"Almost four years."

Tori concealed her surprise, but wondered why his grief was still so sharp after all that time. "And you haven't been to church since then?"

He shifted in his seat. "I go occasionally. It's not like I'm mad at God or anything. I never miss a day with my Bible, and I'm still tithing. But seeing another man address the congregation when it should be my dad up there…" Sam's voice deepened to the extent that his next words were barely audible. "Well, it just hurts, that's all."

"But don't you miss the fellowship of other believers?" Tori asked gently. When Sam didn't reply, she offered a suggestion. "You could try a different church. Start fresh with a new bunch of people." Maybe he would consider visiting her church.

He shook his head. "I don't see how that would be much different. Besides, for the past four years I've been traveling constantly. I'm just not a church-every-Sunday kind of guy."

The truck's heater was going full blast, but a stream of cold air was hitting Tori's right side. She adjusted her jacket and slid her hands into its pockets, then pushed her feet against the floor vent that was blowing hot air.

Sam noticed the movement. "I'm sorry this truck is so drafty."

"I'm fine," Tori lied, not wanting him to feel bad about something he couldn't help. "What do you do for a living, Sam?"

He glanced over his left shoulder and signaled for a lane change. "You could call me a professional adventurer."

"Could I? And what would I mean by that?"

"Reid and I started an adventure travel business five years ago. He runs things in the office and I'm the field guy."

"Adventure travel." Dismay slid through Tori as she repeated the words. Wasn't *adventure* a euphemism for *dangerous*?

Sam smiled. "If you ever want to swim with sharks or skydive off a cliff or test your survival skills on a desert island, give us a call. Basically, if it's legal somewhere in the world, Extreme Adventures can set it up for you."

She dearly hoped he was kidding. "You *encourage* people to risk their lives?"

He threw her a surprised look. "We don't tolerate stupidity. And we don't allow our clients to use anything but the best guides and the very latest in safety gear."

And he thought that made it okay? "That must get expensive," Tori said carefully.

"Yeah. But you'd be surprised how many middle-class types will skimp on other areas of their lives in order to finance an occasional thrill. I'm a great example of that. My apartment's not much bigger than a doghouse and this truck's ten years old." He tossed her a boyish grin. "But honey, you should see my sports equipment!"

Tori didn't smile back. She was quickly revising her good opinion of Sam McGarry's sense.

"Something wrong?" he asked.

She shook her head. "It's just that I've never understood why anyone would want to flirt with death."

"I wouldn't call it flirting with death." A car passed them, throwing light into the truck's cab and revealing Sam's troubled expression as he pushed his fingers through his hair. "Maybe some of us just need more of a thrill than a quick roller-coaster ride at an amusement park."

"Is Reid a daredevil, too?" Tori regretted using the word when she saw Sam wince, but what was he so sensitive about? What did *he* call people who sought thrills by engaging in dangerous activities?

"Reid was a firefighter until a brick wall fell on his back. He can't lift anything heavy now, which is why I was helping him move his stuff. But he's a bona fide hero."

"So are you," Tori reminded him.

"Me?" He shot her a surprised look. "No. I walked into your apartment by mistake. That's completely different from running into a burning building to rescue somebody's kid. Reid's whole job was about saving lives." Sam twitched a shoulder. "Although he says he's had enough excitement to last him for a while, so he stays in the office and leaves all of the fun stuff to me."

The fun stuff. In other words: the crazy, dangerous stuff. She should have known Sam was too good to be true. "So stepping in front of that gun was just another thrill."

"No, Victoria." As they passed through a brightly lit interchange, Tori saw his hands tighten on the steering wheel. "I honestly thought you were going to be shot to death right before my eyes. There was nothing thrilling about that."

"I'm sorry," she said quickly. "I don't know what made me say something so awful." But she actually had a pretty good idea. Since that encounter in Corinne's kitchen, she'd been looking at Sam with stars in her eyes, and he had just thrown a cold bucket of reality over her head. She should be grateful for that because a daredevil was the absolute last person she could ever get involved with.

"You've been through a lot," he said mildly. "But we've been talking a lot about me. Why don't you tell me about *your* job?"

"I'm a college archivist."

Sam gave her a sideways glance. "You organize dusty old papers and things?"

"I appreciate order," she said, a little defensively.

He smiled. "You're probably one of those people who alphabetizes the little jars in your spice rack."

No, a daredevil wouldn't find her work at all fascinating. "That's right," she said, confirming his guess about her spice rack and silently daring him to laugh at her ordinariness. "I'm about as interesting as dryer lint."

"Hey, I'm nowhere near bored," he protested. "So tell me who you do all this archiving for."

"Wheldon College." She didn't expect him to recognize the name of the small, private school.

"Is that the place with that little jewel of a pond?"

"Yes," Tori said, pleased that he knew it. A real-estate anomaly just north of downtown Chicago, the college green took up a full two acres, offering a grassy field, a sprinkling of mature trees and a teardrop-shaped pond that reflected the tall buildings surrounding it. "The white domed building by the pond is my library."

Sam nodded. "I'm not sure exactly how an archivist is different from a librarian."

"We're professional cousins, so our duties can overlap. But in general, librarians are concerned only with published materials, while archivists select and preserve records of historic significance. That can include things like unpublished journals and letters as well as photographs, scrapbooks and all kinds of recordings. We describe and catalogue those items and make them available to researchers."

"You love your job." Sam's tone was thoughtful, but he gave his head the tiniest shake.

Was he making fun of her? Yes, she loved her job. Maybe Captain Adrenalin didn't understand that, but so what? It was her dream job.

And she was in danger of losing it. The cash-strapped college had already made some staff cuts and Tori was probably next on the list. Between that worry and the awful situation with Bill, it was no wonder Tori had spent the past year in a state of constant anxiety.

Sam glanced at her as she wriggled into a more comfortable position and rested her head against the seat back, but he said nothing. Tori shut her eyes and concentrated on the soothing drone of the heater that blew warm air on her feet.

Some time later, she was startled awake by the thump-thump-thumping bass of the too-loud stereo in a passing car. She rubbed her eyes and sat up just as Sam pulled into her parking lot.

"Reid's SUV is gone," he remarked. "He must have decided to pick up the last load of furniture."

"Should he be doing that?" Tori asked, slipping effortlessly into worry mode. "With his bad back?"

"He's fine." Sam parked the truck and shut off the engine. "He knows what he can handle and what he can't."

"Use my phone," Tori urged, reaching for her bag. "Let's make sure he's okay."

Sam gave her an odd look. "Thanks, but I have a

phone. If Reid needs me, he'll call. If I don't hear from him, he's fine."

Experience had taught Tori differently. When her father had been shot, her mother hadn't known for three full hours because she'd been out shopping with friends. When something awful happened, you didn't always know it right away, so it was smart to keep close tabs on your loved ones. But Tori couldn't make Sam worry about his brother if he was determined not to, so she dropped the phone back into her purse and fished out her keys.

"Reid wouldn't have left without securing your place," Sam said. "But let me come in and make extra sure."

Extra sure. Finally, the man was speaking a language Tori understood. "I'd appreciate that," she said.

They found the broken window neatly boarded up and Tori's lace curtains pulled together in front of it. Reid had swept up the glass shards and straightened the room. He had even folded the quilt—although he'd put it on the wrong chair. Tori's heart hummed with gratitude and she made a mental note to bake him a pie and buy the nicest potted plant she could find for his new apartment.

But what about Sam? What could she do for the man who had saved her life? How did you thank somebody for *that*?

Feeling his gaze on her, she turned to look at him. He stepped closer.

"Hey." Regarding her with a strange intensity, Sam grasped her chin with a gentle hand and tipped her face up. "There's a bruise right at your hairline." His fingers slid into her hair and moved over her scalp, exploring her goose egg with a whispery touch. "And you have a bump."

"Bill hit me," she admitted. "With the gun."

Sam's chin jerked back and he sucked air through his teeth, making a long hiss.

"It doesn't hurt anymore," Tori assured him. "I took some aspirin."

"I hate what he did to you," Sam said in a fierce whisper.

Tori bit her lip hard. She was *not* going to cry again.

Sam studied her face for several more seconds, then lowered his hand. "You're the bravest woman I've ever seen."

Well, *that* certainly lightened the moment. Tori *humphed* in amusement. "You must not have seen a lot of women, then, because I happen to be the world's biggest coward."

He just smiled at that. "Mind if I call you tomorrow?"

Tori experienced a tingle of relief. A phone call, she could handle. The way he'd been looking at her just now, she'd been afraid he was about to ask for a date. She did owe Sam her life, but she had enough to worry about without getting involved with a daredevil. Responding to his question with a nod, she reached into her bag for a pen and some paper.

"Just tell me," he said, laying a restraining hand on her arm. "I never write down phone numbers."

Tori recited her number. He repeated it. Tori commented that he must have an excellent memory.

Smiling again, he tweaked her nose with the tip of his finger. "Some things are worth remembering, brown eyes."

When he had gone, Tori locked the door and placed a quick call to let Corinne know she had arrived home safely. Then she finished tidying up, checked the door again and went to run a hot bath. A little while later, ready for bed, she checked the door one last time.

She knew it was locked, but lately she'd fallen into the habit of making extra sure. "You can't be too careful," her mother always said, and tonight that was an easy thing to believe.

Chapter Three

At seven-fifteen on Monday morning, Tori braced herself and phoned her father. As she had expected, he chided her for not calling him the night before. He was a retired Chicago cop, he reminded her stiffly; his presence might have been useful. But Tori knew what really bothered him, apart from the fact that his baby girl had been threatened. He hated knowing that when she'd needed help and comfort she had turned to a stranger—a strange *man*—instead of her father.

Holding back a sigh, Tori dropped a tea bag into a deep china cup and poured boiling water over it. It was pointless to remind her father that she was twenty-seven years old. The only calendar Blake Talcott recognized was the one in his heart. And according to that, Tori was still his little girl.

He said he'd check on Bill and call her back. Tori slumped at her kitchen table, forgetting her tea as she stared unseeing out the window and into a murky morning, her sluggish brain registering little apart from the rhythmic splatting of rain on her brick patio.

"They say Bill put on quite a show," her father reported a few minutes later. "They took him straight to the mental ward."

Remembering what Bill had promised to do when he was free, Tori shivered. "Will they let him out on bail?"

"He's looking at assault and battery with a dangerous weapon, armed assault with intent to murder and a string of other charges, so if the judge sets bail, it'll be high. But things haven't gone that far yet. For now he's being held pending a full psych evaluation."

Tori released the breath she'd been holding. "Thanks, Daddy. You should call Corinne now."

"I will. And then your mother and I will head over to your place to get that window taken care of."

No. Tori was determined to deal with this like the grown-up she was. "Thanks, but I can handle it."

"Baby, I know you can handle it. But your mother's worrying herself ragged, so just let me do it, all right?"

"I need to get to the office," Tori argued. "I'll call my apartment manager from there."

"You're going to work?" Her father's deep voice pulsed with disapproval.

Tori closed her eyes. "Daddy, I'm okay." At least, she would be, just as soon as she got back into her routine.

After a tense silence, her father relented. "Well, call your mother when you get there, so she'll know you made it safely."

Tori arrived at the college just as a full-blown thunderstorm broke. She'd forgotten her umbrella, so she got a good soaking as she dashed from the staff parking lot to the library. She bounded up the shallow stone steps, whipped open one of the big glass doors and had just reached the curved marble staircase leading to the second floor when lightning struck nearby, its brilliant flash occurring at the same instant as a deafening crack of thunder.

It sounded exactly like gunshots.

"Girl, you're white as a sheet," Francine Blanton observed from behind her desk when Tori entered the reception area.

Chilled and breathless, Tori just shook her head at her assistant as she struggled with clumsy fingers to work her coat buttons.

Francine jumped up to help peel off the sodden garment, then swept Tori with the assessing look of a concerned friend. "You need coffee," she declared, and she went to get some.

Tori pushed wet ropes of hair away from her face, then sank onto one of the hard-bottomed, armless chairs in front of Francine's desk. Moments later a toasty ceramic mug was pressed into her hands and Francine sat down beside her, apprehension furrowing the smooth dark skin of her forehead as she waited for an explanation. Between bracing sips of the coffee, Tori related what Bill had done.

"And you're sure he'll stay locked up?" Francine's chocolate-brown eyes were wide with concern.

Tori nodded. "For the time being. If they even think about releasing him, somebody will call my dad." Her sentence was punctuated by an earsplitting boom of thunder, and the lights went out.

"That was the transformer," Francine said with an air of resignation. "Remember last year? It took them four hours to bring the power back."

Tori sighed over the rim of her coffee mug. "My dad tried to get me to take the day off."

"You should have," Francine said staunchly. "Being threatened at gunpoint would knock anyone sideways." Grinning suddenly, she dug a playful elbow into Tori's ribs. "But I want to hear more about Sam the Hero. Is he handsome?"

Tori tapped her fingernails against her coffee mug and considered the question. Her definition of "handsome" had always been Julian, and Sam wasn't like Julian in any way. "He has streaky blond hair, wild green eyes and a chipped front tooth," she said finally. Francine could draw her own conclusions.

"Mmm-mm." Francine shook her head, sending her mass of tiny, shoulder-length braids swinging. "I just adore those scruffy guys," she teased. "What does he do for a living?"

"He's a thrill-seeker," Tori said flatly. "He runs an adventure-travel service." She swallowed one last mouthful of coffee and turned her mind to business. "There's no telling how long the power will be out, so let's grab some work and go home. We can check back at lunchtime and see where we stand."

"Sounds like a plan." Francine's expression turned grave as she laid a hand on Tori's arm. "Although *you* should take the whole day off. That was an awful thing that happened to you."

Tori blew out her cheeks. "I need to work, Francine. Just as soon as things get back to normal, I'll be fine." The words slipped easily out of her mouth, but were they true? What if her world had been knocked so far out of its orbit that it had trouble slipping back into its proper path?

She checked in with her mother as soon as she got home, then made arrangements to have her window replaced. Shortly after noon, she was doing paperwork at the kitchen table when her doorbell rang.

Instead of offering a polite greeting when Tori opened the door, Reid McGarry raked her with a frankly assessing look, then nodded. "So you're all right."

Touched that he'd wanted to check on her, Tori invited him in. Reid was a bit taciturn, but he had a kind heart and Tori liked him. On learning he was taking the day off to unpack and settle into his new place, she persuaded him to join her for a simple lunch of sandwiches and reheated chicken soup.

They had just begun eating when Tori's phone rang. Excusing herself and urging Reid not to let his soup get cold, she got up to answer it.

It was Sam. And he had a great telephone voice: deep and thrilling. After trying in vain to flatten her foolish grin, Tori turned her back before Reid got the idea—the very *wrong* idea—that she was interested in his brother.

Sam asked how she was feeling. Then he said he'd prayed for her, Corinne, the babies and even Bill after he got home. Tori's heart was melting fast, right in front of Reid, who was politely pretending to be deaf and blind, when she was saved by the doorbell.

"Sam, the window people are here," she said, grateful for the interruption. "Reid's here, too, so I have to go. But thanks for—"

"Reid's there?" Sam asked sharply. "Could I talk to him?"

"Yes, I'll put him on. Thanks again, for everything." Mortified by the amusement twinkling in Reid's hazel eyes, she thrust the phone at him and made her escape.

* * *

Sam sat at his desk hooking paper clips into a chain and wondering how a phone call that had begun with Victoria Talcott's dulcet *hello* could have gone so horribly wrong. How had he ended up talking to his brother? And what was Reid *doing* there, anyway?

"Just having lunch," Reid said airily.

Sam dropped his paper clips. "Go have lunch somewhere else."

Reid snorted. "Relax, Romeo. I've seen nothing here that interests me. Nothing except this grilled ham and cheese sandwich you're preventing me from enjoying."

Sam shot out of his chair. "Have you lost your mind?" Gesturing wildly with his free hand, he paced behind his desk. "She's beautiful. She's amazing. She's—" He realized what he was saying and shut up.

"I thought we discussed this," Reid said with his mouth full. "You weren't supposed to—"

"Funny," Sam interrupted. "You seem to be under the impression that you have a say over who I date."

"I mean it, Sam." All levity had drained from Reid's voice. "This is a bad idea. Like I said before—"

"I heard you." Sam flopped back into his chair. "Just tell Tori I'll be tied up for the rest of the day, but I'll call her tomorrow."

"You *should* be tied up," Reid muttered.

Reid was right about most things, Sam reflected as he jabbed his end-call button, but he was wrong about Tori. Last night something had clicked between her and Sam, and it had had nothing to do with her seeing him as a hero.

Sam had never met such a fascinating woman. She was

sweet and intelligent and he could listen to her talk for hours. Her voice was deep for a woman's, but melodious; her words were deliberate and unhurried, as if she thought carefully before releasing each one. She did appear to be wound pretty tight, but that was hardly surprising in light of what she'd been through.

No doubt it was true, what Reid had said about her being vulnerable, but Sam had never hurt a woman in his life. Sure, he'd ticked off a few of them. But he was no heartbreaker.

He could hardly wait to see Tori again. Leaning back in his chair, he drummed his fingers on the armrests and smiled. He had no idea where this might be headed, but he was always up for a new adventure.

Tori had been at work for less than two hours on Tuesday morning when Corinne surprised her and persuaded her to steal away to a favorite French bakery for a treat.

"I was desperate to get out," Corinne said as she chose a table next to the bakery's front window and began unloading coffees and pastries from a tray. "And Aunt Bev wanted some time with the girls."

Tori draped her coat over the back of a chair and sat down, but she couldn't help fretting as she watched people rush past on the sidewalk. "What if somebody sees you and it gets back to Bill?" Corinne's husband might be locked up, but they had no guarantee he'd stay that way. Tori laid a hand on her sister's arm and spoke urgently. "He doesn't know Aunt Bev has moved back to Chicago. He's got it into his head that you're somewhere in California, with her. He's not even looking for you here."

Corinne pointed a teaspoon at her. "You worry too much."

"Look who's talking," Tori shot back, stung by that criticism from her sister, of all people. "You got just as many of Mom's worry genes as I did."

"I know." Corinne stirred her coffee. "But I've been thinking about the way Sam prayed the other night. He was so calm and confident. I want to be like that, Tori. I want to worry less and trust God more."

Ignoring the reference to Sam, Tori pinched off the corner of a warm croissant. "There's nothing wrong with being careful."

"We're not *careful*, Tori." Corinne's straight blond hair swung as she shook her head. "We're neurotic." She raised a hand to forestall Tori's response. "Yes, we have to take precautions because of Bill. But right now he's locked up and I'm tired of cowering in my little house. Yesterday I almost jumped out of my skin when the mail carrier rang my doorbell."

"That's not surprising," Tori murmured. "Considering what you've been through this past year."

"You're missing my point." Corinne gave her a level look. "Being careful is one thing, Tori, but all this nail biting over things we can't control is making us sick. This can't be how God wants us to live. I keep thinking about Matthew 6:27, remember that one? 'Who of you by worrying can add a single hour to his life?'"

Tori sipped her coffee, unwilling to confess that she'd been extra worried lately—about the way she worried. What scared her the most was her growing obsession with the lock on her front door. Even when she knew it was secure, she had to go and *look*, often as many as three times before she went to bed.

Yes, she was neurotic. And what she'd been through on Sunday had exacerbated the problem. "Let's talk about this later," she said, dodging the discussion she wasn't ready for.

"Okay." A smile tugged at Corinne's mouth as she waggled her eyebrows. "Tell me everything about that dishy Sam."

Absolutely not. Tori had been spending entirely too much time thinking about that dishy Sam. "There's nothing to tell."

"Give me a break, Tori. As upset as I was the other night, it was impossible to miss how cute he was. And he's obviously interested in you." Corinne sat back in her chair, a triumphant gleam in her brown eyes. "Maybe now you'll stop trying to make yourself fall in love with Julian."

Tori felt her cheeks heat up. "Julian is a good man."

"Oh, Julian's a *wonderful* man. He always says and does exactly the right thing." Corinne lifted her coffee cup and shuddered delicately. "Just like a Stepford boyfriend."

He wasn't her boyfriend, exactly, but correcting Corinne's assumption didn't seem like the best move right now. Tori sat up straighter. "I happen to appreciate knowing exactly what to expect from a man."

"Well, you've never looked at Julian the way you were looking at Sam the other night," Corinne retorted.

An image of Sam's chipped-tooth grin flashed through Tori's mind, but she pushed it aside. "That was gratitude."

The teasing light faded from Corinne's eyes. "Julian's great, Tori, but something's missing between you two. And you've known that for a long time."

True. But while she wasn't "in love" with Julian, she

had long cherished a deep respect for him. Tori was ready for marriage and Julian would make a steady, reliable husband and father.

Unlike Sam. Tori couldn't picture *him* sitting placidly by the fireside, looking up from his literary magazine to answer one of the children's questions. No, Sam would be standing in the doorway, his emerald eyes snapping with excitement: "Forget the homework, kids. Daddy's going to take you bungee jumping!"

"Over my dead body," Tori whispered into her coffee cup as Corinne bent to retrieve the car keys she had accidentally brushed off the table's edge.

"So," Corinne said as she sat upright again. "About Sam."

"I'm *grateful* to him," Tori reiterated, then she deftly changed the subject by asking about the babies.

Minutes later, mindful of all the work waiting for her at the office, Tori hugged her sister goodbye. "Call me when you get home," she urged. "Or I'll worry about you all day."

Back at the library, Tori deposited a white bakery sack on Francine's desk, right next to a tissue-wrapped floral arrangement which she eyed with open curiosity. "I brought you a croissant."

"Mind reader." Francine grinned her thanks, then handed Tori a small pink envelope and slanted a meaningful look at the flowers. "I thought Julian was still in Italy."

"He is." Tori made no attempt to conceal her surprise that the delivery was for her. "He's not due back for a couple of weeks."

"He hasn't done anything stupid, I hope?"

"Julian?" Tori huffed in amusement. "Julian has never done anything stupid in his life."

He'd never done anything impulsive or unexpected, either, she reflected as she slipped a finger under the envelope's flap and broke the seal. But Julian's mother and Tori's were best friends, so maybe he'd heard about Sunday night and was sending a thinking-of-you bouquet.

As Francine ripped tissue paper and revealed a bunch of graceful white lilies in a glass vase, Tori removed the card from its envelope.

Francine wadded up the tissue paper and disposed of it, then looked expectantly at Tori. "Well?"

"They're from Sam." Dazed, Tori surrendered the card.

"You are infinitely more interesting than dryer lint," Francine read aloud, "and I'd like to see you again." Her dark eyebrows shot up. "Dryer lint?"

Tori snatched back the card. "I told him I'm an archivist."

Francine rolled her eyes.

With Francine on her heels, Tori carried the fragrant bouquet into her office and surveyed the possibilities. There weren't many, as every flat surface was covered with neatly stacked boxes and folders. With an elbow Tori gestured toward her credenza, which stood next to the window. "Shove some of this stuff out of the way, will you, Francine?"

"What's he like?" Francine asked, as she moved some things aside on the credenza.

"Dangerous." Tori set the vase down and resolutely shifted her mind back to business. "We're running low on the cubic-foot archival boxes. You'd better order some."

Francine leaned over to sniff the lilies. "What kind of dangerous?" she asked, still in best-friend mode. "Dangerously charming?"

Yes. Which was why Tori had to banish him from her

thoughts. "I told you yesterday," she said, answering Francine's question with more patience than she felt. "He's not my kind of man."

"Well, exactly who *is* your kind of man?" Francine's braids swung rhythmically as she shook her head in disgust. "Except for the occasional dull evening with Julian—and I'm not sure those count—you haven't had a single date in the three years I've known you."

"I've been busy. And my evenings with Julian aren't dull. You know very well that he's an old family friend and we have a lot in common. Now, would you please get your nose out of my love life and go order those boxes?"

"I did it last week," Francine said, waving a hand to dismiss that subject. "And your love life needs serious work. You should go out with Sam before you actually *become* as dull as dryer lint. I don't get what you're so afraid of."

"I'm afraid I'll *like* him," Tori blurted, frustration getting the better of her. "Then next month he'll fall off a mountain and his friends will bring home little pieces of him on a stretcher."

Francine pursed her lips and appeared to think about that. Suddenly, she brightened. "You can go out with him three times. That's enough to loosen you up without having to worry about either of you falling in love."

"I don't want to be loosened up," Tori grumbled. "And what kind of ditz falls in love on the fourth date?"

"Girl, when it comes to dangerous men, we're *all* ditzes. That's why you're going to limit this to three dates."

"Francine," Tori said witheringly, "I do not play games with men."

"I'm not talking about playing games," Francine said

in apparent exasperation. "Remember the last time I was on a diet? If I craved something forbidden, I allowed myself three bites of it. Giving myself permission to savor those three bites is what kept me from totally blowing my diet."

It worried Tori that she actually had an inkling of where Francine was headed with that.

"So instead of trying to convince yourself that you're not interested in Sam, go ahead and explore that interest." Francine nodded sagely. "That's the best way to cure it."

"What if he doesn't ask me out?" Tori nibbled her bottom lip, barely able to believe she was actually considering this ridiculous plan.

"The man sent you flowers. He'll call." Francine stabbed a finger at Tori's breastbone. "See that you're in when he does."

No. Tori searched for an excuse and turned up a good one. "Julian and I have never said anything about dating exclusively, but after all this time—"

"*Julian.*" Francine put her hands on her hips. "Could we please stop pretending the love bug's going to bite you and Professor Knowles? You've been friends forever. If something was going to happen, it would have happened by now, don't you think?"

But Julian was her ideal man. Tori could always count on him to be who and what and where he was supposed to be; no surprises. That kind of dependability meant a lot to Tori, so she didn't understand her profound interest in Sam. Why did her heart skip every time she thought about him?

And why had her heart never skipped for Julian?

All right. If Sam asked, she'd say yes to a date. That would give her a chance to investigate the cause of all this pesky heartbeat-skipping. And once she figured it out, maybe she could make it happen with Julian.

Yes. At his desk, Sam banged his phone into its cradle, then grabbed two pencils and played a short drum riff on a stack of rock-climbing magazines.

Victoria Talcott had just agreed to meet him for lunch.

What he needed now was a plan. He thought for a moment, then placed a call to Jackie, the wife of his old sky-diving instructor. Jackie was a caterer who specialized in small, elegant parties; after a brief consultation she agreed to fill Sam's impromptu request.

Now all he had to do was kill two hours.

Picking up a letter that lay on his desk, he took a deep breath and began reading. The first sentence was tricky, so he backed up and started over, but it was no use. The tiny black letters jumped and ducked under Sam's squinty gaze until he groaned in frustration.

"Give it here." Willa Traynor, Sam's cousin and the world's worst receptionist, strode into the office like a cat-walk model on her sky-high heels. Her platinum curls bounced against her shoulders as she approached Sam with one hand extended.

He surrendered the letter. "I hate it when they use those tiny fonts," he grumbled, pushing his chair back from the desk and rubbing his eyes.

"Poor Sammy." Willa ruffled his hair with her free hand. Sam jerked his head away. "Knock it off," he said mildly.

Undaunted, Willa perched on the arm of his chair and draped one of her own slender arms around Sam. "If you don't like the way I talk, you can always fire me."

"I'd love to," he said, provoked into stretching the truth. "But Reid would just hire you back."

Willa was so bright she'd finished high school early and was devoting this year to "enjoying life," as she put it, before starting college. She certainly wasn't *working*, at least as far as Sam could tell, but somehow she managed to charm the young, hip clientele of Extreme Adventures. People were actually asking for the brat if she wasn't at her desk when they came in.

"You're crowding me." Sam nudged her off his chair.

Watching as she perused the letter, he wondered for the zillionth time why printed words always had to play leapfrog whenever he tried to read them.

"Andrea Fields wants to thank you for the best vacation of her life," Willa reported. "You delivered even more than promised, blah, blah, blah, and she's recommending you to all her friends." Willa looked up. "She's almost as bad a speller as you are."

"Thank you," Sam said. "Now go show it to Reid. He might want to use it for the new satisfied-customers brochure."

As she walked away, Sam frowned at the tiny black skirt that exposed almost every inch of her long legs. "Willa."

In the doorway, she turned.

Maybe it wasn't his business, but she was only seventeen and she'd grown up without a father. Sam cleared his throat. "That skirt's a little short."

She propped a hand on one slim hip and tilted her head

at him. "You know I love you, Sam, but you're not my dad, okay?" She blew him a kiss and flounced out of the office.

Sam sighed and mentally moved her back to the top of his prayer list, where she stayed most of the time.

"Oh, I forgot," she called from the hallway. "Have fun on your lunch date!"

Sam's jaw clenched in annoyance, but he knew chiding her for listening to his private phone call was more likely to elicit a laugh than an apology. He reached for the phone again, thinking that if he could bump one of his skydiving students back an hour, he'd have more time with Tori.

"Sam?" Angie Bowers, a widow who had lived next door to the McGarrys for years and who now kept the books for Extreme Adventures, stood in the doorway looking sweet and grandmotherly as she peered at Sam over her reading glasses.

Sam put down his phone and waited.

Angie gave him a sly smile. "I hear you have a lunch date."

Sam expelled a long, loud breath. "I'm trying to work here," he said, picking up his phone to prove it.

Angie sighed her disappointment and drifted away. A moment later, Reid poked *his* head in.

"You have a lunch date?"

Once again, Sam replaced the phone. Then he stood up, threw his arms wide and roared, "I am a man! I date women! This is not a new thing!"

"You haven't had a date in months." Willa's sassy rejoinder floated in from the hall. "Reid's back goes out more often than you do."

Defeated, Sam collapsed onto his chair. It *had* been a while since he'd had a date. But he'd grown tired of soothing the ruffled feathers of women who dragged him into relationships and then complained that he traveled too much and didn't lavish enough attention on them. Was it his fault they never listened when he tried to explain his priorities? Although he never put it quite so bluntly, having dinner with a beautiful woman was nice, but it didn't beat screaming down a forty-degree slope on a snow-covered mountain. *That* was *fun*.

Given his history with women, Sam was a little surprised by his strong interest in Victoria Talcott. But although she was a worrier, she didn't appear to be the demanding type, so Sam was willing to risk some involvement to discover why she fascinated him.

Reid folded his arms and leaned a shoulder against the door frame and sighed the way he always did when he thought his brother was making a big mistake. "Please tell me this lunch date isn't with my next-door neighbor."

"The bald guy with the enormous tattooed arms?" Sam shook his head. "No. He seems very nice, Reid, but I—"

"My *other* neighbor." Reid cast a hopeless glance at the ceiling. "Sam, forget that Chinese proverb. You are not responsible for that woman's life."

"I know that," Sam snapped. "I just like her, that's all."

Reid closed his eyes. "Well, I have to live next door to her. So if you even come close to breaking her heart, I'm going to make your life miserable."

"And that would differ from our present arrangement, exactly *how*?" Sam shook his head, disgusted. "It's just lunch, Reid. I'm not quite so irresistible that women fall for me over lunch." Firmly closing that subject, Sam introduced a new one. "Gray called a little while ago. It's snowing in Utah."

Reid's eyebrows rose. "It's awfully early."

"Yeah, but they've got good cover already, so Gray's having a ski party. Can you handle things here on Friday and Monday?"

"Do I have a choice? We can't say no to our best client." Reid huffed out a breath. "Although it annoys me that I'm the only one who ever does any sacrificing around here."

"Close the shop and come with us," Sam suggested.

"Can't. I'm meeting a new client on Monday. A guy who wants to winter at the South Pole. Alone."

"Not possible," Sam said. "There are usually more than fifty scientists wintering over at South Pole Station."

"He wants his own shelter, a few miles away. He wants a guide to take him in and set him up in a one-man camp."

Sam gaped. "That is just about the dumbest thing I've ever heard."

Reid's face remained impassive. "Cost is not an issue for this guy. And yes, he knows the extreme weather conditions make flying impossible in the wintertime. He realizes he won't be able to call a taxi if he gets a sudden urge to leave early."

"Or even if he has a medical emergency," Sam said. "What does he think he's going to *do* for six months?"

"Read books, he says. And write one."

Sam cringed at the thought of spending an Antarctic winter with nothing to do but read books. What would Victoria Talcott think, he wondered, if she knew he'd rather have bamboo splinters shoved under his fingernails than open a book?

"Our guy doesn't want any contact with the outside world," Reid added.

Sam tugged on his ear, thinking. "Reid, this thing has just plain stupidly dangerous written all over it."

"Yeah. Maybe."

It didn't happen often, but occasionally a client would ask Extreme Adventures to organize something that was illegal or just plain stupidly dangerous. In those cases, Reid and Sam had no trouble saying no.

"I haven't promised anything," Reid said now. "Just that we'd look into it."

Sam laced his fingers together behind his head and nodded absently. The South Pole guy sounded nutty, but Sam knew people said the same about *him*.

He knew he wasn't normal. He suspected his craving for adventure had become an unhealthy addiction to the adrenaline highs he experienced when he engaged in risky activities. He might draw the line at setting up stupidly dangerous adventures for clients, but hadn't he crossed that line plenty of times on his own?

Physically strong and uncommonly agile, Sam excelled at outdoor sports. He was an expert skier and a certified skydiving instructor. But since losing his best friend in a mountain-climbing accident five months ago, he'd begun to wonder if he was holding too lightly the life God had given him.

Reid turned to go, then looked back over his shoulder to fire a parting shot. "Don't overdo the charm at lunch. Tori deserves better than you."

The words had been meant as a brotherly gibe, but as Sam stared at the empty doorway he began to suspect they might hold a great deal of truth.

Chapter Four

Standing just outside the library's main entrance, Tori concealed her dismay as she watched Sam bound up the wide arc of limestone steps to meet her. With a bulky patchwork quilt clutched to his chest and a wicker picnic basket swinging from his free hand, he took the steps two and three at a time, holding Tori's gaze as she held her breath, afraid that he'd trip. But Sam was as sure-footed as a mountain goat, even when he had to dodge an inattentive student on her way down the steps.

All smiles and bouncy enthusiasm, he came to a stop in front of Tori and held up his unwelcome surprise—the picnic basket. "I was thinking we could eat by the pond."

But it was October. And the temperature was hovering around fifty degrees beneath a menacing gray sky. Tori lifted her eyes to the swollen clouds. "What if it rains?"

Sam appeared genuinely puzzled by the question. "Uh…we'll get a little wet?"

Tori was tempted to tell Nature Boy about the bone-chilling deluge she had endured just yesterday morning. But she quickly discarded the notion because he looked so eager, so adorably proud of himself and his picnic basket. "To the pond, then," she said brightly, starting down the steps.

At least Francine would be happy. Francine was always pestering Tori to deviate from her routine, try something adventurous. And if having a picnic on a cold, wet day in October with a man she'd known less than forty-eight hours wasn't wildly adventurous, Tori couldn't imagine what might be.

They had nearly reached their destination when Sam stopped abruptly and asked if Tori would mind waiting a moment. Before she could ask what was wrong, he had set the basket and quilt on the ground and was moving away from her with long, purposeful strides that quickened to a graceful lope.

He approached a foursome of young women seated under the willow tree that grew by the water's edge. At this distance Tori was unable to hear the brief exchange, but when Sam gestured in her direction, the students grinned and stole glances at Tori, then gathered up their books and stuffed them into backpacks.

Jogging backward for a few steps, Sam threw the women a friendly wave, then pivoted and ran back to Tori, his sun-kissed hair flopping rhythmically with each long, effortless stride.

"You asked them to leave," Tori guessed when he bent to retrieve the basket and quilt. "Why were they so cheerful about it?"

"Oh, I just explained that this is our first date and I planned a picnic under the willow tree so you'd think I'm classy and romantic, but they were in our spot." He shrugged. "They were very understanding."

He looked perfectly serious, so Tori suppressed the laugh that bubbled to her lips. When Sam started back toward the pond, she gave her head a bemused little shake before falling in beside him. Could a man *be* this ingenuous?

As they walked, Tori pulled a silk scarf from her coat pocket and wound it around her neck. She was freezing, but she tried not to look it because she didn't want to disappoint Sam. She watched him spread the quilt on the grassy bank, where the willow had already dropped many of its slender autumn-yellowed leaves, and then she sat down. Folding her legs close to her body, she tugged her long skirt and her coat over them for warmth.

Sam dropped to his knees beside her and reached into the basket. Withdrawing an insulated serving dish, he removed its cover to reveal a roasted chicken that smelled of lemons and rosemary and made Tori's mouth water.

"I thought picnics were ham sandwiches and potato chips," she said as she watched Sam uncover a luscious-looking antipasto salad.

"You deserve better." He held up a see-through container of beautiful mixed berries for her to admire.

An odd warmth stole over Tori. "Were you born with all this charm," she teased, "or is it something you have to work at?"

"Oh, I'm working at it," Sam said, nodding vigorously as he set two coffee mugs on the quilt. "Women usually find me fairly easy to resist."

Tori chuckled. "I don't believe that."

"Oh, I guess they're interested in the beginning," he conceded. "But it wears off fast."

"Why does it wear off?" Tori couldn't believe they were having this conversation.

"I'd better not say." Sam's tawny eyebrows rose a little, giving him a look of appealing earnestness. "I'm trying to get you to like me."

"I like you," Tori said, making no effort to hide her amusement. "Why does it wear off?"

He sighed. "Well, at first they think it's glamorous to date a guy who travels all over the world. But after they sit home alone for a few Saturday nights, I stop looking so good." His mouth curved into a sheepish grin. "Not much of a sales pitch, is it?"

Tori had never heard of anyone being this honest. And she could hardly believe she was so attracted to a man who freely admitted he was *trying* to charm her.

"Let's pray," Sam said. He grasped Tori's hand and offered a brief expression of gratitude for the meal they were about to share in this peaceful setting. Then he squeezed Tori's hand and let it go and poured her a cup of coffee.

She murmured a distracted thanks and sipped the steaming beverage. Three dates? She'd be doing well to make it through lunch without falling for this guy. She drank some more coffee, hoping a good jolt of caffeine would bring her to her senses.

Sam spooned marinated mozzarella balls, sun-dried tomatoes, wine-colored olives and other savory goodies onto a plate. "That's a beautiful building," he said, nodding toward the library. "What's it like inside?"

Tori felt the familiar rush of pride as she gazed at the

graceful limestone edifice. "I'll give you a tour. Are you a book lover?"

"No." He sounded amused. "I'm not a reader."

"You must be very busy with your work," Tori said politely.

"It isn't that." He finished filling the plate and handed it to Tori along with a knife and fork and a blue cotton napkin. "I'm dyslexic. Severely. I barely made it through high school."

He didn't sound at all embarrassed about it and Tori was curious, so she asked. "How do you cope?"

"I ask for help when I need it. And I have a good memory."

That explained why he'd memorized Tori's phone number rather than letting her write it down. "Did anyone ever work with you on reading?"

"Yeah." He picked up another plate and began filling it for himself. "I'll give it another shot someday, because the experts insist that even people like me can learn. But it's an enormous challenge for me to sit still, so right now I'm focusing on what I do best."

"Sports," Tori guessed. She speared an olive with her fork. "Which ones, in particular?"

"Skiing in the winter, skydiving in the summer. I do a lot of other things, but those are my favorites."

Tori figured skiing couldn't be too dangerous since Julian and his parents did it. One time Julian's mother had broken her foot, but she'd gone right back to Aspen the next winter. So there was nothing shocking about the fact that Sam skied.

The penchant for skydiving, on the other hand, proved he was insane.

"I imagine an archivist has to be pretty well educated," he said, offering her the baguette. "What do you have, a master's degree?"

"Yes." She broke off a chunk of bread and handed the slender loaf back to him. "That's usually the minimum requirement for a college archivist. Many hold doctorates and are faculty members. It was that way here at Wheldon until last year. I was just an archival assistant until my boss had to retire for health reasons. Now they call me the archivist, but I'm really just a placeholder. If the college wasn't struggling financially, they'd be working to attract someone as qualified and experienced as Dr. Grant was."

Sam looked thoughtful as he balanced his plate on one blue-jeaned thigh and leaned back on his hands. His leather jacket parted to reveal a crisp yellow T-shirt that set off the blond streaks in his hair; his shoulders twitched as though keeping time to music. "But the longer you hold the position, the more inclined they'll be to keep you."

Tori acknowledged that with a brief nod. "But if they make another round of staff cuts, I could be the next to go." No doubt they'd dump Francine, too, and put the college's overworked librarian in charge of the archives. And all that glorious history would be locked up and forgotten.

Sam stopped twitching. "You love this school," he said quietly.

Tori nodded. "I did my undergrad work here. History."

Sam remained still, watching her face.

"I was eighteen when I first came here." Tori's gaze drifted to the dark, mirror-smooth surface of the pond. "I was so scared." She pointed to an ornate cast-iron bench by the water's edge. "I sat right there and prayed. And when I opened my eyes, five Canada geese flew over my shoulder and landed in the water right in front of me, not six feet away."

Sam's rapt expression encouraged her to continue.

"They looked right at me and they weren't afraid." Tori had never told this story to anyone, not even Corinne, but it felt right to share it now. "It was a little fanciful, I guess, but I took their acceptance as a sign that I belonged here."

Sam's only response was a brief smile of understanding before he turned to watch three mallards cruise silently by, their passage making V-shaped ridges on the pond's glassy surface.

Moisture from the ground had wicked through the quilt and Tori felt a cold mist on her face, but those little discomforts seemed insignificant now. She had never been all that wild about picnics, but she would remember this one for a very long time.

She and Sam ate in silence for a few minutes and then she asked where *he* belonged.

"At this particular moment?" He tore a piece from the baguette and tossed it to a duck who quacked excitedly over the windfall. "I belong under this willow tree beside this pond with this endlessly fascinating woman."

Not sure what to make of that comment, Tori smiled it away. "Tell me about Extreme Adventures. How did you get started with that?"

Sam straightened his legs and began shifting his feet like a pair of windshield wipers, left-right, left-right. "The concept was mine, but we'd never have made it off the ground without Reid. He's the brains of the operation."

Tori didn't believe that, but she liked his modesty. "Do you go on all the adventures?"

"No. It's usually safer to use local guides. But I help out sometimes and I'm always traveling to check out new locations and guides. And I do a fair amount of interpreting. My Spanish comes in handy on some of the Central and South American trips."

"Your Spanish?" Tori wondered how a man who was unable to read had managed to learn a foreign language.

"I don't read or write it," he explained. "But Rich, my best friend since the second grade, was Mexican. His English was so awful that I finally just gave up and learned *his* language."

Tori smiled, then she and Sam happened to lift their coffee cups at the same moment. Their eyes met as they drank, but the strange intimacy of the connection disturbed Tori, so she quickly broke it.

"Hey." Sam gestured with his cup. "Would you like to meet my mother?"

Tori blinked. Everything about him was so unexpected. Apparently, his brain was as restless as his body, and whatever was on his mind just popped right out of his mouth.

"She lives about a mile from here." There was an odd urgency in his tone and his eyes seemed almost to be pleading with Tori. "It wouldn't take long. We'd just say a quick hello."

Tori hesitated. She wouldn't have minded meeting Sam's mother, but when she thought of all the work on her desk....

"I promised I'd stop by today," Sam said. "Not that she'll remember that." He looked into his cup and sighed. "She has Alzheimer's, and she doesn't know me anymore.

I just thought maybe if I showed up with somebody she *really* doesn't know, I might look familiar by comparison."

"Oh, Sam." Compassionate tears gathered in Tori's eyes. "I don't know what to say."

"That's okay." He flung the remaining coffee out of his cup. "It wasn't one of my better ideas."

"*No,*" Tori protested, appalled that he'd misunderstood. After what he'd done for her, did he really think she'd deny him this small favor? "I meant, I'm sorry she has Alzheimer's." She rose to her knees and began repacking the wicker basket. "Come on. I want to meet her."

They took Sam's truck and within minutes had arrived at the Alzheimer's unit of an assisted-living community. Sam led Tori past the reception desk and down a carpeted corridor where they met a nurse coming out of one of the rooms. Sam greeted her, but would have kept walking if she hadn't touched his arm.

He stopped abruptly. "Is everything okay?"

The nurse offered a fleeting smile to Tori, then looked back at Sam. "I just thought you should know the florist delivered *red* roses this time. And forgot the card."

Sam blew out a breath. "Thanks for letting me know. Is she having a good day?"

"She's as cheerful as ever, which is remarkable for someone at her stage of the disease." The nurse looked at Tori. "Everything scares and frustrates them, so most of them turn nasty. Just last night, we had a man screaming that there was a naked stranger in his bathroom. We had to move him to a room with no mirrors. And one lady—"

"Thank you," Sam said, cutting her off. "I'll follow up with the florist."

The nurse nodded pleasantly and turned away.

"Dad used to give her pink roses," Sam explained as he and Tori started walking again. "The church kept him busy, but he always made a point of spending Saturdays with Mom. And as often as he could afford it, he'd buy her pink roses. So a couple of months ago, Reid arranged to have a half-dozen delivered to her every Saturday."

Tori's heart ached at the sweetness of that. "And does she remember?"

"No. But the flowers still come with a card that says, 'I'll love you forever. Robert.'" Sam stopped in front of a partially open door and rapped softly on its frame. "Hello," he called. "Would you mind some company?"

The door was opened by a slight woman in a green shirtwaist dress that was buttoned crookedly. Tori had been expecting an old lady, but Mrs. McGarry appeared to be only in her mid-fifties. There were hints of gray in the light brown curls that didn't appear to have seen a brush that morning, but Sam's mother was still lovely. She had high cheekbones, pretty if somewhat vacant hazel eyes and a smile that was timid yet hopeful.

She invited them in, then looked uncertainly at Tori. "I'll order coffee and cookies, shall I?"

"No, don't go to any trouble." Sam gave his mother a gentle smile. "We just had lunch."

The long, narrow apartment had no kitchen and reminded Tori of an upscale hotel room. The floral wallpaper was a pleasant surprise, as were the tall corner windows behind a plump sofa covered in green-and-white-striped chintz. "What a pretty room," Tori said, settling onto the sofa beside Sam's mother. "It's like being in a garden."

Sam took a chair adjacent to them. "That's what I said the first time I saw it."

His mother looked startled. "You've been here before?"

A spasm of pain shot across his face. "A few times."

"I'm so sorry." His mother put her hands to her cheeks, obviously distressed. "I forget things."

"It's all right." There was a tenderness in Sam's voice that made Tori's throat swell. "We're just a couple of friends."

Tori had been waiting for Sam to introduce her, but she now understood he was avoiding names to keep from upsetting his mother.

Mrs. McGarry brightened suddenly. "Let's have coffee."

"No, thank you," Sam said. "We can't stay long."

Tori was trying to decide whether to comment on the bouquet of roses on the table beside her when she noticed a silver-framed wedding photograph under the crimson canopy of blooms. "What a handsome man," she said, reaching for the picture.

Sam's mother squinted at it. "Who is that, dear?"

Alarmed, Tori looked at Sam, but he rose abruptly and strode toward the windows. "That's Robert," Tori said, remembering what Sam had told her about the card that always accompanied the roses. "It's you and Robert. A long time ago."

Two deep lines appeared in Mrs. McGarry's forehead as she stared at the photograph. "Robert," she repeated as though tasting the name for the first time. With an index finger she outlined her late husband's face, searching for the memory.

Tori looked again at Sam. His shoulders sagged as he

stared out the window and she grieved for him, with him. She turned back to his mother and spoke with fierce conviction. "You and Robert were very happy. You had two sons who grew up to be strong, fine men. Just like Robert."

"Two boys," Mrs. McGarry echoed wonderingly.

"I know them." Acutely aware of Sam's startled regard, Tori didn't dare look at him now. "Reid and Sam." She hoped she hadn't omitted any siblings.

"Reid and Sam," Mrs. McGarry repeated without expression.

"Your family adored you," Tori declared. "You must have been the happiest woman in the world."

Sam's mother smiled wistfully, then asked if Tori would like some coffee and cookies.

"No, thank you," Sam said as gently as before. He moved to stand beside the sofa. "We have to be going now."

Tori rose, then submitted to yet another impulse and bent down to kiss Mrs. McGarry's satiny cheek. Noting that Sam's mother seemed pleased by the gesture, she dared further. "Would it be all right if my friend kissed you, too?"

Sam's mother looked at him sideways. "Do I know him?" she asked in an agitated whisper.

Swamped by sadness, Tori was unable to reply.

"My name is Sam," came the deep voice from behind her.

"Sam!" His mother's face changed in an instant, and she gazed up at him as raptly as a child on Christmas morning. "Like my second boy."

Tori stared. She had guessed Sam was younger than Reid, but she'd said nothing about that to his mother.

"Just like him," Sam said faintly.

"He was a handful," his mother said in worried tones. "He used to crawl out his bedroom window and climb up on the roof."

"He liked to sit with his back against the chimney and look at magazines," Sam explained. "He was always happiest outside and it was quiet up there."

Mrs. McGarry twisted her fingers together. "But it was dangerous."

"Not for Sam. He used to climb up there with a stack of magazines under one arm and an apple in his mouth."

Hearing Sam speak of himself in the third person cracked Tori's heart. How many times had he been through this? How many times had he stood here and looked into his mother's eyes hoping that *this* time, she would know him?

"We have to go," he said. "May I kiss you goodbye?"

His mother tilted her cheek toward him. As Sam bent down, Tori turned away, clamping her lips together just in time to muffle the small sob that caught in her throat.

She and Sam walked out to his truck without speaking. When he opened the passenger door, Tori breached the painful silence with a question: "You took magazines up to the roof?"

"Sports magazines." With a hand under her elbow, Sam guided her up to the seat. "Lots of pictures." He started to close the door, but Tori touched his arm.

"How often do you come here?" she asked.

"Every week."

He put himself through this torture every week? "And does she ever…"

"No."

Emboldened by her compassion, Tori lifted her hand

and smoothed back a wavy lock of straw-colored hair that had fallen over his right eye. "I hurt for you, Sam."

Avoiding her eyes, he closed the door and walked around to his side. "I shouldn't have dragged you off to meet my mother in the middle of our first date," he grumbled as he climbed into the driver's seat.

Tori gave him the simple truth. "It felt right to me, Sam."

He still wouldn't look at her, but the tense line of his jaw relaxed. That was good, but it wasn't enough.

"Come see my library," Tori urged. "I'll give you a tour."

He glanced at his watch. "Don't you have to get back?"

After the morning coffee break with Corinne and the long lunch with Sam, Tori was already planning to work late tonight. But she couldn't let Sam go until he smiled again, so she insisted on the tour.

They started with the main floor of the hundred-year-old building. "This is Elmira Wheldon Danvers," Tori said, stopping in front of the life-size, full-length oil painting of a lithe blond woman in a pale blue dress. "She dreamed of going to college, but when she was eighteen her parents forced her to marry one of her father's business associates. She was widowed less than two years later and she used her husband's fortune to build this college." Tori shook her head in admiration. She always loved telling this part of the story. "Elmira herself was the first student to enroll. She was a member of the first graduating class."

"Good for Elmira," Sam said warmly.

Tori led him up the marble staircase to the second floor. When his steps slowed and he stretched out a hand to touch the exquisite mahogany paneling, Tori stopped. "We have all this beautiful brass and marble and carved wood, but no money to maintain it."

Sam traced a joint in the wall with his thumb. "This was real craftsmanship."

"Elmira believed a college's library was its heart," Tori explained as they continued up the steps. "So it should be the grandest building."

Tori introduced Sam to Francine, then showed Sam into her own office and pointed to the window overlooking the willow tree and the pond. Sam's face lit up when he saw his white lilies on the credenza.

"They smell like you," he said, moving closer to sniff one. His voice deepened as he turned back to Tori. "Did you notice that?"

Her favorite perfume did include a note of lilies. Tori was surprised and flustered that Sam had made that connection. "Come on," she said, taking his arm and leading him away from the dangerously romantic flowers. She took him up another staircase, this one of scarred oak, to show him the third floor.

"Welcome to my world." With a broad sweep of one arm she indicated the rows and rows of shelves stacked with neat boxes, all behind floor-to-ceiling steel bars and a locked gate.

Sam emitted a long, low whistle.

"We have some extremely rare and valuable items here," Tori said, explaining the barricade. "Also, many of these records are confidential, at least for a certain number of years. There are all sorts of rules about accessibility."

"So people can't just wander in here and nose around," Sam said.

"No. If you want something, I'll find it for you."

"It looks very neat," Sam said politely.

"I love the order of it," Tori said. "I love knowing all this history is right here at my fingertips." She walked away from Sam, absently trailing her fingers over the bars.

"Amazing," he said, following her.

"Many of our students have gone on to make names for themselves, especially in the world of literature and politics," Tori said. "We get a lot of their papers. That's one of the best parts of this job, accessioning new materials and—"

"Accessioning?"

She turned to look at him. "Adding items to the archives. We can't possibly store everything that's offered to us, so each item must be evaluated in light of its historic significance and its relevance to our collections."

Sam wrapped his hands around two of the bars and tested their strength. "So you decide what gets accessioned."

"Yes. It can be very exciting work. Right now I'm waiting for some papers from the estate of Senator Adam Danvers. He—"

"Senator Danvers?" Sam's head snapped in her direction.

It was hardly surprising that Sam recognized the name. Barely a decade had passed since the senator's failed presidential campaign. "He was Elmira's son," Tori explained. "She married George Danvers when she was thirty-nine. And Adam—the senator—was their only child. You probably heard that he died a few months ago. Well, he willed us some papers."

Tori had an idea she was talking too much, but this was a favorite subject. "Elmira destroyed her personal journals and letters, so we've never known much about her. But the senator promised to bequeath to the college any of his papers that contained references to his mother. I can't wait to get my hands on them because the college's centennial is coming up next year and I'd love to be able to fill in some of the gaps in our knowledge of—" Tori stopped when she noticed Sam staring hard at the floor, looking as though he was about to bite right through his bottom lip.

The words *dryer lint* popped into her head. Sam must be bored silly by this conversation. "I'm sorry," she said with a self-conscious little laugh. "You shouldn't have asked about my work."

He captured her hand with his. When he lifted his gaze, it rested briefly on her mouth before continuing up to meet her eyes. "When can I see you again?"

Tori looked away from him. This morning Francine's three-date plan had sounded almost reasonable, but Tori hadn't sufficiently considered Sam's devastating charm. Now she was scrambling to construct a coherent sentence that included the words "no" and "thank you."

"Dinner," Sam said, squeezing her fingers. "Tomorrow."

"I...don't think so," Tori managed.

"Another time, then?"

It wasn't wise to continue seeing him, but she owed him her life and as yet had done nothing to express her gratitude. Stalling, she looked down at their joined hands and was suddenly struck by an idea so good it nearly took her breath away. She pulled her hand out of his and blurted, "Sam, let me work with you on your reading."

He looked startled. "Thanks, but I—"

"Please." Tori's mind was already busy making plans. She had no experience with dyslexia, but she was a fairly intelligent person and hardly a stranger to research. She could probably find most of what she needed on the Internet, but she also had a cousin who homeschooled her 13-year-old son who was learning-disabled. Beth could offer some helpful advice, Tori was certain.

Sam lowered his head and gave Tori a stern look from under his eyebrows. "You don't owe me anything."

She would get nowhere by contradicting him, so she stressed what *she* would gain from the experience. It was a sneaky approach, but she believed his innate generosity would prevent him from disappointing her. "I have a friend who volunteers with an adult literacy program and all she ever talks about is how good she feels when her students succeed. Sam, I'd love to share your excitement when everything clicks and you finally discover the joys of reading. Please let me."

He smiled suddenly. "All right. I guess I wouldn't mind seeing you on a regular basis."

A warning bell clanged in Tori's head. "These wouldn't be dates, Sam."

"Okay." He shrugged. "But if we're going to meet in the evenings, we might as well have dinner together."

Tori backed up a step, lest he take her hand again. "Let's just stick to the reading."

"Problem." Mischief glinted in his clear green eyes. "I can't concentrate when I'm hungry."

Tori was determined to give him this gift, but he seemed equally bent on carrying on a flirtation. Well, let him try. He was completely wrong for her and as long as she kept reminding herself of that, she'd be safe.

"I'll cook for you," she decided. Otherwise, he'd probably drag her to some romantic, candlelit restaurant and squander their valuable time. "Tomorrow night. We'll eat and then we'll work." She'd get on the Internet tonight and learn all she could about dyslexia. "How does that sound?"

"Perfect." Sam disarmed her with that chipped-tooth grin. As Tori's heart completed its second somersault, she admitted to herself that for such a well-educated woman, sometimes she had no sense at all.

Chapter Five

After letting Sam into her apartment the next evening, Tori closed the door and turned the dead bolt with such alacrity that her guest couldn't help smiling.

"Victoria," he drawled, "let me assure you that escape was the very last thing on my mind."

She considered trying to laugh it off. With a little encouragement, Sam would chalk this up to ordinary second-date nervousness. But she couldn't deceive anyone as honest as Sam, so she confessed. "I'm...a little obsessed with that door."

His amused expression faded as he studied her face. "You're a woman alone in the city. Isn't it a good idea to keep the door locked?"

Tori refused the lifeline he'd thrown to her pride. "Yes, but I have a problem." She stared down at the fingers she was twisting together. "When I got my first apartment, my mother called every night to make sure I'd locked my door. That's what started me off."

"Started you off?"

Still staring at her hands, she nodded miserably. "I always locked it when I came in, but she made me double-check and it got to be a habit. I've always been a worrier and in the last year I've gotten worse because of all the trouble with Bill. Last night I checked the door three times." She braced herself and looked up for Sam's reaction.

"Um…okay." He frowned, seeming baffled by her agitation. "So you're a little weird."

"You don't understand," Tori said impatiently. "It's not *normal*, how much I worry."

Sam laid his hands on her shoulders, blatantly amused yet oddly tender. "You're really something else, brown eyes. I've never known anyone who worries about how much she worries." He made a show of looking at his watch. "I'd love to talk more about your neuroses, but could we do it over dinner? I'm starving."

Tori was stunned. She had just revealed her awful secret and Sam had shrugged it off. He *accepted* her, warts and all. And by poking gentle fun at her, he was encouraging her to relax and accept herself.

She resolved to try. Her answering smile felt a bit wobbly, but it was a start.

She led Sam to the kitchen, where she had already set the table and arranged a picture-perfect basket of fruit for the centerpiece. The rice and vegetables were ready, so Tori had only to stir-fry the shrimp and steep the jasmine tea. "Do you like Szechuan?" she asked as she turned on a gas flame and pulled her still-warm wok over it.

"Hot stuff? Love it." Sam plucked two apples and a pear from the basket and began juggling them.

Tori was a little dismayed that he'd spoiled her arrangement, but she was *seriously* dismayed when he flashed a crooked grin that made her giddy. She had never known a man so full of enthusiasm and sweetness. How she was going to work closely with him on his reading without succumbing to his charm?

When the shrimp turned pink, Tori added her crisp-cooked vegetables and poured her sauce mixture into the wok. Sam stopped juggling to watch her toss the steamy, hissing shrimp and vegetables, glazing them with the thickening sauce. As the piquant aroma filled the kitchen, he sniffed appreciatively.

He loved the meal and told her so at least half a dozen times. After they finished the stir-fry, Tori made a second pot of jasmine tea and they broke open crisp almond-scented cookies that contained Scripture verses instead of the usual silly fortunes.

Sam withdrew a narrow slip of paper from the folds of a cookie. He frowned at it, then handed it to Tori. "I don't do fine print. The letters dance."

She was glad to read it for him. "Because you are my help, I sing in the shadow of your wings. My soul clings to you; your right hand upholds me. Psalm—"

"Sixty-three," Sam said. When Tori glanced up in surprise, he shrugged. "I listen to the Bible on CD when I work out. But they just say the chapter numbers, so I don't know what verse that is."

"Verses seven and eight," Tori said, just as her phone rang. When she excused herself and answered the call, a man with an unusually deep, compelling voice apologized for disturbing her and asked to speak to Sam.

"Tell him it's Gray," the caller added.

Tori offered the phone to Sam. "It's a Mr. Gray."

Sam folded his arms across his chest and looked disgusted. "Tell him I'm not accepting calls from eccentric billionaires this evening."

Confused, Tori stared at him, waiting for more.

He sighed and got up. He took the phone, giving it a look of utter distaste before raising it to his ear. "Yes, my cell phone is turned off," he said between his teeth. After a brief pause, he said, "Because I'm having dinner with a beautiful woman, you jerk. Do I interrupt *your* dates?" He listened for a moment, then said, "Not *now*, Gray. I'll call you when I get home."

He handed the phone back to Tori. "I apologize for that," he said, resuming his seat at the table. "He's buying some new ski boots and wanted my advice."

Flustered by the beautiful woman comment, Tori settled back into her chair and did her best to move the conversation along. "Oh, that's right. You mentioned yesterday that you liked skiing."

"I don't like it," Sam said as he reached for another cookie. "I'm a fanatic." His green eyes took on a faraway look as he broke his cookie in half. He popped a piece into his mouth and then mumbled around it, "I especially love hucking."

"Hucking?"

"Jumping," he translated. "I love being in the air. Back flips are my specialty."

Tori didn't care for the visual she was getting on that. "You can't just swoosh down the hill like a normal person?"

Sam's eyes widened and he sucked in his bottom lip, looking adorably boyish as he shook his head.

Lifting her teacup, Tori nodded toward the phone. "Was that really an eccentric billionaire?"

"That was *the* eccentric billionaire. Grayson Traynor."

Tori nearly choked on a mouthful of hot tea. "You mean I just spoke to the man who owns half of downtown Chicago?"

"I'm afraid so." Sam drummed his fingers on the table's edge. "I don't know how he got your number, but Gray moves in mysterious ways."

"Wow," Tori breathed.

"Hey, do you ski?" Sam folded his arms on the table and leaned forward, his eyes alive with eagerness. "Could I interest you in a free trip to Utah this weekend?"

Still a bit stunned that a famous billionaire had just phoned her residence to ask for Sam's advice on ski boots, Tori shook her head. "I don't ski."

"Excellent. It'll be fun teaching you."

Imagining herself cartwheeling down the side of a frozen mountain, skis and poles flying in all directions, Tori shivered. "Thanks, but I have no desire to learn."

"Okay." The light in Sam's eyes hadn't dimmed. "You can watch from the terrace at Gray's place. It's outfitted with telescopes and you can have lunch outside. Gray's planning a Friday-to-Monday weekend, but if you can't take time off work, we'll go late and come home early. We don't have to fly out with the others in Gray's jet, we can just do the regular airline thing. I have lots of frequent-flier miles. How about it?"

With more reasons to say no than she could even count, there seemed little point in confessing her fear of flying. Tori shook her head vigorously. "I couldn't."

"You wouldn't be the only one not skiing. Gray will be sitting on the terrace knocking back espressos and making phone calls while he watches us."

Tori tried to imagine herself drinking espresso with Grayson Traynor. "He doesn't ski?"

"Oh, Gray's a fairly advanced skier. But he broke his ankle last month in a skydiving accident. Nothing serious, he was just having trouble with his flare. That's where you put on the brakes at the end for a stand-up landing. He came in too fast, then tripped over his big feet." Sam twitched a shoulder. "He's very tall. But he's a good student, otherwise."

This had to be the most bizarre conversation Tori had ever participated in. "You're teaching Grayson Traynor to skydive?"

"Doing my best. Please come, Tori."

"Don't you have to be a licensed instructor for that?"

"For the skydiving? Yeah, I'm certified. Come to Utah, Tori. You won't believe how beautiful it is."

"No, I'd just spoil your fun," she said firmly. "How did you meet Grayson Traynor?"

"We're cousins. We were never really close because there's almost twenty years between us. But a few years ago he decided to take his son on a white-water kayaking trip. I lined up a guide, but I happened to have some experience on that particular river, so I tagged along. Things got a little hairy and we sort of bonded." Sam shrugged as if that explained everything.

"What happened on the trip?"

Sam's gaze dropped to the table and he pushed some cookie crumbs around with his thumb. "Well, Austin—that's Gray's son—didn't have much kayaking experience and his cocky attitude worried me. And Heather, the guide, couldn't seem to peel her eyes off Gray. We knew about the falls and meant to carry around them, but when Gray and Heather climbed out of the river, Austin decided to give us a little scare by flirting with the falls. When he tried to turn back, he couldn't paddle hard enough. So I followed him over."

Tori stared. "You *followed* him over a waterfall?"

"It wasn't a bad little drop." Sam shifted in his chair and pulled a ring of keys out of his pocket. "Maybe twenty feet, and I had run it before."

"On purpose?"

He looked at her in apparent surprise. "Well, *yeah*." He dropped the key ring over his raised index finger and began swinging the keys around and around. "The thing that had me worried about Austin was the rocks just beyond the pool. If Austin didn't drown by the time he reached them, I was afraid he'd be ripped to shreds."

Tori watched Sam's wrist work, twirling the keys faster and faster, and worried that they'd slip off the end of his finger and fly across the kitchen and break something. "Was he hurt?"

"No. The kid surprised me." Sam caught the keys in his fist. "He flipped when he hit the pool, but even though he was scared out of his mind, he executed a perfect Eskimo roll. He popped up like a cork and I was down there just in time to get between him and the rocks."

So Sam had put himself between Grayson Traynor's son and the dangerous rocks. Just as he had put himself between Tori and the gun. But while she was impressed by Sam's heroism, she couldn't help wondering how much he valued his *own* life.

"He swallowed half the river," Sam continued, "but he was fine after he stopped vomiting and Gray finished alternately hugging him and screaming at him. But Gray said no more white-water adventures, so now we mostly ski and skydive."

Tori seriously doubted that skydiving was any safer than kayaking over twenty-foot waterfalls, but she kept that to herself. "Is Austin still a show-off?"

"Not so much. We think he's finally started growing a brain. And he's a natural on skis. Daddy Gray is very proud." Sam returned the keys to his pocket. "Please come this weekend. Gray's sister Kath will be there. You'll love Kath."

"No, I'm sorry."

"Just try it once."

Tori shook her head. She wanted to shake *him* until he let go of this terrible idea. "Sam, you and I are very different."

"Yeah." His head bobbed enthusiastically. "Different is fun."

"No." The word came out a little more sharply than she'd intended, but she was determined to clear this up once and for all. "I want to get married and have a family. Maybe you want that, too—someday. But you'll never want it with a woman like me, so what's the point in all this?"

He looked surprised and a little hurt. "I like being with you," he said quietly. "That's all. I just like being with you."

His words went straight to Tori's heart and in that unguarded moment she forgot her resolution to keep him at a distance. "I like being with you, too."

Satisfaction lit his eyes. "So you'll let me take you out to dinner when I get back from Utah." When Tori opened her mouth, he lifted a hand to stop her protest. "And then we'll come back here and read," he said virtuously, nodding at her until her traitorous head mimicked the movement.

His mouth curved into a knowing smile. "Tuesday."

One of these days, Tori promised herself, she was going to say no to Sam McGarry and make it stick. But for now she gave in because they were already a full hour behind the schedule she'd mapped out for this evening.

The night before, she'd phoned Beth, who explained some of the challenges facing dyslexics and helped outline a plan for evaluating Sam's needs. Following that conversation, Tori had spent two hours on the Internet, educating herself about dyslexia and bookmarking three home-learning programs she thought might be good for Sam.

She was eager to get started, but she couldn't think straight unless everything around her was in perfect order, which meant the kitchen had to be addressed first. She was grateful when Sam pitched in, carrying dishes to the sink while Tori rinsed them and stacked them in the dishwasher.

During dinner, a light rain had begun to fall, but suddenly the pleasant patter changed to a ferocious roar. Scooping leftover rice into a plastic container, Sam glanced toward the window, interested but obviously unconcerned. Tori, on the other hand, had begun to worry. As she poured detergent into the dishwasher's dispenser cup, she wondered if any of her loved ones had been caught driving in this awful weather.

"I'm going to shake up your system." Sam stood next to the wall-mounted spice rack, a mischievous smile playing on his mouth. He plucked two little jars from a shelf and switched their places, then turned to look at Tori. "Hey, why don't we get you a pet? That would be a great way to break up your routine."

Tori stiffened. "There's nothing wrong with my routine."

Sam picked up two more jars and shook them like a pair of maracas. "C'mon, Tori," he coaxed. "What kind of pet have you always wanted?"

His artless enthusiasm was impossible to resist. "A fish," she said, warming to the idea as she turned on the tap and dampened a clean dishcloth. "I like those pretty blue ones with the swishy fins and tails. Bettas, I think they're called."

"There you go." Sam nodded encouragingly. "I was hoping you'd think a little broader than that, but a fish would be a start. Maybe you could build up to an aquarium. That's more like having a hobby than a pet, but it might accomplish the same thing. Loosen you up a little."

He was just like Francine, pressuring her to loosen up. "I'd like to have a fish," she said with some irritation. "But that isn't going to make me a different person."

Sam looked confused. "I'm not trying to make you a different person. But that was some scary stuff you went through with Bill and I'd just like to see you relax a little."

"I'm relaxed," she snapped, viciously wringing water out of the dishcloth. "Why does everybody think I need to loosen up? This is *me*. This is who I *am*."

"Okay." Sam's gaze dropped to the floor. "Let's save the reading for next time." He glanced up and smiled fleetingly. "Thank you for dinner."

He was halfway to the front door before Tori realized what she had done.

"Sam, wait!" She threw the cloth into the sink and rushed after him, ashamed of herself. What was she going to do next, find a puppy to kick? "I'm sorry. You're right, I *do* need to loosen up. I just—" She faltered.

She just didn't know how to do it.

"Don't apologize," he said gently. "I'm not going away mad. I just think you've had enough of me for one evening and I want to leave while there's still a chance I'll be invited back."

Tori couldn't stop her smile. He was so ridiculously honest. "Please forgive me, Sam. I've been under a lot of stress lately and what happened with Bill has just started to catch up with me. Maybe it's a good idea to cut this evening short, but please wait a few minutes, until this awful rain lets up."

"I like driving in the rain," he said, reaching for the doorknob.

"Well, at least call me when you—" Tori caught herself. Sam didn't owe her that or anything else.

He regarded her soberly. "You want me to call when I get home so you'll know I'm not lying dead in a ditch somewhere."

Tori sighed. Did he have to know *all* of her embarrassing secrets? Soon she wouldn't have a scrap of pride left.

"Victoria." He made a loose fist and with the backs of his fingers, traced the line of her jaw from her left ear down to her chin. "You are so much stronger than you realize."

Before she could respond to that cryptic comment, he'd slipped out the door and closed it. Sighing again, Tori turned the dead bolt.

The doorknob rattled. "It's locked." Sam's muffled voice came through the door. "See? Now you won't have to come back later and check it."

Too embarrassed to reply, Tori backed away from the door and returned to the kitchen, wondering for the umpteenth time why she never worried about the locks on the patio door or the windows.

Maybe those were different. She hated hearing city traffic, so she never used her little patio or opened any windows. She supposed locks that were never *un*locked weren't worth worrying about.

She finished the cleanup and looked around her spotless kitchen, not quite at ease. Her hands itched to put the little jars of bay leaves and rosemary back where they belonged, but she was determined to leave them.

Slumping onto a kitchen chair, she dropped her head into her hands. Why was she so desperate to control every detail of her life? "Lord," she whispered as rain pelted the windows. "I want to relax and trust You, but it's just so hard. Please help me let go of these awful little obsessions."

The phone rang, interrupting her prayer. Certain that it was her mother calling to make sure she was in for the night, safe and snug, Tori picked it up without checking her caller ID.

"I made it home," Sam said. "I'm also calling to remind you that your front door is locked. Can you trust me on that without going to check it?"

"Yes," she said weakly. It was worth a try.

"Thanks again for dinner," he said. "Good night, Victoria."

As was her habit, she turned off the kitchen lights first, and then those in the living room. After switching off the floor lamp next to the sofa, she started toward the front door.

And stopped, remembering Sam.

She didn't look. Turning her back on the door, she felt a little thrill of satisfaction.

The phone rang, and she hurried to snatch it up. "I didn't look, Sam," she said, not caring that she sounded like a first-grader begging for a gold star. "Honest, I didn't even—"

"What didn't you look at?" her mother asked.

Tori's excitement dissolved in an instant. "Sorry, Mom. Sam just left here and I thought he was calling to tease me about something."

"Sam who?" Her mother's tone was faintly disapproving.

"Sam McGarry. The guy who stopped Bill from—" Tori was unable to finish that sentence, but her mother would realize where it had been headed. "I cooked dinner for him."

"Well, that was a lovely gesture," her mother said. After a brief pause, she added, "Have you talked to Julian lately?"

"He called a few days ago. He'll be home soon."

"Good. Maybe you two will finally start making some plans."

Tori sighed. "Mom, I won't be making any plans with Julian. Not the kind you're hoping for."

"You two were always so close," her mother said wistfully.

Had they been especially close? There was something about Tori's remarkable rapport with Sam, a man she had just met, that made her long-term friendship with Julian look almost superficial. But she didn't want to get into that with her mother. "I was just going to bed, Mom."

"Good night, then. Is your door locked?"

Tori closed her eyes. "Mom, I'm twenty-seven years old. I know to lock the door before I go to bed."

"I'm sorry, sweetheart, but you know how I worry about my girls. The one time you forget could be the time—"

"It's *locked*," Tori interrupted, squeezing her eyes more tightly shut. She was *not* going to check.

But a few minutes later, she did. Just to be extra sure.

Chapter Six

"You just missed Sam," Francine said late the next morning when Tori returned to the second floor after a two-hour stint at the library's reference desk. A dimple flashed in Francine's cheek as she pointed to the open doorway of Tori's office. "He left something for you."

More flowers? Tori hurried into her office, then stopped so abruptly that Francine ran into her. Enchanted by Sam's gift, she barely heard her assistant's apology.

A glass sphere rested on one corner of Tori's desk. Filled with water, it also contained a handful of sparkling pink marbles, an aquatic plant and an electric-blue fish that stared straight at Tori, blowing kisses as it fluttered its fins and tail.

"Flowers, I understand," Francine said. "But what kind of man gives a woman fish?"

"A man like Sam, apparently." Tori pressed her lips together to keep from looking inordinately pleased.

"His name's Theophilus," Francine said. "Sam says it's from the Bible."

Next to the fish bowl, Tori spotted a bottle of food, a

booklet of care instructions and Sam's business card. She picked up the card and turned it over, finding a message that looked as if it had been scrawled by one of her first-grade Sunday school students. It read, Mising you alredy. Sam.

Tori sat down at her desk and opened the middle drawer until she could see the pink card that had come with her lilies. That message, in which Sam had assured her she was "infinitely more interesting than dryer lint," had obviously been dictated to someone at the florist's shop. But this one, Sam had written himself. It contained just four words, two of them misspelled, one of them his name. Yet somehow it was the most engaging piece of correspondence Tori had ever received. She placed it on top of the pink card and shut the drawer.

"We're having dinner on Tuesday," she said to Francine. She hadn't yet explained about the tutoring. She told herself that was because she didn't want to violate Sam's privacy, but it probably had more to do with her reluctance to see Francine thrilled about Tori's continued contact with Sam.

"That will be your third date," Francine pointed out. "Where do you plan to go from there?"

"Nowhere," Tori said firmly. Except for the tutoring, of course. "I've enjoyed getting to know him, but he's not the man for me. You know I'm looking for a husband."

Francine nodded thoughtfully. "At least you gave it a try. I'm proud of you for that. You *were* in a rut, you know."

As a ringing telephone summoned Francine back to her own desk, Tori tapped the glass bowl with a fingernail and watched her fish respond. It was sweet that Sam had remembered she'd wanted a blue betta. He was an incredibly thoughtful person.

Propping her elbows on the desk, Tori rested her chin on her hands and stared at the fish. "I could fall for him, Theo," she whispered. "If I'm not careful, I could fall for Sam."

But she *would* be careful. She was an intelligent woman who knew exactly what she wanted out of life. Sam McGarry had briefly captured her attention, but she was too smart to allow him to disturb the calm waters of the future she envisioned for herself and—well, maybe not Julian, but somebody just like him. So as long as she kept her goals firmly in mind and exercised some caution, she wouldn't have a thing to worry about.

Sam had been working with some skydiving students on Thursday, so he didn't make it to the office until late afternoon. Willa was on the phone when he entered the reception area, and she was not merely chomping her usual wad of gum, but applying lipstick as she ended what sounded like a business call. Sam stopped to stare pointedly at her.

She hung up the phone and shook her blond curls back from her face. "That was your four o'clock," she said, peering at her reflection in a small mirror. She pressed her too-red lips together, then opened them again, reminding Sam of the fish he'd bought for Tori. "He's running twenty minutes late."

"When you start college, we're getting a *real* receptionist," Sam grumbled as he helped himself to a couple of lemon drops from the crystal bowl on her desk. When Willa flashed an unrepentant grin, he added, "Don't forget I'm going to Utah tomorrow."

She recapped the lipstick and dropped it into a drawer. "Give cousin Gray a kiss for me."

"Yeah," Sam grunted. "Like he'd hold still for that."

Willa smirked. "I bet Victoria would hold still for it."

Probably not, but a man could always hope.

Heading to his office, Sam heard his name called as he passed Angie's cluttered little domain. He backed up and looked in her doorway.

The grandmotherly bookkeeper waved a slip of paper. "I took a message for you when Willa was at lunch." She tilted her head back to better view the paper through her half glasses. "Rafe called from Starwood Lodge."

"Rafe Gunderson?" Sam rolled the sour candies into his cheek and leaned against the door frame. "What did he want?"

"He'd just like you to call him some evening. He said he's been reading the book you gave him."

Swamped by gratitude, Sam shut his eyes. So the crusty old mountain guide was finally reading the New Testament Sam had given him last winter. "What's his number?"

Angie read it off the paper and Sam repeated it. He thanked her and was about to leave when she spoke again. "Reid says you talk to the clients and the guides about God."

Sam shrugged. "The subject comes up." His father had taught him never to be shy about discussing his faith.

Angie nailed him with a penetrating look. "So the book you gave Rafe Gunderson was a Bible."

"Just a paperback New Testament." They were cheap, so Sam bought them by the stack. Even when he traveled light, he could always wedge a couple into his backpack, just in case he ran into somebody who wanted one.

"That's quite a ministry you have, Sam."

He bit down on the lemon drops, crushing them between his molars. Telling people what he believed and why was hardly a ministry. He would never be anything like his father. Robert McGarry had been a spiritual giant: a gifted evangelist and an amazing pastor and teacher.

"I'm not my dad," Sam said shortly. He turned to go.

"You're more like him than you realize." Something in Angie's tone made Sam turn around. She pulled off her glasses and laid them on her desk. "What's wrong, Sammy?"

He wondered how many times she'd said those words over the years. Since the first time he'd toddled to her house next door for a cookie, this generous woman had loved him like her own. Could she help him now? Could she answer the question that had been bouncing around in his mind for the past few days?

He walked over to her desk and slid into the chair next to it. "Explain something to me about Mom and Dad. They were…" He had to search for the word. "They were different, right?"

"A penniless seminary student and a sought-after debutante?" Angie's smile was wistful. "I'd say *different* barely begins to cover it. But they loved each other, so they made it work."

Sam wrenched his body out of the chair and strolled over to the window.

"Is this about the woman you took to lunch the other day?" Angie asked.

Sam grasped the cord attached to the mini-blinds and tugged, just for something to do. "She's different," he said, and then he lowered the blinds again and pushed his hands into his pockets to keep from fidgeting. "She's…fascinating." He regretted that last word when he turned and caught Angie's rapt expression.

"Sam. Are you trying to tell me you're in love?"

"No, nothing like that," he said quickly. "I just met her."

His mother's old friend chuckled. "Well, tell me what's so fascinating about her."

Sam returned to the chair and slumped into it. "Everything." Sure, she worried too much, but it was kind of cute the way she'd fretted about Reid's weak back and about Sam driving in the rain. And although she believed she was a coward, Sam had never seen a gutsier woman than the one who had stood up to Bill, determined to protect her sister even at the cost of her own life.

"What's she like?" Angie pressed.

"Indoorsy," Sam said, remembering the panicked look on her face when he had invited her skiing. "Bookish." He could see her passing up a hike in the woods in favor of an afternoon on the sofa with *Anna Karenina*. "And she's a chronic worrier."

Angie folded her hands on her desk and looked down at them.

"I know," Sam said, guessing the direction her thoughts had taken. "But I'm never bored when I'm with her. She's just so—"

"Fascinating," Angie said, drawing out the word.

"Angie?" Willa spoke from the doorway. "I have to run an errand for Reid, so you've got the phones, okay?"

"I've got the phones," Angie confirmed.

"Well, they're ringing." Willa pointed to Angie's phone, on which two lights were flashing.

Angie slid an apologetic look in Sam's direction. "We'll talk later."

"No, that's okay." He pushed himself out of the chair.

Why had he brought this up? Tori was looking for a husband, and Sam didn't stand a chance of making her short list—not that he wanted to. Family meant a lot to Sam, but he wasn't anywhere near ready to sign up for one of his own. He needed to figure out his own life before he got all tangled up in somebody else's.

But couldn't they just enjoy each other's company for a while? Where would be the harm in that?

Late on Friday afternoon, the package Wheldon College's archivists had been awaiting for three decades finally arrived. Tori's eager fingers trembled as she took the cutting tool Francine offered. About the size of her computer monitor, the box was much smaller and lighter than Tori had expected. But at least it was here.

"I don't get why the senator didn't leave us any money," Francine said. "His wife was gone and he had no children. Couldn't he have bequeathed something to the school?"

Tori slid her blade along a taped seam. "I'm just glad he kept his promise about these papers."

"Did you tell Dr. Goodman they were coming?"

"Last week." Tori sighed as she cut through more tape. "He didn't seem particularly interested."

"I don't know why I expected the college president to care," Francine said morosely. "Nobody does. Not anymore."

Tori put down her box cutter and gave her assistant a stern look. "We'll make them care again. We're going to bring the glory back to Wheldon College, Francine, and we're going to start with whatever is inside this box."

She hoped.

"You're right." Francine squared her shoulders and looked so fiercely determined that Tori had to suppress a smile.

Few people were aware that Wheldon College had been built by a plucky twenty-year-old woman. Tori was certain that once people were made aware of the college's history, they'd admire the founder just as Tori did—and they'd be eager to make donations to the school. To that end, Tori planned to celebrate the college's centennial next spring with a tribute to Elmira. In addition to a lavish display in the library, she and Francine were putting together a Web site detailing the founder's remarkable achievements.

Whatever was inside this box—Tori was hoping for a hefty stack of personal letters and perhaps even a few photographs—would be a welcome addition to the archive's Elmira Wheldon Danvers collection.

Tori's excitement rose as she folded back the four cardboard flaps, then drew a deep breath and removed the wad of bubble wrap that had kept the box's contents from shifting.

Francine leaned past her and peered into the box. "That's *all*?"

Tori swallowed her disappointment and pulled out the thin brown accordion file folder. "Something is better than nothing, right? And there must be *something* in here."

Tori laid the folder on her desk and carefully untied its fabric ribbon. She pulled out a stack of letters, all unfolded, their tops and left edges neatly aligned and held together by a large clip. A quick perusal showed that most of the letters were addressed to the senator. Only a few had been written by him and sent to others. There did not appear to be any letters written to or by Elmira.

Tori's excitement had evaporated, but she still intended to read every word of these letters. Surely she would learn something about Elmira's hobbies and interests or about her friendships and other associations. There had to be *something* here that would breathe a little life into the planned centennial exhibit.

"I'll leave you to it," Francine said as she gathered up the empty box and the packing tissue.

Two hours later, Francine had gone home and Tori was reading a letter from one of the senator's childhood friends when she turned a page and found something stuck to the back of it. Since all of the other papers had been neatly stacked and clipped together, Tori concluded that the thin ecru envelope had been caught behind the letter and not intentionally inserted there.

She turned the envelope over and frowned at it, surprised and puzzled. Hand-addressed to the senator at his Washington home, it was marked Personal. The envelope bore a Chicago postmark from eighteen years ago, but no return address.

It had never been opened.

Why would the senator have included an unopened envelope with this collection of letters that mentioned his mother? There was only one way to find out, so Tori reached for her brass letter opener and carefully slitted the top of the envelope.

With cautious fingers, she removed a single sheet of expensive-looking stationery and unfolded it. The note wasn't dated, and there was no salutation or closing. The message was brief and shocking. Tori read it a second time, whispering the words as if that would help her understand them better.

"I know you weren't expecting to hear from me again, but you have a right to know I'm pregnant. G. knows, and is supporting me. I don't want or need anything from you, and I will always be ashamed of what we did. K."

Tori gaped at the letter she held. Who had written it? And who was G.? A friend? A relative? That part about G. "supporting" the woman seemed to indicate she hadn't chosen an abortion. But if she had carried the baby to term, then—

Tori's heartbeat quickened. What if the senator was not Elmira's only descendant? He and his wife had been childless, and at the time this letter was written he would have been almost sixty-four years old. But what if this mysterious woman had actually given birth to his son or daughter?

Tori bit down hard on her bottom lip, quelling her mounting excitement by reminding herself that she was a professional. She dealt in facts, not speculation. This was probably nothing.

But what if Elmira *did* have a living grandchild?

Eighteen years ago, news of a married U.S. senator fathering another woman's child would have been scandalous. But both the senator and his wife were now deceased. And the child—if there *was* a child—would be an adult. Might he or she be eager to publicly acknowledge a blood relationship to a U.S. senator and to noted philanthropist Elmira Wheldon Danvers? And if so, wouldn't that garner some priceless publicity for the college?

Indulging in a moment's fantasy, Tori conjured up a lovely young woman, flaxen-haired, pale-eyed and slim; just like Elmira in the portrait that hung on the library's main floor. On a perfect spring day, the founder's grand-daughter stood before a microphone next to the old willow tree and exhorted the graduating class to pursue their dreams with the same single-minded devotion Elmira Wheldon Danvers had demonstrated.

Reason intruded on Tori's daydream, insisting that she might just as well expect to find a pot of gold at the end of the rainbow. And yet...

Was it completely outside the realm of possibility that God had entrusted her with a very special mission? In the college's darkest hour, this letter had fallen into the hands of its archivist. Surely that was significant.

Maybe the child had grown up unaware of her—or his— relationship to the senator and Elmira. But she—or he— would be eighteen now, according to the letter's postmark. An adult. And didn't a large number of adopted children eventually seek the truth of their biological parentage?

Tori rubbed a finger along one edge of the brittle pa-per. "Lord," she whispered. "Is there something here that You want me to find?" She carefully refolded the letter, then returned it to its envelope and locked it in one of her desk drawers.

"I knew there would be something in that box," she said to Theophilus as she opened his bottle of fish food. She sprinkled a few flakes into the fishbowl. "But we'll keep this to ourselves," she murmured as her new pet attacked his food. "Until we're sure there's a real story here and that nobody will be hurt if we tell it."

* * *

"You must get this all the time," Sam said in the middle of dinner on Tuesday evening, "but you're really beautiful."

Stunned, Tori paused in the act of twirling linguine with clam sauce onto her fork. "I never get that," she said with perfect sincerity. In face and figure she was as average as they came, so if she looked good tonight it was because she was wearing her favorite dress. It was deep red and lent her skin a rosy glow while playing up the highlights in her chestnut hair. Its light fabric skimmed her body in a way that flattered without being indecent. But although Tori felt almost pretty tonight, *beautiful* was quite a stretch.

"Nobody *tells* you that?" Sam put his fork down and shook his head in apparent amazement. "I don't mean to criticize, Victoria, but it sounds like you've been dating some spectacularly stupid men." He shook his head again and went back to his seared tuna.

Tori was glad for the restaurant's dim light because she had to be blushing furiously. She forked up a clam and decided that if they didn't get serious about Sam's reading lessons tonight, she would simply refuse to see him again. She had no choice. No woman could hold up under this kind of siege.

Tonight he had taken charming to a whole new level. First, instead of his usual T-shirt and jeans, he'd shown up in black dress pants with a crisp blue shirt under a sport coat. If it hadn't been for that sun-kissed, too-long hair and those wild green eyes, Tori wouldn't have recognized him. Now his eyes were starry in the candlelight, his voice had become deep and honey-rich and he was saying she was beautiful.

"You didn't tell me about your weekend," he said.

Tori seized the opportunity to quash his inexplicable fascination with her by demonstrating her ordinariness. "On Saturday I watched the babies so Corinne could get out for a while and on Sunday I taught John 3:16 to a bunch of rowdy six-year-olds. I also made a special dinner for my dad's birthday. Oh, and I did the crossword in the *Tribune* and missed only two words. That's my personal best."

"Congratulations." Sam's eyes hadn't glazed over. In fact, he was bobbing his head and looking positively interested. "How's everything at the library?"

Tori hadn't planned on telling anyone about the letter she'd found, but Sam had her so rattled, she blurted out the news. "Something exciting has happened, but I can't share it with Francine or anyone at the college. I don't want to stir up hopes and then disappoint everyone. But I just have a feeling, you know?"

Sam put down his fork. "Tell me."

Regretting her outburst, Tori gave a self-deprecating shrug. "It will probably turn out to be nothing."

"Maybe not." Sam raised his eyebrows and tipped his head forward, encouraging her to go on.

"Okay." She drew a steadying breath. "I want to commemorate the college's centennial next spring by spotlighting our founder's life. I'm planning to put a display in the library and also develop a Web site that'll be linked to other sites celebrating women's achievements. The problem is, although Elmira was a renowned philanthropist, her private life was largely a mystery. Since the mid-seventies, our archivists have been hoping that Senator Danvers, her only child, would—" Tori stopped, wondering at the sudden widening of Sam's eyes.

"Senator Danvers," he repeated in a pinched voice as he reached for his iced tea. "You mentioned him once before."

"Yes," Tori said, puzzled by Sam's odd reaction to the name. "He was Elmira's son." She watched Sam gulp some tea. "What's wrong?"

"Nothing." He smiled, but there was an unmistakable wariness in his eyes and he returned his glass to the table in a clumsy move that wasn't like him at all. "Go on."

"No." Tori shook her head. "I really shouldn't have—"

"Please," he interrupted in a voice as soft as midnight.

Tori assured herself that she was imagining things, and her excitement came back in a rush. "We just received some papers the senator willed to us. And here's the exciting part, Sam: based on a letter I found, I'm pretty sure that eighteen years ago, Senator Danvers fathered a child out of wedlock."

Oh dear, that hadn't come out right at all. No wonder Sam's mouth was hanging open and he was staring at her as if she'd just sprouted an extra head. Tori flapped her hands, pushing her foolish words away. "I didn't mean that the way it sounded! Of course I'm not *excited* about the senator having a physical relationship with a woman he wasn't married to. That's not romantic or admirable in any way."

Sam had closed his mouth, but his jaw was flexing and he wouldn't meet Tori's eyes. She watched in amazement as the man who was as transparent as a freshly-washed window struggled against his very nature and attempted to conceal his reaction to her news.

But what was wrong? If the senator had fathered a child outside of his marriage, what could it possibly matter to Sam?

Chapter Seven

Sam focused all of his energy on breathing normally. Everything was fine. Tori couldn't possibly know about—

He stopped himself, afraid to even think the name, lest he somehow transmit it to her brain. He was no good at secrets and lies, so he had no idea how he was going to pull this off. He swallowed hard and tried desperately to look and sound only mildly curious. "Why would you be interested in a scandal like that?"

Uncertainty flickered in Tori's sweet brown eyes. "I'm not interested in a scandal," she answered in a subdued tone that made Sam feel lower than dirt. "I'm just going to do some discreet research and find out if Elmira has a living descendant."

"And then what?" Sam thought his voice sounded surprisingly natural for a man whose heart and lungs had ceased operating.

"That depends on what I learn. But Sam, you know a lot of adopted children go looking for their birth parents after coming of age." Her excitement returned in a flash and she reached across the table and grasped Sam's wrist. "And *this* child would be eighteen now."

Not yet, Sam thought bleakly. Not for another three months.

Tori's dark eyes shone. "All I have to go on is a brief handwritten letter from a woman who told the senator she was pregnant with his child. She signed it with just an initial, K. The envelope has a Chicago postmark with a clear date on it. That's all I know, but I'm feeling very optimistic."

Good for her. Sam was feeling sick. What a horrible, unbelievable coincidence. How had Tori stumbled onto this?

She squeezed his wrist. "I don't intend to out anybody, Sam. But if Elmira's grandchild chooses to acknowledge the relationship, the publicity could generate donations and save the college. And if that happens, the college will hardly go looking for a more experienced archivist. Not if it's my initiative that ushers in the new prosperity."

What was he supposed to say? He couldn't admit he was keeping a confidence, but *not* telling her felt dishonest. Sam wasn't anywhere near the Christian he ought to be, but deceit wasn't one of the temptations he struggled with. He had never learned how to lie. He couldn't even manage those little polite lies everyone else told so easily.

Despair gripped his heart as he looked down at the graceful hand covering his wrist. What did God want him to do?

Tori followed his gaze and withdrew her hand. "I'm getting carried away. I don't even know that there *was* a baby. Something might have happened. Which is why I'm not going to mention this to anyone else."

"Good plan," Sam said, a little more heartily than he'd meant to. "Get all the facts first." If God answered the urgent, silent prayers Sam was shooting toward heaven right now, Tori would never get anywhere with her investigation.

"I know it's an impossibly big dream." Her shoulders slumped and her voice turned husky as she looked down at her plate. "But sometimes even impossible dreams come true."

"Sometimes." Sam kept his tone noncommittal.

She looked up and caught him with a soft brown gaze that pleaded with him to be on her side, to root for her. "This could be very wonderful for me, Sam."

And horrible for an innocent kid. If only he could explain that Tori would understand and she'd stop digging around in this minefield before it was too late.

With a fingertip she traced small patterns in the condensation on her water glass. "I shouldn't have said anything."

He caught her hand in his. When she looked up, startled, he gave her as much as he could. "I get that you're excited about where this might lead." He cleared his throat, dislodging some of the fear that had stuck there. "I'll be praying about it," he added with perfect sincerity.

She beamed him a smile of gratitude that made the back of his neck tingle. "Thank you, Sam."

He squeezed her hand and let it go. "Save room for dessert," he said, relief lightening his tone. "They serve a killer tiramisu here."

"Let's get it to go," she said. "We can have it with coffee at my place."

Now that they'd made it out of the minefield, Sam relaxed and grinned at her. "You're going to make me read."

He'd been hoping they could skip that tonight and just enjoy each other's company.

She gave him an arch look. "That's what this is all about."

Sam just smiled. He'd be grateful for any help she could give him on the reading, but that was *not* what this was all about.

Naturally, Francine wanted to know everything about what she believed was Tori's third and final date with Sam. Tori wasn't ready to talk about it, so she shooed her assistant out of her office, then propped her elbows on her desk and rested her chin on her clasped hands and tried again to organize her jumbled thoughts, starting with the ones about Sam asking for a kiss last night.

Just before leaving her apartment, he'd bent his head to Tori's and asked in a bone-melting voice if he might kiss her. Fortunately, Tori had studied for that particular test, so she answered with the stark honesty she'd learned from Sam: no, because she'd probably *like* kissing him, and they both knew they weren't headed for a serious relationship.

He'd gone ahead and pressed his lips against her cheek, which seemed harmless enough, but then he'd given her an enigmatic smile. Having grown accustomed to his guilelessness, Tori felt at a distinct disadvantage; just when she'd boldly decided to match Sam's candor, he had turned inscrutable.

Which brought her back to all that dissembling he'd done at the restaurant. He'd been upset about something, no question. But he hadn't owned up to it and that wasn't like him.

She shouldn't have told him about that castle she'd built

in the air, in any case. Even if Elmira *did* have a grand-child—and that was a very big *if*—the chances of every-thing coming together as Tori hoped were ludicrously slim.

She shook her head at her brilliant blue fish, who was waving his fins and blowing kisses. "Maybe it is a ridicu-lous dream, Theo. But right now, it's all I have."

"Beg pardon?" Francine bustled into the office with an armload of folders.

Tori smiled ruefully but didn't look up. "You caught me talking to my fish."

"Not my business," her assistant said with a theatrical air of unconcern.

"I like having a pet," Tori said, still watching Theophi-lus swish around in his bowl. "I've never had one before."

Francine grunted as she deposited the folders on Tori's credenza. "Girl, that's not a pet. It's a desk decoration."

Tori cupped protective hands around the fish bowl. "Don't listen to the mean lady, Theo."

Francine snorted her amusement and left the room.

Tori continued to study her fish. She wasn't really talking to him, just thinking out loud. She liked doing that and she liked watching the graceful undulation of his fins and tail.

Sam had been right. Having a pet was good for her.

But Sam wasn't. At least, not in the romantic sense. But while the date portion of last night had been troubling, the tutoring session had gone extremely well. Tori had given Sam a few preliminary tests and identified his strengths and weaknesses. Confident that she could help him, she had entered his credit card number on an Internet order form and purchased a learning program. The materials would arrive in two business days, so Sam had agreed to return to Tori's apartment on Friday evening. They would order a pizza and make it a working dinner.

Tori's chair squeaked as she leaned back in it and stared at an ancient crack in the ceiling's dingy white plaster. There would be no more meals at romantic restaurants. If Sam insisted on dinner, they would have something delivered. From now on, their meetings would be strictly business.

Tori felt a slow, satisfied smile curve her lips. It felt good to be back in control.

Behind the massive mahogany desk in his spacious Sears Tower office, Grayson Traynor looked every one of his forty-eight years as he closed his pale blue eyes and massaged his temples with long fingers. "Does anyone else know?"

Sam halted his energetic pacing on the thin Oriental rug and slid his hands into his pockets. "I don't think so."

"It's an unbelievable coincidence." Gray ran a hand through his prematurely white hair. "What were the odds that a woman you're dating would just happen across that letter?" He shook his head. "Astronomical."

"I don't think in terms of odds," Sam said, echoing the standard reply his father had made whenever Sam or Reid slipped and mentioned something about luck or chance. "I believe in the sovereignty of God."

Gray snorted. He prided himself on his clear thinking and he'd never had much use for what he called God talk.

"God *allowed* this," Sam insisted, returning to his pacing with renewed vigor. "There was a reason for it."

"It couldn't have been a *good* reason," Gray muttered.

Sam glanced at the floor, sparing a brief thought for the possibility that he might be wearing a path along the edge of what was surely a priceless antique carpet. Figuring the polished parquet floor could better stand his abuse, he shifted his path a couple of feet closer to the wall of windows. "Did you know she'd written to him?"

Gray's answer came after a brief hesitation. "Yes."

A horrible thought brought Sam to another halt. "Do you think there might be any other letters?"

Gray plucked a golf ball off his desk and rolled it between his finger and thumb, studying it. "There weren't any others." After a moment he raised his eyes to Sam, his expression calculating. "What's Victoria like?"

"Tenderhearted. Fiercely loyal. You can't buy her, Gray."

Gray squinted one eye and aimed, then whipped back his arm and fired the golf ball across the room. With an angry *ping* it struck a small brass sculpture, knocking it off a marble-topped table.

Sam folded his arms and waited.

Gray rested his elbows on his desk and rubbed his temples again. "This has been eating at me for years. Was I wrong to make that promise? Am I wrong to keep it?"

"I don't know," Sam said wearily. "But when this house of cards comes crashing down, I'm not going to let you blame Tori."

The phone on Gray's desk buzzed. He ignored it and leveled a penetrating gaze at Sam. "You're falling for her."

"She's teaching me how to read," Sam corrected.

"I'll just bet she is," Gray said, looking smug.

Sam walked across the room and picked up the sculpture Gray had knocked to the floor. He weighed the brass piece in his hand for a moment, then replaced it on the table. "Nothing's happening with Tori." That was what she kept telling him, anyway. Did he believe it?

He tilted his head to one side, considering, then he flipped the little sculpture over to see if it looked right *that* way. He couldn't tell. He didn't know what the jumble of metal was supposed to *be*, so how could he know which end was up?

And if he couldn't figure out a stupid little piece of art, what hope did he have of sorting out his confused feelings for Tori? "We're too different," he said finally.

Leaning back in his enormous leather chair, Gray waved a hand, dismissing that. "If she's important to you, you'll work things out."

Sam wandered over to the windows and gazed out at the sapphire expanse of Lake Michigan. Even if he could somehow get Tori to accept what he did for a living—and, okay, what he did just for the fun of it—they'd still have this other problem. How could he build a relationship on top of a lie?

Maybe it wasn't a lie, exactly. But it had sure felt like one when she'd looked into his eyes and he'd had to look away before she guessed he was hiding something.

Gray's irritated sigh broke the stillness. "The senator's *dead*. Why does Victoria care what happened all those years ago?"

"This isn't about the senator," Sam said. "Tori's not looking for a scandal, just a spokesperson. She's convinced that trotting out a living descendant of her college's founder will attract publicity and bring in donations to save the school."

"Oh, it'll attract publicity, all right." Gray's tone was resentful.

"She doesn't realize where this is headed, Gray. She's just caught up in her dreams." Was it so difficult to understand she was grasping at straws to save her college? "If she knew what was at stake, she'd let this go. So if I could just tell her—"

"*No.*"

"All right." Sam closed his eyes briefly. He had given his word and he would keep it.

Gray eased out of his chair and walked around to the front of his desk. Leaning a hip against it, he pushed a hand through his hair. "I'm sorry, Sam. I do realize you're caught in the middle."

He was. And if Tori ever found out that he had known the truth all along… Well, he couldn't bear to think about how hurt she'd be.

"We won't mention this to Kath," Gray said. "I don't want her worrying about this, not on top of losing Rich."

Rich. As always, Sam's gut twisted as he pictured his best friend's body lying at the bottom of a rocky ravine. Not that he blamed the other climbers for leaving it there. Recovering Rich's body from the "death zone" of Mount Everest had never been an option.

Everyone who ventured up to that barely survivable altitude knew the score: even if you were ill or injured, you had to make it back under your own power. Any climber who sacrificed part of his own strength to help you was ensuring *two* deaths. Heroism wasn't unheard of, but those risks were undertaken only for the living. The dead had to be left on the mountain.

It had been hard on Kath, not having a body to bury. And it had been hard on Sam, who knew exactly where Rich's body rested on the windswept mountain they had once climbed together.

Gray stared at his shoes. "She hasn't accepted it yet."

Who had? They'd lost Rich five months ago, just a month before he and Gray's sister had planned to be married. The tragic irony was that after years of pursuing Kath, Rich had finally convinced her that being ten years his senior was no barrier to their love. And then he had died.

Sam shook off those sad thoughts and returned to the matter at hand. "Are you absolutely sure about—"

"I'm sure." Gray rubbed the top of one shoe against the back of his pant leg, polishing it, then held his foot out to study his work. "What, exactly, did the letter say?"

"Just that she was pregnant. And she didn't sign her name, just her first initial."

Gray's head jerked up. "That's all? Just her initial?" When Sam nodded, Gray looked profoundly relieved. "Then you're worrying for nothing. Nobody can prove anything, Sam. The press sure never smelled any scandal. So if your Victoria doesn't even have a name, she's not going to uncover anything."

Sam wasn't so sure. "She's smart, Gray. And motivated."

Gray's phone buzzed again, and this time he reached for the receiver. "We'll be fine," he said, and then he turned his attention back to business.

A glance at the wall calendar next to Tori's desk told her Christmas was just two months away. Humming the first few notes of "Silver Bells," she opened her appointment book and penned a note on Saturday's page: *Start making Christmas lists.*

She adored every one of the traditions that drew people together to celebrate the birth of the Savior. Christmas was the sweetest, best season of the year—and Tori had long cherished a dream of being a Christmas bride. In her imagination, she had often hung glossy holly and big satin bows on the ends of the pews in her church. And more than once she had pictured herself clutching a bouquet of scarlet roses as she floated up the aisle on her father's arm.

As she doodled a wreath of pointy-tipped holly leaves around the note she'd just made, she reflected that her thirtieth birthday was less than three years away. She was eager to have children, so it was time to get serious about finding a husband. If she didn't get married by next Christmas or the Christmas after that…

A throat was cleared sharply and Tori looked up to find Alice Richer, the college's eternally grumpy head librarian, standing in the doorway.

"Good morning," Tori said in a fairly chirpy tone, considering that her spirits had just taken a nosedive. Alice's rare visits to the second floor were never pleasant occasions.

As though she had just read that thought, the head librarian's eyes narrowed to slits and her pruney lips pursed even tighter. A wisp of gray hair escaped from her tight little ponytail and she ruthlessly shoved it away from her face so it wouldn't interfere with the glare she was giving Tori. "I would appreciate it if you would come downstairs occasionally and give us a hand at the reference desk," she said.

That comment was unfair, as Tori spent two hours at the reference desk every morning. She loved interacting with the students and steering them toward the research materials they were looking for. But she had other work to do, as well.

"I'm sorry, Alice. Ten hours a week is all I can manage right now. Unlike Dr. Grant, I have just one assistant."

"We're all making sacrifices," Alice retorted.

Tori instantly regretted mentioning her predecessor's name. Dr. Grant had been a faculty member and as such reported to the vice president of academics, not the head librarian. When he'd retired and budget cuts had prevented a replacement from being sought, Tori had assumed his title along with most of his responsibilities, if not a commensurate salary. But Alice felt Tori should have been placed under her supervision rather than being made an equal who reported to the same boss she did.

She was probably right, but at present they were all doing well to keep their jobs. What was the point in quibbling about titles and power structures *now*?

"I don't know why I'm bothering," Alice grumbled. "You won't be around here much longer, anyway."

So that was why Alice had come upstairs. Tori's heart sank another few inches. "Have you heard something?"

Alice's wrinkly mouth curled into a tight smile. "You might want to start polishing your résumé."

Alice wouldn't say any more. When she left, Tori looked at her fish and sighed. "What's going to happen to us, Theo?"

Francine appeared in the doorway. "What did the old harridan want?"

"She was hinting at staff cuts," Tori said wearily. Alice wasn't exactly a sweetheart, but she wasn't a liar, either, and she'd just intimated that she knew something. "If you want to start job hunting, Francine, I'll understand. In fact,

I'd better write your glowing reference this week, while I can still sign it as Wheldon College's archivist."

Francine sagged against the door frame. "What about you?"

"Me?" Tori drummed her fingers on her desktop. Thanks to her careful spending habits and that worried eye she kept on the future, she had three months' salary in the bank. "I'll go down with the ship," she said.

Her gaze drifted to the window. Even seated at her desk, she could see the top of the old willow tree. "A hundred years," she said glumly, thinking about Elmira, the feisty young woman who hadn't let go of her dream. "For a hundred years, this was a great school."

"It's still a great school," Francine said with spirit. A phone rang in the outer office, but as she backed away, Francine stabbed a finger in Tori's direction. "This isn't over yet. Don't forget that with God, all things are possible."

Yes, but Tori couldn't help worrying. She hated not being in control, not knowing what awful thing might happen next. If only she could *do* something.

Well, maybe she could. Just as soon as she could manage it, she would carve out some time to play detective and find out where the senator's mysterious letter had come from.

Maybe her dream would come true, just as Elmira's had. Maybe she wouldn't go down with the ship, after all.

Maybe God would help her *save* the ship.

Just after midnight on Wednesday, Tori sighed and turned away from her front door. Of course it was locked. She'd locked it when she'd come in, and she'd double-checked it while waiting for her bathtub to fill. But after climbing into bed she'd popped right back up and headed for the living room, needing to reassure herself that she was safe.

"Lord," she whispered into the darkness as she again pulled the quilt up to her chin, "I hate living this way. Please help me let go of these foolish worries."

She tossed and turned for a while and had just drifted to sleep when a shrill ringing jolted her awake and threw her into a panic. Middle-of-the-night phone calls were always bad news, so as she rolled to her side and fumbled in the darkness for the phone, she braced herself to hear that one of her loved ones had suffered some kind of accident.

"Hi, honey." The masculine voice that responded to her breathless hello was warm and familiar. But who...

"Turns out they don't keep such a close eye on the loonies at this place," her caller remarked cheerfully.

Tori gasped and sat up. "Bill?"

"I know it's late," her brother-in-law said. "But I need to talk to you."

"Where are you?" she squeaked. He was still locked up, wasn't he? They couldn't possibly have let him go.

He ignored the question. "I just want to talk," he said in a perfectly normal tone.

"I d-don't think that's a g-good idea," Tori stammered.

"Tori, this is breaking my heart. I'm sorry about what I did. Can't we just talk?"

Tori attempted to moisten her lips, but her tongue was as dry as paper. "I don't think your...um, your doctors would advise that right now." She gulped a mouthful of air and the next batch of words came out sounding fairly calm. "But if they say it's all right, I'll come and visit you."

"No need for that. I'm coming to see *you*." A click on the line told Tori he'd hung up.

Stunned, she replaced the phone on her bedside table. Why would he have this free access to a telephone so late at night? And what had he meant about coming to see her?

The answer was obvious.

Tori clapped a hand over her mouth, cutting off a shriek of terror. Her first thought was to call the police, but what if Bill had phoned from somewhere nearby? What if he was watching her apartment at this very moment?

Reid. He would come and stay with her until the police arrived. But Tori didn't have his phone number and she wasn't about to step out her front door and stand there in the open while she leaned on his doorbell.

She flipped over to her knees and with her fist, pounded on the wall above her bed's brass headboard. "Reid!" she shouted. "Reid, wake up!" She pounded again.

"Tori?" His muffled voice was husky with sleep and confusion.

"Reid! Can you come over here? It's an emergency!"

"On my way!" he yelled back, sounding fully alert.

Tori reached for the lamp, then changed her mind. The dark felt safer. As she stabbed her arms into the sleeves of her chenille bathrobe and fumbled to tie the sash, she remembered that Reid had been a firefighter. Surely he would be quick.

He was. He knocked on Tori's door just as she reached it.

"I think Bill has escaped," she said as she grabbed his arm and pulled him inside and locked the door. "He just called and said he was coming to see me. He sounded normal, not crazy at all, but I don't think they'd allow him to make phone calls in the middle of the night, so I'm really scared. I don't remember what he said, exactly, but it sent chills up my spine, and…oh, Reid, what if—"

"Okay," he interrupted, sliding an arm around her shoulders and giving her a light squeeze. "Stop talking for a minute and breathe. You did the right thing, banging on the wall. Have you called the police?"

She shook her head. "I'll do it now. I just didn't want to be alone for another minute."

"Don't turn on any lights," Reid said grimly. "And don't walk past any windows." He paused. "Give me your cell phone. I'll call Sam while you call 911 from your house line. He lives nearby, so he might even beat the police here."

"Sam?"

Reid was only a dark shape beside the front door, but somehow Tori was aware that he stiffened. "You don't want him?"

Yes, she wanted him, but she was afraid of what that might mean. "Yes, call him," she said, and was shocked to hear the words leap out of her mouth when her mind had been heading in the opposite direction.

She located her bag and felt inside it for her phone. "Call him," she said again, pushing the phone at Reid. "Please."

She'd deal with the ramifications of this decision later. Right now, she was just too frightened to pretend that she didn't want Sam.

Sam had friends all over the world, so being awakened by a ringing phone in the middle of the night was a fairly common occurrence. But he knew something was wrong when he switched on the lamp next to his bed and saw Tori's cell phone number—or something very close to it; he couldn't always count on his brain to provide the correct information when it came to reading numbers—on his caller ID display. Worry zinged through his gut as he grabbed the phone. *"Tori?"*

"It's me," Reid said. "Calling from her place. She's okay, but you should get over here."

Sam felt a sharp stab of fear. But Tori was *okay*, wasn't she? Hadn't Reid just said she was okay?

"She's on the phone with the police right now," Reid said. "Sam, her crazy brother-in-law just called. It sounds like he might be on his way over here."

"You keep her safe," Sam ordered as he snatched up his jeans from the floor. "I'll be right there."

He ended the call, confident that his brother would protect her even if it meant risking his own life. Nothing was going to happen to Tori. But *she* didn't know that, and right now she must be frantic. So with every cell in his body straining toward her, Sam grabbed his keys and his wallet and tore out of his apartment, praying as he ran.

Chapter Eight

Moonlight filtered through Tori's lace curtains, throwing shadows on the bare wood floor of her living room as she huddled on the sofa, her gaze fixed on Reid's reassuring silhouette.

Standing to one side of a window, he'd nudged back the curtain just enough to peek out. "They'll be here soon," he said.

Tori was glad the police were coming, but theirs wasn't the arrival she was so anxiously awaiting. She wasn't going to feel safe until Sam got there and looked into her eyes and told her she was all right.

She'd still been stammering at the police dispatcher when Reid had gently taken the phone from her and spoken to the woman himself. He'd given Sam's name, then described him and his truck. "We don't want the cops mistaking him for Bill," he'd explained to Tori as he hung up the phone. Now Reid stood beside the window, a silent sentinel watching the front walk, while Tori sat on the sofa hugging her knees and trying to pray.

"I see a police car," Reid said. "And here comes Sam."

Tori leaped to her feet.

"Don't open the door," Reid said quickly. "He's still in the parking lot. Wait until I give you the okay."

It seemed like years before he did that. But finally Sam was inside and Tori locked the door and fell into his arms.

"We're not going to let anything happen to you," he said against her hair. "Try not to worry." He eased her back a little, supporting her with one arm while he groped the wall behind him. "Which of these is the outside light?"

"The switch on the left," she answered.

She heard a soft click and light filtered through the curtains, enabling her to see his face. He looked down and smiled some courage into her.

"Did you make some new friends in the parking lot?" Reid asked.

Sam nodded. "They just got here. They checked my ID, then told me to come in and turn on this light, but no others. They're taking a look around the building."

"We've been staying away from the windows," Tori said.

"Good." Sam pressed a firm kiss against her temple.

Laying her head on his shoulder, Tori relaxed in his solid embrace. "Thank you for coming."

"Oh, he had no choice," Reid said dryly. "It's that Chinese thing."

"Shut up," Sam said without heat.

As Reid snorted in amusement, Tori burrowed deeper into the shelter of Sam's arms, not caring that the brothers appeared to be sharing some kind of joke.

"Bill won't get in here tonight," Sam said. "But you'll have to stay somewhere else until they catch him."

Tori understood that and was already working on a plan. "He knows my car, so I don't dare leave in it," she said, thinking out loud because she was so rattled.

Sam leaned away from her to give her an incredulous look. "You think I'd *let* you?"

She shook her head, not in answer to his question, but because she was still working things out. "My dad can be here in forty minutes. Will you stay until then?"

"No." Now he looked hurt. "I'll drive you."

Afraid that she was becoming dangerously dependent on him, Tori shook her head again. "It's really not necessary."

"Don't wait for your father," Reid advised. "If Bill shows up here, the cops will handle it. But I don't think you want to stick around and witness that."

No, she didn't. So after she changed into jeans and a sweater, she tossed a few things into an overnight bag and the men hustled her out to the parking lot. There they met two police officers who reported having taken a good look around the apartment building and found no suspicious activity. But Bill *had* escaped, so Tori was questioned about the phone call.

As she recounted her conversation with Bill, Sam and Reid shifted to stand slightly behind her; Sam at her right shoulder and Reid at left. That seemed odd until Tori realized they were guarding her back, shielding her with their own bodies from whatever evil might be lurking in the shadows.

Reid confirmed that in his usual blunt fashion. "We'd better get her out of sight," he said to the officers. "The last time Bill came to see her, he brought a gun. And he's too crazy to care that she's standing here with—"

Tori felt a lightning-quick movement behind her and heard a solid *thump*. Terrified as she was, she smiled when she realized Sam had just smacked his brother into silence.

"We'd better get going," Sam said.

Tori was shepherded to Sam's truck, where Reid helped her up to the passenger seat. When he stashed her bag behind it, Tori thanked him for all he had done, then grasped his shoulder and planted an impulsive kiss on his cheek.

He gave her a warm look, then smirked at his brother.

"Why is it," Sam grumbled, "that women are always so eager to kiss firemen?"

Reid laughed and closed Tori's door.

When they were safely on the road, Tori phoned her parents' house. Her sleepy-voiced father became instantly alert when she told him what had happened.

"You're sure you're okay?" he boomed.

"I'm fine, Daddy. I know you would have come after me, but Sam insisted on driving me home. And that seemed like a better idea than waiting around my apartment with Bill—" She closed her eyes and made herself say it. "With him *out* there."

Her father grunted his agreement, then added, "Sounds like this Sam might actually have a brain in his head."

Why did his voice have to be so loud? Tori glanced nervously at Sam, who had just stopped for a red light. He was staring straight ahead, but his mouth was twitching.

"How old is he?" Tori's father demanded.

"I don't know." Tori sealed the phone tightly against her ear, hoping that would prevent the sound waves from escaping. She'd probably burst an eardrum, but at least she might retain some dignity.

"I'm twenty-nine," Sam said, leaning toward her so the phone would pick up his voice. "I don't drink or smoke and I'm driving the speed limit."

Her father coughed. Tori widened her eyes at Sam, signaling him to be quiet.

He just grinned. "I've never been arrested," he practically yelled. "I'm a pastor's kid."

Tori's father made an odd strangling noise that turned into another cough. Was he laughing? Sam certainly was.

All this masculine jocularity was too much for Tori. She told her father she'd see him soon and she dropped the phone into her bag.

"Let me guess." Sam's voice quaked with amusement. "You weren't allowed to date until you were twenty-one."

"He's a little overprotective," Tori admitted. Eager to change the subject, she asked the first question that popped into her mind. "How did you chip your front tooth?"

Sam threw back his head and laughed again. "You *would* have to ask me that tonight." He rubbed a hand over the lower portion of his face, wiping off his smile. "It happened on a Ferris wheel when I was seventeen."

Tori rolled her eyes. "Sam, only you would try to climb a Ferris wheel."

"I wasn't climbing it," he said with a slightly aggrieved air. "I was *riding* it."

"What did it do," she asked sweetly, "buck you off?"

He gave her a long, patient look. "I was stuck at the top. With a girl. And just as I made my move to kiss her, the wheel jerked and started turning again and we got banged together."

The memory must have been especially vivid, because Sam shuddered. "I just about fainted when I had to face that

300-pound gorilla she called Daddy and explain why I brought his princess home with a split lip and a bloody shirt."

"*My* father has killed men for less," Tori deadpanned.

"I'm sure he has," Sam said with apparent feeling. The light changed and he proceeded through the intersection.

Tori eased up on him. "Sam, I'm kidding. Daddy's a sweetheart. Especially to anyone who asks about his worms."

Sam flicked a concerned glance in her direction. "Your father has worms?"

"He raises them. He sells them to bait shops."

Sam nodded thoughtfully. "Thanks for the tip."

Tori dipped her head, allowing her hair to swing forward and conceal her smile.

"You're so far away," Sam complained. "Come sit by me."

Yes. She needed to do that. Tori unfastened her seat belt and scooted across the bench seat. She pulled the other belt around her hips and clicked it, then leaned her head against Sam's solid shoulder, marveling that she felt so calm after that horrible scare with Bill. As she rubbed her cheek against the supple leather of Sam's jacket and inhaled its now-familiar scent, she wished with all her heart that the man who had saved her life would place a higher value on his own.

"Why do you do it?" she asked suddenly. "The adventuring."

His shoulder shifted under her as he reached to adjust the heater controls. "I like the challenge. Pushing my mind and body right to the edge of what's possible."

"But aren't you ever scared?" she asked, settling against him again.

"All the time. But scared is good. Scared is what gets your adrenaline moving, and that sharpens your focus." Stopping for another traffic light, he turned his head toward her, until his face was mere inches from her own. "Time slows down." His voice deepened as his gaze settled on her mouth. "Leaving you suspended in that single…perfect moment."

That sounded very poetic, but it was still crazy. "Doesn't it ever occur to you that you might be killed?"

If he'd been about to kiss her, those words had surely put it out of his mind. He turned his head and rested it on top of hers. "There have been a couple of times when I thought I wasn't going to make it. And five months ago my best friend was killed on Mount Everest."

"Oh, how awful!" Tori breathed. "I'm sorry, Sam."

He was silent for a minute and when he finally spoke, his voice went right through Tori's skin and made her bones vibrate. "Rich didn't do anything stupid. Sometimes bad things just happen."

"But didn't that make you stop and think?"

"Yeah." He sighed the word, then he lifted his head and eased his foot back onto the gas pedal. "It sure did."

Hope flared in Tori. "So you're thinking about quitting?"

"No." Illuminated by the blue-white light from under the dash, his lean jaw seemed to tighten. "I could park myself in a rocking chair and maybe live to see a hundred birthdays, but what would be the point? There'd be no joy in it."

An awful weight pressed on Tori's spirit. Nobody could take the risks Sam did without one day paying the ultimate price for his thrills. Tori was determined that when the inevitable occurred, she was not going to be the woman who received the phone call.

"Is this where I turn?" Sam asked a few minutes later.

Tori gave the necessary directions and soon saw her father pacing on the lighted front porch of his brick colonial-style house. As Sam's truck rolled to a smooth stop in the driveway, Blake Talcott tightened the belt of his robe and strode to Tori's door. He flung it open and pulled her into a fierce hug. "Are you okay?"

"I'm fine," she squeaked, barely able to breathe.

"I tried to call you back," he scolded. "Your phone was off."

"Was it?" She must have hit the wrong button when she ended their call. "I'm sorry."

"Mr. Talcott." Sam walked around the truck and thrust out his right hand. "I'm Sam McGarry."

Tori saw the speculative gleam in her father's eyes and knew Sam was in for a bone-crushing handshake. But he would be expecting this test, wouldn't he?

"Do you know if they've found Bill yet?" Sam asked a moment later. If his hand was pulverized, he had borne it manfully.

Tori's father looked at her. "That's what I was calling you about. He showed up at your place five minutes after you left."

"Five minutes," Sam echoed. "Praise God it wasn't any sooner."

"He didn't have any weapons on him," Tori's father said. "And he didn't fight this time. He said he just wanted to talk."

"I've seen how Bill *talks* to her," Sam said with surprising vehemence. "If he ever tries to get near her again, I'll—"

"Okay," her father interrupted, pushing a hand through

his bristly salt-and-pepper hair. "I understand the sentiment, but Bill's part of our family. This situation's complicated, Sam, and it's been hard on all of us. But we're grateful for all you've done."

They climbed the porch steps and entered the house.

"Is Mom up?" Tori asked in the foyer when her father pulled her into his arms for another of his lung-bursting squeezes.

"No," he said against her hair. "She didn't wake up when you called, and that was just as well because she'd have worried herself sick waiting for you to get here."

"Let her sleep," Tori said against his broad shoulder. "I'm fine, Daddy." Inhaling his familiar, spicy scent, she closed her eyes. "I just want to go to bed now, okay?"

"All right," he said, releasing her. "We'll tell your mother and call Corinne in the morning." He turned to Sam. "It's late. You can bunk in the guest room."

"Thanks." Sam's gaze swung to Tori. "Would that be okay with you?"

He wasn't sure of his welcome? That was a laugh, because Tori didn't see how she was ever going to let him go. Even now that she was safe in her father's house, she wanted Sam nearby. "Please stay," she said. "It's a long drive back."

Minutes later, when her father had gone back to bed and she had shown Sam to the guest room, Tori stood awkwardly in the upstairs hall, craving the comfort of a hug but afraid Sam would take it the wrong way. She was his friend and his reading tutor; she didn't want him thinking there was any chance she would ever—

He swayed toward her and covered her mouth with his.

Oh, the man knew how to kiss. Not that Tori was an expert. She'd never kissed anyone but Julian. Not that it had happened all that often, and not that it had ever made her see stars like this.

Sam pulled her closer. She went, promising herself she'd be sensible tomorrow. She'd stop feeling this way and she'd explain in language he couldn't possibly misunderstand that she could never be involved with a man who lived the way he did.

His warm mouth slid across her cheek. "You're safe now," he whispered in her ear. "Praise God, you're safe."

The words brought Tori to her senses. She pushed herself out of Sam's arms and pressed her fingers against her lips to stop their tingling. Too alarmed by her reaction to Sam's kiss to form a coherent apology, she just shook her head as she backed away.

Somehow, her boneless legs carried her to her old room, where she closed the door and collapsed onto the bed, stunned. She *wasn't* safe. She wasn't safe at all.

She was falling.

It was almost eight o'clock when Tori shrugged into her pink chenille robe, finger-combed her hair, and shuffled out to the upstairs hallway. Passing the guest room, she was unsurprised to find its door open and the quilt pulled neatly over the bed. This was a workday, so last night Tori had told Sam not to wait for her. She planned to check in with Francine and then take the morning off.

She was halfway down the carpeted stairway when the low rumble of a masculine chuckle—not her father's—drifted up to meet her, lightening her heart and quickening her step until she reminded herself that last night's kiss had been a terrible mistake. She padded silently through the family room and paused in the kitchen doorway.

In a pretty blue housecoat and slippers, with her soft brown hair in a charmingly-mussed ponytail, Tori's mother stood at the gas range pouring batter into an iron skillet. Sitting at his usual place with one beefy hand wrapped around a coffee mug and his face concealed behind a newspaper, Tori's father was grousing about the political news. And Sam sat in a pool of yellow sunlight, looking happy and perfectly at home as he pushed his fork into a thick stack of pancakes.

When he spotted Tori, his mouth curved into a devastating smile. He didn't rise from the table, as Julian would have done. He just sat there and smiled, so transparently glad to see her that her knees went weak with the wonder of it.

"Good morning," her mother sang from somewhere far away.

"Good morning," Tori murmured, still struggling to un-hitch her gaze from Sam's.

"You're not awake," Sam accused, his green eyes twinkling in the sunlight.

Oh, she was awake. She'd never been more awake in her life and she was noticing everything. Like the way the dark brown stubble covering his jaw made his teeth look even whiter. And how one wavy lock of sun-streaked hair flopped across his forehead, covering his left eyebrow and making her fingers itch to brush it back. And how his plain gray T-shirt hugged his shoulders and clung to his muscular chest.

Her mother saved her from Sam's blinding charm by

stepping in front of her and holding out a steaming mug of tea.

"Thank you," Tori said with real feeling, and then she remembered and lowered her voice. "Did Daddy tell you?"

Her mother's mouth tightened as she nodded. "It's over now and you're safe. Let's not think about it anymore."

That was Regina Talcott. She fretted constantly and talked endlessly about all the bad things that could happen, but when something awful *did* happen, she refused to discuss it.

Tori eased into the chair next to Sam's. "Morning, Daddy."

"Back at you, baby." He gave her a warm look over the top of his newspaper.

"Regina." Sam pushed his chair back. "Let me cook pancakes for a while so you can sit down and eat."

She demurred. Sam insisted. He was a guest, she said. Her pancakes were as good as his mother's, he said, and Regina gave up and sat down. Sam took over in the kitchen, making pancakes and refilling coffee cups as naturally as if he'd been part of these family breakfasts for years.

When he caught Tori watching him, he winked. She took a sip of tea to hide her involuntary smile.

Sam's eyes shone with mischief. "Wish I had one of those Kiss the Cook aprons."

Tori's mother, oblivious to Sam's innuendo, paused in the act of dragging a forkful of pancake through a puddle of maple syrup to beam a smile at him. But Blake's newspaper rustled and he shot an inquisitive glance at Tori. She dodged it by dropping her napkin, giving herself an excuse to slink under the table.

When the last pancake had been flipped, Sam sat down

and ate two more. He talked quietly with Tori's mother, but Tori noticed he was keeping an eye on her father. When Blake finally closed his newspaper and began to refold it, Sam sat up straighter and said in a deep, man-to-man voice, "Blake, I understand you raise worms."

"I sure do." Always eager to discuss his favorite subject, Tori's father tossed his paper onto an empty chair. "I started slow, just last year, but I'm having some real success. Did you know that under ideal conditions a thousand breeding worms can produce one and a quarter *million* offspring in just one year?"

"Wow." Sam shook his head in apparent admiration. "Are all worms the same or are there different kinds?"

Having just taken a long drink of coffee, Tori's father gestured with his cup as he swallowed. "Oh, there are different worms for different uses."

"Please, Dad." With the side of her fork, Tori cut off a bite of pancake. "Not at the breakfast table."

He gave her a brief, indulgent smile and went right back to his worm talk. "You take your Belgian Reds. Those are the ones for compost. Gardeners love those babies because they'll eat garbage faster than you can throw it out."

Tori put her fork down with a clatter. *"Daddy."*

He flicked her an apologetic glance and turned back to Sam, undaunted. "But those don't make the best bait. For bait, you want Red Wigglers."

Sam gave Tori a sympathetic look. "Blake, maybe we should continue this discussion somewhere else. I'd love to see your operation."

Tori exchanged an amused glance with her mother.

Calling that mess in the basement an *operation* had just won Sam her father's friendship for life.

"Sam's a charmer," her mother said as the men's footsteps receded down the basement steps.

"Mmm," Tori agreed, staring morosely into her tea.

"Honey." Regina cleared her throat. "I'm a little concerned about the way you're looking at him."

Join the club, Tori wanted to say, but she swirled the tea in her cup and remained silent. Sam's reckless flirting had unnerved her. She'd been hoping they could just forget about last night's kiss, but Sam was giving every indication of wanting to repeat it.

Too bad they couldn't. Tori was looking for a husband and she couldn't afford to get sidetracked by Sam.

"You just met him," her mother pointed out. "You can't know very much about him."

Tori knew he was brave, intelligent, compassionate and funny. She knew he was a Christian and a praying man. Wasn't that a lot to know about someone?

They'd known each other for only a short time, but they'd been through a lot together. Tori had laughed, cried, prayed and shared secrets with Sam. But while he was hardly a stranger, there was a part of him that Tori would never understand.

"Mom?" she asked suddenly. "How did you stand Dad's being a cop?"

Her mother looked startled by the question, but then she gave her head a sad little shake. "Not very well. If he was twenty minutes late getting home, I'd fly into a panic. You'd think after all those years I'd have gotten used to it, but I never did."

Tori sighed. "I could never get used to it, either."

Her mother's eyes widened in dismay. "Sam's a cop," she guessed.

"No," Tori said quickly. "He isn't."

The worry lines between Regina's eyebrows only deepened. "Honey," she said urgently. "When you walked into this room and saw him, your face—" She stopped, her gaze shifting to the basement door, which had been left ajar. She got up and closed it, then lowered her voice for good measure. "I know he saved your life, but—"

"Don't worry, Mom." Tori heaved herself out of her chair and went to stand before the bay windows, where she could toast her bare feet over the warm air blowing from the floor register. "I'm not in love with Sam." She was confident of that, if nothing else. Love was more than tingly feelings, her pastor always said. Real love was always accompanied by commitment. And Tori wasn't about to cross that line where Sam was concerned.

She folded her arms, hugging herself. "I refuse to worry myself sick over a man who risks his life for no good reason."

"What does he *do*?"

"Sam does extreme sports," Tori said bitterly. "He's a thrill-seeker. An adrenaline junkie. Sam goes over waterfalls in kayaks and he jumps out of airplanes and he does backflips on skis. And one of these days, he's going to get himself killed!"

Her mother looked horrified. "Oh, *honey*."

Tori dashed angry tears from her eyes and explained the rest. "Maybe if he had a job like Daddy's, where he was out there every day trying to make the world a safer place, I could learn to accept it. But I am *not* going to waste a single day of my life sitting by the phone, waiting to find out whether Sam has lived through his latest stupid adventure!"

In the basement, Sam's heart pounded nearly as hard as Tori's feet did on the floor above him as she ran through the family room and up the stairs to the second floor.

"These old houses," Blake said, casting a rueful glance at a heating duct in the unfinished ceiling. "The walls are solid, but you can hear all sorts of things through the vents." He turned to Sam and asked almost casually, "What exactly do you do for a living, son?"

Every bit of moisture in Sam's mouth had evaporated. "What she said," he rasped. He wasn't out there trying to make the world a safer place. He wasn't a cop like Blake or a firefighter like Reid had been. Tori had nailed it. Sam was no hero. He was nothing but a self-absorbed adrenaline junkie.

"I see." Blake tucked his chin against his chest and stared at the bare concrete floor. Long moments passed before he spoke again. "When I married Regina, I was a man with a dangerous job and she was a worrier. I thought she could learn to accept my being a cop and she thought she could get me to quit the Force." He looked up and drilled Sam with a look. "We were both wrong."

He appeared to be waiting for a response, so Sam nodded miserably.

"What I'm telling you, son, is that Tori is her mother all over again. And that's never going to change."

"Yeah." Sam cleared his throat, not that it did any good.

Suddenly desperate to get away, to be alone, he pushed out some more sandpapery words. "I guess I'd better be going." He offered his right hand to Tori's father. "I'm sorry."

Blake took his hand in a crushing grip. "Sam, it's not for me to judge how you spend your life. But my daughter *is* my business and you're not right for her." He squeezed the last of the blood out of Sam's hand, then let go. "I think you know that."

Yeah, Sam knew that. She'd been telling him that from the beginning. He just hadn't wanted to hear it.

"All I want is to see her settled and happy," Blake said. "And to be perfectly honest, Regina and I are hoping for some kind of announcement when Julian returns from—"

"Who's Julian?" Sam interrupted, his brain stumbling over the reference to another man.

Blake hesitated. "Julian Knowles. They've been dating off and on for years. I think it's always been a little more serious on *his* side, but she's never been interested in anyone else and that has to mean something."

Did it? She'd never said anything about any Julian.

"He's a good man," Blake said. "Solid. Dependable."

Oh, really. Well, if good old Julian was so solid and dependable, why hadn't Tori called him that first night, when Bill had almost killed her? And where had he been *last* night?

"He's a history professor," Blake continued. "He's been in Italy for the past several months, doing research for a book."

Several months? This guy could stay away from Tori for *months* at a time? Sam had been having trouble with mere days.

If Tori's father imagined she was pining for old Julian, he was mistaken. Last night she had been plenty glad to see Sam. She'd thrown herself into his arms and she hadn't been shy about snuggling next to him in the truck. And when he'd kissed her, she hadn't exactly run away.

No, she sure hadn't been thinking about any dusty old history professor last night, Sam reflected with grim satisfaction. Then he remembered the aftermath of that kiss; the shocked look in her eyes. And suddenly his jealousy was swamped by regret.

Why hadn't this Julian jerk caught the first plane back to Chicago after Bill assaulted Tori? If Julian had been a better boyfriend, Sam wouldn't be standing here right now watching all the color drain out of his world.

And Tori wouldn't be upstairs crying.

"He's good for her," Blake said.

Yeah, even inattentive Julian was probably better for Tori than Sam could ever hope to be. "I understand," he said, because he really did.

He just had one thing to settle before he could get out of here. "I was supposed to see her tomorrow night."

"I'll take care of it," Blake said, not unkindly. "You'd better just go."

Sam's feet felt like they were encased in iron boots as he trudged up the basement steps and opened the door at the top. Relieved to find the kitchen empty, he walked straight to the front door and then out to his truck. He didn't look back.

Tori showered and dressed, then dabbed some concealer around her eyes before applying a bit more makeup than usual. Looking into the bathroom mirror, she smiled hard and made herself hold it for a full minute. When she was certain Sam wouldn't guess she'd been crying, she went back downstairs.

She found her parents in the kitchen. Her mother sat at the table looking agitated and her father stood grim-faced by the window.

"Excuse me," Tori said, thinking she had interrupted a private disagreement. "I'm just looking for Sam. We should be going."

"He's gone," her father said. "Baby, sit down."

Confused, Tori sank onto a chair beside her mother. Why had Sam stayed for breakfast and then left without her?

"Victoria." Her father's voice held a note of apology as he sat down across from her. "Sam and I overheard what you said about him."

Tori stopped breathing. "How much did he hear?"

"Enough to understand there's no future for the two of you. He did the right thing, leaving."

Not like this, she thought wildly. It couldn't end on this ugly note. She had said some harsh things to her mother, but she could have explained herself to Sam if she'd had the chance. She turned a mutinous look on her father. "I suppose you opened the front door and *invited* him to leave."

"Victoria," her mother said quietly, reminding her to use a respectful tone when addressing her father.

"He saved my life," Tori said. "And he's done other good things I haven't even told you about. You don't understand how much I owe him."

"You don't owe him your heart," her father said bluntly. "Baby, he's not right for you."

But he *was* right, in so many ways. Sam comforted her and encouraged her and made her laugh. He listened to her crazy dreams. He had even bought her a fish.

"It's easy to see why you're attracted to him," Tori's mother said. "And Julian's been gone for... What? Four months now?"

Tori clenched her hands and reined in her temper. "Mom, this has nothing to do with Julian."

"All right." The legs of her father's chair squeaked against the floor as he pushed away from the table and got to his feet. "There's no point in talking this thing to death. We had an awkward moment, but Sam took it like a man, so let's move on. How about I take you ladies out for some Thai food tomorrow night?"

Tori tossed her head in defiance. "I'm having dinner with Sam." Of course it was just a tutoring session, not an actual date. They were just going to order pizza, but Tori wasn't in any mood to explain that.

"Sam won't be able to make it," her father said.

"Dad." Tori gaped at him. "You can't cancel my dates."

"I didn't cancel your date. Sam did."

"He wouldn't have done that," Tori said, upset enough to hint that her father wasn't being completely truthful about the extent of his involvement. "Not without a good reason."

Her mother laid a hand on Tori's arm, another gentle reminder, but her father's gray eyes held the glimmer of an apology as he posed a quiet question: "Well, baby, didn't you *give* him a good reason?"

Chapter Nine

The blustery wind that rattled her office window every minute or two was doing nothing to soothe Tori's nerves. How was she ever going to apologize to Sam for what he had overheard earlier?

Giving her head an impatient shake, she pulled a legal pad off her credenza and slapped it onto her desk. She reached for a ballpoint pen, determined to map out a strategy for discovering the identity of the woman who had written to Senator Danvers.

She tapped the pen against her bottom lip, thinking. During his bid for the presidency more than a decade ago, he'd been a married man running on a family values platform, so even the slightest suspicion that the senator had once been involved in an illicit affair would have made front-page news. But as far as Tori knew, no scandal had ever been attached to his name.

"Which means this woman won't be easy to find," Tori mused aloud as she watched Theo swim in circles.

She wrote a single letter on her pad. *K* wasn't much to

go on, but it would help narrow the field of possibilities. Tori could rule out anyone whose first name or nickname didn't begin with that letter.

The wind howled again, scattering her thoughts. Frustrated, Tori threw down her pen and walked over to the window. Leaning both hands on the sill, she watched the willow tree writhe in the gusting wind, its slender branches whipping and twisting back on themselves just as Tori's thoughts were doing now.

Exactly how much of her conversation with her mother had Sam overheard?

Behind her, the old wood floor creaked. Tori turned to see who had come into her office.

"More flowers for you," Francine sang. "I don't know about you, but I'm in love with Sam. At least, I'm assuming that's who these are from." She set the tissue-wrapped vase on a corner of Tori's desk and peeked at the flowers. "Red roses!" she squealed, immediately setting to work unwrapping them. She detached a small pink envelope and thrust it at Tori.

Tori's eyes stung as she withdrew a card covered with Sam's now-familiar scrawl and read what he had so painstakingly written: Tory I will miss you but I undrstand. Im sorry for makeing you worry. Sam

So he wasn't holding it against her. She should have known he wouldn't. But rather than bringing relief, Sam's forgiveness intensified her regret.

"You have to keep seeing him," Francine gushed, too excited about the roses to pick up on Tori's depressed mood. "He's the best thing that's ever happened to you."

Tori swallowed, then waved the card at her assistant. "This is a goodbye note."

"He's *dumping* you?" Francine's voice rose in outrage.

"No. I chased him off."

"Are you *insane*?" Francine shrieked.

"Not yet. And I'm trying hard to keep from ending up that way." Tori inhaled deeply. "He kissed me last night."

"Hold on." Francine raised a hand. "Last night? You didn't tell me you were going to see him last night."

"I can't talk about it, Francine. Just let it go."

Francine studied her face for a moment and then spoke with a quiet intensity. "Girl, that must have been some kiss."

Fighting off the too-vivid memory, Tori shut her eyes. "Let it go. Please."

After a long, compassionate silence, Francine left the office, pulling the door shut behind her.

Tori caressed one perfect rosebud with a fingertip. Whenever she'd dreamed of her Christmas wedding, she had always pictured herself carrying scarlet blooms just like these. But she would have to design a new bouquet now; she would never again see red roses without thinking of Sam.

She walked around the desk and plopped wearily into her chair, then opened her middle desk drawer and dropped Sam's card inside.

This was for the best. Sam McGarry was an amazing man and she didn't want to forget him. But she couldn't see him ever again.

Since Sam's Friday evening plans had fallen through, he agreed to join Reid and some friends for a weekend fishing trip. Reid had left the office early on Friday, so at five o'clock Sam saw Angie and Willa out, then locked the front door, pocketed his keys and called Reid from his cell phone.

"I'm leaving now," he said, heading down the sidewalk to where his truck was parked at a meter. "Pick me up as soon as you can get away."

"Go ahead and swing by here," Reid said. "The cable guy just finished, so I'm ready to go."

"It's not—" Sam sidestepped three giggling girls who weren't looking where they were going. "—Uh, convenient for me to pick you up."

"It's on your way home," Reid pointed out. He paused for three seconds, then asked, "Are you hiding from Tori?"

"No." Sam unlocked his truck. "I'm just doing my best not to run into her."

"Why?"

"It's complicated." Sam heaved himself up into his seat.

Reid paused again. "You haven't known her long enough for things to have gotten complicated."

Sam pinched the bridge of his nose, where a tension headache was beginning to make itself felt. "I'm afraid I have."

"I knew it," Reid said with palpable disgust. "Sam, I *warned* you about this. I told you to leave that sweet woman alone."

"I know," Sam said, automatically lifting his free hand in a weary, give-it-a-rest gesture. "I just didn't think it could get this serious, so I—"

"*How* serious?"

Sam dropped his hand. "Serious enough for her father to warn me off."

"Why? What's wrong with *you*?" Loyal Reid aborted his tirade to take offense on Sam's behalf.

"I don't have a safe, nine-to-five job," Sam said flatly.

"Oh. That." Reid, always so sure about everything, seemed at a loss for words. "No, I guess that wouldn't endear you to a woman's father," he said finally.

No. And Sam couldn't fault Blake for wanting better for his daughter.

"I'll call when I get to your place," Sam said. "I won't come to the door, so be ready."

The visitors' lot was full when Sam arrived at the apartment complex, so he borrowed a reserved space and phoned his brother. Reid was on another call, but promised to be right out. Sam dropped the phone into his pocket, then leaned his head back and closed his eyes. His headache had just reasserted itself, so he felt for the button and lowered his window, hoping some cold air would revive him.

When a chilly breeze carried a familiar floral scent to his nostrils, Sam's eyes flew open and he jerked upright in his seat.

"Hi." Tori's smile was the polite kind she might have bestowed on a stranger. "You're in my spot."

Sam blinked at her, wondering why she was wearing sunglasses at dusk. "Your spot," he repeated stupidly.

Her smile seemed frozen on her face. "My parking spot."

Sam glanced at his side mirror and saw her car stopped behind him, its driver-side door ajar. When he looked back at her, she kicked her artificial smile up a notch and he realized what the sunglasses were for.

"Tori," he said wearily, "Could we please not do this?"

Her silky hair swung over her shoulder as she tilted her head to one side. "Could we not do what?"

Sam made an impatient gesture with his hand. "This awkward, polite thing."

Her eyebrows rose over the glasses. "You would prefer to be graceful and rude?"

Sam was in no mood for jokes. "What I would prefer is for us to be friends."

"We *are* friends."

"Then why are you hiding from me? How about losing the shades?"

She pushed the glasses up on her head, pulling her hair back in a way that showed off her pretty cheekbones. Then she just stood there, looking beautiful and making Sam's chest hurt.

"Satisfied?" she asked in that low, musical voice.

"Not anywhere near," he muttered, staring at her mouth.

"Stop it, Sam."

He shifted his attention to her eyes. "I suppose I'd better," he said, allowing a dash of sarcasm to darken his tone. "You don't want to get in trouble with your boyfriend."

She looked startled. "What boyfriend?"

"Julian." The name tasted sour in Sam's mouth. "Somehow you never got around to mentioning him."

Her dark eyes flashed. "I guess that explains why you left without saying goodbye."

"It seemed like the smart thing to do," he said evenly.

"Daddy chased you off." She shook her head in disgust.

"It wasn't like that." Sam's body needed to twitch, but he held still. "Your father just explained a few things, that's all. Some things I think *you* might have explained."

"There was nothing to explain," she snapped. "Julian has nothing to do with—" She stopped and gave an exhausted little sigh. Sliding her hands into her pockets, she stared at the pavement. "I don't want to argue with you, Sam. I just want to thank you for the roses and tell you I'm sorry about the way everything happened."

"Yeah." Fairness compelled him to admit this wasn't anything she could have helped. "I'm sorry, too."

"We met under unusual circumstances," she said. "In the normal course of things, you and I might have crossed paths, but we'd never have…um…"

"Gotten involved?"

"I'm not sure *involved* is the right word, but—"

"It is for me," he said. It was absolutely the right word. He'd been involved since the moment she'd fainted in his arms. And the more he saw her, talked to her, thought about her, the more deeply involved he got.

And the more she pretended not to see it, not to *feel* it.

"You know what I'm saying, Sam." Her impatient tone rekindled his annoyance. "If we'd met in a different time and place, you would never have asked me out. And this—" She pulled a hand out of her pocket and gestured vaguely. "This would never have gone anywhere. Just admit that, please."

"No. I don't play what-if games. Let's deal with what happened."

"Fine," she shot back. "What *happened* has caused a world of regrets and hurt feelings. I'm sorry you overheard my conversation with Mom and I'm sorry Daddy interfered. I wish you and I could have talked things over in private." She paused for a breath, then spoke more gently.

"The end result would have been the same, but it might have been easier on both of us."

"Yeah." Sam realized he was drumming his fingers against the steering wheel and stopped. "Well, I guess we've talked it over now."

Tori nodded emphatically. "And we're still friends." She hesitated, then added, "I hope?"

"Friends." Despair slid through Sam as he participated in the lie. "Absolutely."

They weren't friends. Her orderly mind was already processing their relationship, carefully folding it and tucking it away in a neat little box she would never open again.

"Hey there, neighbor." Reid approached Sam's side of the truck with a tackle box in one hand and three fishing rods in the other, a battered nylon backpack swinging from one shoulder.

Tori had no trouble finding a genuine smile for *him*.

Coming to a stop beside her, Reid flashed a concerned look at Sam. "Am I interrupting something?"

"No," Sam said, his eyes steady on Tori's. "Just two *friends* talking." He saw her wince at the emphasis he placed on *friends* and immediately regretted his snide tone.

She slid her sunglasses back on, hiding her eyes, and then she brightened her smile for Reid. "Looks like a fishing trip."

"Yep." Reid moved past her to stow his gear in the truck bed. "We're going out on a friend's boat."

"Well, you guys be careful."

Sam stared at her glasses, frustrated by his inability to penetrate the dark plastic. "Tori…"

She shook her head at him and turned away. Sam sat

back in his seat to watch her reflection in his side mirror as she walked to her car.

Reid leaned his hand against the truck's cab, blocking Sam's view. "What's going on?"

"*Move*," Sam growled.

Reid stepped back.

Tori opened her car door and turned. "Hope you catch something good!"

Reid raised one hand in a casual acknowledgement, then he walked around the front of the truck to the passenger side.

Sam closed his eyes briefly. He almost *had* caught something good. But when he'd tried to reel her in, she'd slipped off his line.

"Is she okay?" Reid bounced onto the passenger seat and slammed the door.

"Oh, absolutely." Sam grabbed the Cubs ball cap tucked up under his sun visor and slapped it on his throbbing head. "Tori's just fine." He tugged the cap's bill down and reached for the radio controls.

"But you're not," Reid observed. After a moment he added, "I'm sorry."

Sam found an alternative rock station and cranked up the volume, not caring what it did to his head. "Don't feel sorry for me," he barked over the music. "Save it for the fish."

"I've gone a whole week without seeing him," Tori grumbled to herself one evening as she yanked a brush through her hair. "So why can't I go ten measly minutes without *thinking* about him?" She dropped the brush with a clatter on the bathroom countertop and pulled the cap off a tube of lipstick.

Everything was going to be normal again, she promised herself as she slicked color on her lips. Starting that night.

The night before, she had picked up Julian at the airport, but he had been too exhausted to talk. Tonight they'd have a wonderful dinner and they would discuss the Italian Renaissance or English poets or something equally fascinating that Sam knew nothing about.

"I can talk to Julian about *lots* of things," Tori muttered as she tugged open a drawer, swept the hairbrush and her makeup into it, and banged it shut.

She and Julian were compatible. *They* had similar interests. Which was why she was going to marry somebody exactly like him. She'd have a house in the suburbs and she'd drive the kids to soccer practice and then she'd hurry home to start dinner for somebody just like Julian, because *he* would be home at seven every night, not slamming an ice ax into some frozen mountain on the other side of the world, cheating death for the umpteenth time since breakfast.

That was how Sam's best friend had died. But had Sam taken the hint and scaled back his own risk-taking activities? *No.*

"You seem awfully tense," Julian remarked a few minutes later, when he stood with Tori just inside her front door. "Would you like to talk about it?"

"No." She gazed up into his sky-blue eyes and tried to smile. She needed this evening with Julian. His familiar ways would settle her nerves and help her ease back into her old life. "It just hasn't been a very good day, that's all."

One of Julian's perfect black eyebrows rose slightly, and a dimple appeared in his cheek as he smiled, handsome and urbane as ever. "Let's go make it better," he said, moving behind Tori and holding her coat for her to slide her arms into.

They were on their way out to Julian's car when they met Reid coming up the sidewalk. Tori introduced the men.

"I believe I owe you an enormous debt," Julian said as they shook hands.

Inwardly cringing at the proprietary sound of those words, Tori plastered a smile on her face. Reid shot her a puzzled look and even though she had nothing to feel guilty about, her gaze skittered away from his.

"Actually, it was my brother who saved her life." Cool and assessing, Reid's eyes flicked over Julian.

"Please convey my deepest gratitude," Julian said.

"Glad to." Reid's gaze shifted back to Tori. "He's away on a ski trip right now."

"Ah." Smiling, Julian lifted a hand to smooth his perfectly-styled hair. "I'm something of a skier, myself. I try to make it to Aspen twice a year."

"I've always enjoyed Aspen Mountain." Reid's smile was faintly mocking. "But it's a little tame for Sam."

Knock it off, Tori told him with her eyes. "Julian was the downhill star of his college ski team," she said proudly.

Modest Julian inclined his head. "That was fourteen years ago, Tori."

"Sam's in British Columbia," Reid said, forgoing any comment on Julian's accomplishments. "Heli-skiing," he added in a tone clearly meant to provoke Tori.

It did. "Heli-skiing," she echoed in dismay. Was Sam *trying* to kill himself? Needing some physical support, Tori threaded her arm through Julian's.

Apparently thinking she was asking for a definition, he patted her hand and explained. "They take helicopters to remote mountain peaks and then ski down. There are a lot of unknowns in the backcountry, so it's risky. And avalanches are such a serious threat that each skier has to carry a snow shovel and a rescue beacon."

Reid reached into his coat pocket and produced a business card for Julian. "If you ever want to try it, give me a call."

Tori gave Reid a hard look. He ignored it.

"Thank you," Julian said, tucking the card inside his own coat. Then he put his arm around Tori, smiling down at her as he pulled her close to his side. "But I imagine this lady would worry if I did something that dangerous." He dropped a swift kiss on the top of her head. "Wouldn't you, sweetheart?"

Sweetheart? Tori just looked at him, stunned.

He turned back to Reid wearing a distressed look that didn't appear quite genuine. "Oh, I beg your pardon, Reid. I'm sure your brother knows what he's doing."

Reid's eyes narrowed dangerously. "He does."

"He's flirting with disaster," Tori snapped.

"He'll be fine." Reid's flashing eyes added a silent *stop pretending that you care.*

Tori understood his fierce loyalty to his brother because she felt the same way about Corinne. But how could Reid blame her for backing away from Sam? What sensible woman wouldn't? People got hurt doing the things Sam did. Sometimes they even got killed.

"I'm keeping you two from something." Now coldly polite, Reid offered his hand to Julian and said it had been a pleasure to meet him. Then his gaze swung back to Tori. "I'll tell Sam you asked after him," he said pointedly.

Tori sizzled as she watched him walk away.

"Interesting man," Julian commented a minute later as he helped Tori into his gleaming black BMW. "What's Sam like?"

Like no man I've ever known, her heart answered, but she lifted one shoulder in a casual shrug. "He saved my life. I'm grateful to him, naturally."

"I'm not a fool, Tori." Julian's face darkened. "The subtext of that conversation was crystal clear."

Tori reached for her seat belt. "Let it go, Julian. Please. It doesn't matter anymore."

He made sure her coat was tucked inside the car, then he closed her door and walked around to his own side. He slid into the tan leather seat and stared hard through the windshield. "I did a lot of thinking in Italy," he said.

It was close, but Tori managed to hold back a groan of dismay. She knew exactly what Julian was about to say, so she racked her brain to find some way to prevent this proposal and save his pride.

"I'm thirty-four years old," he said. "And it's time for me to settle down."

"Oh, Julian, I—"

"Please." He held up a hand, but still didn't look at her. "Just let me say this."

He was going to be hurt whether Tori let him speak or not, so she nodded and waited for him to continue.

"I'm not a wildly romantic man," he said. "But I never got the impression you were looking for that. I always thought we'd be a comfortable fit, given our common interests and career goals and the fact that our families are so close. We're both Christians and we both want children. That's a stronger foundation than most marriages are built on."

There. He'd said it. And to Tori's immense relief he hadn't said anything about being in love with her. She laced her fingers together and stared down at them. "I'm sorry, Julian. I've often thought that if I made a list of all the qualities I wanted in a husband, I'd have a perfect description of you." She hesitated for a moment, then gave him the truth. "But there's always been something missing."

"Excitement?" he asked, finally turning his head in her direction.

She opened her mouth to say no, that wasn't it, she'd meant romantic love. But then it occurred to her that Julian might have meant that, too, so she closed her mouth and tried to bend her lips into a smile that would tell him how much she cared for him and how sorry she was.

She had admired him for years, but what she felt for him wasn't at all like what she felt for—

No. There was no point in completing that thought.

"I see." Julian's scornful inflection caught her by surprise. "So you're infatuated with Sam."

Infatuated. That was it. And that was *all* it was.

"A lot of women are drawn to reckless men." Julian's mouth twisted unattractively over the words. "But I'm surprised that *you* are. You've always been so sensible."

"Could we please not talk about Sam?" Frustration had sharpened her tone and she regretted that when she saw Julian's wounded look. She patted his arm to soften her rejection. "Nothing's changed between us, Julian." She looked him straight in the eye, meaning every word. "You're as dear to me as ever."

He looked only slightly mollified, so Tori went on. "I don't love Sam," she said slowly and distinctly, praying that it wasn't a lie. "He's not what I want and he never will be."

Julian placed a finger under her chin and lifted her face. "What about me?" he asked, studying her expression with an unnerving intensity. "Are you so certain I'm not what you want?"

Her gaze dropped like a stone. "I'm sorry, Julian."

He let her go. "Maybe I'm more exciting than you think," he said as he started the car. "One of these days, your old predictable friend just might surprise you."

Tori felt a twinge of worry. "What do you mean?"

"I mean," he said patiently, "that maybe you don't know me quite as well as you think you do."

Chapter Ten

❧

Alone on the rooftop of British Columbia, Sam stood knee-deep in sweet powder under a dazzling-blue November sky and whispered a heartfelt Thank You to God. Sam had traveled the world and seen some spectacular scenery in his twenty-nine years, but this Rocky Mountain panorama of jagged granite peaks and softly mounded snow beat out everything else.

The wild mountains were as unpredictable as they were beautiful, so safety demanded that the guides lay down the first tracks. Rafe Gunderson, the revered "old man" of Starwood Lodge, was doing that, ripping a series of crisp, beautiful turns that made snow rise about his waist like the billowing skirt of a ballet dancer. Following him were Matt and Trevor Woods, a pair of inseparable and nearly indistinguishable brothers known to freestyle skiing enthusiasts as the Suicide Twins.

Sam surveyed the blinding-white slope, his gut tightening in the familiar thrill of anticipation, but just as he began to move forward, he thought of Tori and stopped.

It was a good thing she didn't know where he was right now. Victoria call-me-when-you-get-home Talcott, the undisputed queen of worriers, would have a heart attack.

Sam tipped his head back and groaned in frustration. She'd been wrecking his concentration all day long.

How had this happened to him? How had *he*, of all people, fallen for a bookish woman who alphabetized her spices, avoided driving in the rain and checked three times before bed to make sure she had locked her front door?

She was a house-in-the-suburbs kind of woman. A minivan-full-of-kids-and-soccer-balls kind of woman. A dinner-at-seven-every-single-night kind of woman. And she could never be *his* woman unless he became a completely different man.

Sam just didn't see how he could do that.

He was shaking his head in an attempt to fling her out of it when his eyes were drawn to an odd movement on the mountain. Behind Trevor, a slab had just let go. Sam tensed, whispered an urgent prayer and waited. The cloud of sloughing snow caught up to Trevor and for several scary seconds hid the familiar blue jacket from Sam's view. But at last Trevor skied out of trouble and the snow-slide passed harmlessly to his right, presenting no threat to the other two skiers. Sam thanked God and resumed breathing.

Picking out a line just to the left of where Trevor had skied, Sam adjusted his goggles and fought to regain his concentration. With the helicopter gone, his only options besides sitting here and turning into an ice sculpture were to fall off this snow-covered rock or ski down it. He was planning to ski, but with Tori invading his thoughts, he figured he was in for a spectacular wipeout.

It was time to head back to the lodge. They'd started early and had been skiing the steepest slopes. Matt had already mentioned his aching legs and Trevor probably didn't have a lot left, either. If the twins wanted to make one last run, fine. But Sam was finished after this one.

Somehow he made it down the mountain and back to the lodge in one piece. He was dressed for dinner and just about to head downstairs when he decided to place a quick call to his brother.

"Hey," he said when Reid answered. "I was just thinking about that guy who wants to go to the South Pole. Anything happening there?"

"We talked a couple of days ago," Reid said. "He's having second thoughts about wintering alone."

"Excellent. Encourage those." Sam wandered over to his picture window and admired the view as the sun's leading edge touched the peak of a distant mountain and set it on fire.

"Sam." Reid's voice deepened. "I saw Tori just now. She introduced me to Julian Knowles."

Julian. Sam closed his eyes.

Reid was waiting for a response, but Sam had nothing to give him. The silence lengthened and Reid finally broke it with a question. "Did you even know she had a boyfriend?"

Sam pressed the palm of his free hand against the cold glass of the window. "Not in the beginning, no."

"Well, from what I just saw, they're as good as engaged."

"That's…nice." Sam almost choked on the word.

"Is it?" Reid asked sharply.

Sam clutched the phone tighter. "What do you expect me to say, Reid? We're not right for each other."

"Don't be an idiot. I've never seen two people *more* right for each other. And I've never seen you give up without a fight for something you wanted this much."

Sam leaned his forehead against the window. "I've never wanted anything this much."

"Then what are you doing in Canada?"

Whirling away from the window, Sam yanked his straying heart back from the edge of dreamland. "I can't compete with this guy, Reid. He's everything she wants, while I'm—" He gave up. Reid knew what he was. He was a thrill-seeker, a restless wanderer who didn't even go to church. He wasn't a responsible, respectable, *safe* guy like Julian.

"You're making a mistake." Reid sounded utterly disgusted. "But I'll talk to you later."

Sam put the phone down and wilted onto his sofa. He allowed his head to loll back and as he stared at the rustic wood beams in the ceiling, he thought about Tori and her history professor. Realizing that his fists were clenched, he willed himself to uncurl his fingers and release his jealousy.

Tori deserved only the best. And Sam wasn't the best, not by a long shot.

Late the next afternoon on the front steps of Starwood Lodge, Trevor Woods rested a gloved hand on Sam's left shoulder as he stamped snow off his boots. "Dude, that last run was amazing."

"Amazing," Matt Woods agreed. Leaning hard on Sam's right shoulder, he did some snow-stamping of his own, then he thumped Sam hard on the back. "Let's go celebrate not being dead."

Two days of manic skiing with the twins had cleared Sam's head a little. If the weather cooperated and continued allowing the helis to fly, another day or two of wallowing in snow might help him forget Victoria Talcott. If it didn't, he'd just stay a little longer. When his money ran out—and that would happen fairly soon, since his favorite heli-skiing lodge was among the priciest in the Canadian Rockies, although Sam did get a steep discount because he brought so many clients here—he could always shoot down to Gray's place in Utah and invent some new freestyle tricks.

"Did you bring your Bible?" Matt asked as he whipped off his hat and shoved back a tangle of bleached-blond hair.

Trevor snorted. "You know Sam doesn't go anywhere without that Bible of his."

Sam couldn't read much of the Bible, but on trips like this he could often persuade one or two of his fellow adventurers to read a chapter aloud, which usually kicked off a good discussion. Over the years, Sam had been privileged to lead several men to the Lord in just that way. But experience had taught him not to appear too eager, so as he opened the door and held it for the twins, he tossed out a casual invitation. "If you guys are in the mood, we could do a little reading after dinner."

Sam dropped off his boots to be dried and his skis to be waxed for the next day, then headed upstairs to shower and change. In his room, he dumped his backpack on the floor and shucked off his jacket as he listened to a voice mail from Reid. When the message ended, he placed the return call.

"How was it today?" Reid asked.

"Beautiful. I can't believe there's so much snow this early in the season."

"Who are you skiing with?"

Sam looked at the ceiling. "Matt and Trevor."

"The Suicide Twins from Sun Valley?" Reid's voice vibrated with disapproval. "You mean those guys are still *alive*?"

It wasn't exactly news that Reid frowned on the gravity experiments Sam and his friends engaged in, so Sam nudged the conversation along. "They've got a new chef up here, Reid. A French guy. He puts three kinds of sauce on everything."

Reid refused to be sidetracked. "You're not doing anything stupid, are you?"

"I'm just skiing, Reid."

"Nobody 'just skis' with the Suicide Twins."

"I'm just having some fun," Sam retorted. At least he was *trying* to. It wasn't easy when all he could think about was how much he'd rather be back in Chicago, reading books with Tori.

Reid was talking again, but Sam tossed the phone on the bed so he could pull off his sweater. He wasn't going to miss anything; it wasn't as if he didn't know this you've-got-to-be-more-responsible-Sam lecture by heart. Imagining Reid sitting in the wingback chair by the stone fireplace, Sam wadded up his sweater and hurled it at his brother's head.

He retrieved the phone just in time for Reid's big finish.

"—so just don't make the mistake of thinking nobody would care if you got yourself killed."

Sam had been struggling with this ever since they'd lost Rich. Was he properly grateful for the life God had given him? Did his craving for excitement mean he was selfish and reckless, or had God simply made him different from other people?

He'd heard of scientific studies suggesting the brains of thrill-seekers were wired differently from those of normal people. That made sense because even as a very young child, Sam had known this insatiable hunger for *more*. It had never been about showing off and it had never been about cheating death. Quite simply, he just didn't feel alive unless he went all the way to the edge.

His father had understood. But that support had been yanked away from Sam four years ago and now Reid was the only person who had any inkling of Sam's struggle. Not that Reid was unfailingly sympathetic. There were times, and this was one of them, when Reid said things like—

"This craziness has to stop, Sam. I mean it."

Sam sighed. "I hear you."

"*Do* you? The twins had better not be trying to suck you into making another one of those insane videos."

"We're just skiing," Sam repeated. One stunt in a single extreme skiing video and his brother was never going to let him live it down.

It had happened three years ago, when the twins were shooting a video in Alaska. Sam had gone along to watch and one day as the twins and their film crew were enjoying a lunch break, Sam had been seized by the familiar madness. Unaware that an alert cameraman was recording it, Sam pulled off a trick he'd never attempted before or since. Yes, it was stupidly dangerous, but that day Sam had touched perfection and the twins had used the clip.

"I'm sending you a client," Reid said, yanking Sam's attention back to the present. "Julian Knowles."

Sam was so appalled that his knees gave out. Fortunately, he'd been standing beside the bed, so he sank into a fluffy goose-down duvet. "Julian," he repeated tonelessly. If he didn't know better, he might think God was making fun of him.

"He stopped by the office this morning," Reid said. "He wants to give heli-skiing a try. And by a wonderful coincidence, you're already up there."

Sam pinched the bridge of his nose. "By a wonderful coincidence," he muttered. "Reid, even if I wanted to teach Julian to ski, which I emphatically do *not*, you know this would be a stupid place to do it."

"Actually, he might be able to give *you* some pointers." Judging by the way Reid's voice bounced over the words, he was relishing this. "Turns out Julian was the downhill star of his college team."

Reacting blindly, Sam fired his fist at a plump feather pillow.

"He wants to ski with you," Reid said. "So ditch the twins and line up a guide."

Heli-skiing was expensive even at the bargain resorts where skiers went out in large groups, but Starwood was a boutique operation that catered to small parties with deep pockets. Learning what it cost to keep a Starwood heli fueled and at their disposal would quickly cool Julian's enthusiasm, Sam thought with satisfaction. He squirmed out of the duvet's smothering embrace and stood. "Of course you explained that he'd have nobody to share his expenses with."

"I did," Reid confirmed. "He didn't even blink."

Sam flopped back onto the bed. So old Julian was rolling in the green stuff. Didn't that just figure?

"He questioned me closely about avalanches," Reid offered.

Ah, yes. It wasn't something people gave much thought to in the well-traveled ski resorts, but here in the backcountry the danger of being swallowed up by the great white wave was very real and Reid would never soft-pedal that to a client. But was Tori's history professor really up to this? "What does he want from me?" Sam asked, frustrated.

"Isn't it obvious? He's challenging you to a duel."

"But he got the girl. Why can't he just leave me to my skiing?"

"Because he didn't *win* the girl," Reid explained patiently. "He's figured out that you *gave* him the girl and he doesn't want any favors from you."

"What is this?" Sam asked irritably. "High school?"

Reid chuckled. "Unless that place has gotten a lot cheaper since you were up there last winter, it might be wise to turn this trip into a business expense."

Good point. But that was Reid, always seeing the practical side of things.

"Willa just booked his flight," Reid said. "Unless there's some weather delay, you can expect him late tomorrow afternoon." He paused. "And Sam?"

"What."

Reid snickered. "You two kids play nice."

"He went *where*?" Tori stopped just inside the doorway of a Chinese restaurant to stare at her mother.

"Some place called Starwood Lodge, I think his mother said. She didn't mention what city it's near." Regina smoothed back her windblown hair, then took her daughter's arm and propelled her past a gurgling fountain set in the stone wall of the reception area. "All I know is that it's somewhere in British Columbia."

British Columbia? That was where Sam had gone.

"Lenore didn't seem too worried about it," Tori's mother continued as she surveyed the restaurant's elegant peaches-and-cream decor. "And you know Julian always goes first class, so I don't suppose we have to worry about him riding on ski lifts with rusty cables or anything like that."

Tori struggled to conceal her dismay. If her guess was correct, there would be no ski lifts, rusty or otherwise, where Julian was headed. But what about Aspen? Julian always took his parents to Aspen the first week of December and that wasn't far away. So why had he gone to Canada now?

"But so many other things could go wrong," Regina said, turning so Tori could ease her coat off her shoulders. "I'll never understand why that family is so crazy about skiing. One of these days, they're all going to come limping home on broken legs."

Tori shrugged out of her own coat, then handed it and her mother's fake fur to a coat-check attendant. "What about Aspen?" She cringed at the note of desperation that had crept into her voice, but her mother didn't seem to notice.

"Daniel's still recovering from his knee surgery," her mother reminded her. "There was never any question of their making the trip this year." She turned a charming smile on the hostess and requested a table for two, then looked at Tori again. "Lenore didn't know about Julian's trip until this morning. Apparently, he decided on an impulse to meet a friend in Canada."

That didn't make any sense. Julian took two ski trips a year, but he'd never gone to Canada. And he'd never met Sam, so they were hardly friends. And dear, predictable Julian wouldn't know an impulse if it bit his handsome Roman nose. Besides, hadn't he admitted right in front of Tori that heli-skiing was dangerous?

"I'm sure he'll call you tonight," her mother said comfortingly. "I gather he had to snatch this opportunity or lose it and he probably had to make a mad dash to the airport."

Tori needed to sit down, so it was a relief when the hostess led the way to their table. As Tori sank onto a bamboo chair and draped a peach-colored napkin over her lap, her mind flashed back to the previous evening, when Reid had handed Julian a business card.

Reid. She was going to kill him for instigating this.

Tori slapped her napkin back on the table. "Will you excuse me for a minute, Mom? I need to make a phone call."

Concern wrinkled Regina's forehead. "Honey, don't ever leave home without your cell phone. What if your car were to break down?" She reached into her purse. "Here, take mine."

"I have my phone," Tori said, already on her feet. "I just need some privacy. I won't be long."

"Oh." Stretching the tiny word into three syllables, her mother beamed a knowing smile. "Well, don't be too hard on him."

Tori opened her mouth, then decided not to correct her mother's assumption that she was calling Julian. The whole mess was just too complicated to explain right now.

"I'll order for both of us," her mother said. "You just tell Julian to be extra careful up there."

* * *

Sam was making the freestyle tricks of the Suicide Twins look downright sedate as he hucked and hurled himself halfway to oblivion. He was taking extraordinary risks and missing more than a few landings, but the snow was thigh-deep and softer than clouds, so it forgave quite a bit of stupidity.

Too soon, the sun lost its late-afternoon glare and slid toward the mountaintops, leaving Sam no choice but to return to the lodge, where Tori's almost-fiancé was waiting.

When he reached the heavy front door, Sam paused. Holding his skis against his left shoulder, he pulled off his gloves and his hat and stuffed them under his arm. He ran a hand through his sweat-dampened hair and when he couldn't think of any more little ways to postpone the inevitable, he sucked in a breath and yanked on the brass door handle, ready as he was ever going to be to meet Tori's future husband.

"There he is." One of the guides pointed in Sam's direction for the benefit of a dark-haired man who sprawled elegantly in a club chair beside the massive stone fireplace. "That's Sam McGarry."

It irked Sam that Julian possessed the kind of classic good looks women gushed about. With all that perfectly-styled black hair, the guy looked like a TV game-show host. It required all of Sam's concentration not to scowl as Julian uncrossed his long legs, set his drink on the table next to him and stood.

"Julian." Sam's feet did their job and carried him forward. He extended his right hand, just as good manners dictated. He even scrounged up a smile from somewhere.

And then he told a lie. "Glad you could make it."

They sized each other up by exchanging the requisite small talk, both feigning ignorance of the tense undercurrents in their conversation. Julian's counterfeit affability was so annoying that Sam fixed an equally fake smile on his own face and entertained himself with the thought that tomorrow he'd shake up the professor good and send him scampering back to Chicago.

They agreed to meet for dinner and Sam went upstairs to shower and change. In his room, he touched the flashing red button on his telephone, then shrugged off the outer layers of his clothing as he listened to two messages from Tori.

She was in a serious snit. Apparently, her professor was absent without leave. And in that unfathomable way women had of assigning blame, she had determined it was all Sam's fault.

He was still shaking his head over that when the phone rang. He picked it up and barely got the second syllable of *hello* out of his mouth before the object of his affections lit into him.

"Don't do it, Sam," she began without a warm-up. "Don't take him out there tomorrow. He thinks he has to prove something to me, but he doesn't."

"I'm very well," Sam said pointedly. "And you, Victoria?"

That didn't even slow her down. "You know what I'm talking about, Sam. You know Reid goaded him into this. Now he's going to take some stupid risks just because—"

"Now hold on," Sam said, annoyed that she had dragged Reid into this. "There's not a lot my brother can do about it if your boyfriend is determined to—"

"He's jealous of you," she cut in. "He thinks he has to—"

"Victoria." When she stopped, Sam lowered his voice to a menacing softness. "Why would Julian be jealous of me?"

She was so quiet, he thought for a moment that the line had gone dead. Then he actually heard her gulp. "You know why."

"I'm not sure I do." Yes, he was pushing, but why couldn't she just acknowledge the deep emotional connection they shared? Sam understood why they could never act on it, but couldn't she give him the satisfaction of admitting it existed? He affected a silky tone. "Why don't you explain it to me?"

"Don't do this, Sam."

He had to. This ignorant act of hers was making him crazy. "Are you still trying to convince yourself that nothing happened at your parents' house?"

"Nothing happened," she said loftily. "It was just a kiss."

Hah. That brief, chaste contact had rocked her world. Sam hadn't imagined the shocked recognition on her face when she'd pushed herself out of his arms and pressed trembling fingers against her mouth. "That was no ordinary kiss, brown eyes. That was a revelation."

"Yes, and what did it reveal?" she huffed. "That we have no business playing at a relationship!"

"I wasn't playing." And *she* hadn't been, either. But she wasn't going to concede that point, so Sam moved on. "If you're so worried about Julian, why don't you just call him and ask him to come home? He's in room number six."

Dead silence.

Sam pressed harder. "You don't think it's a little odd that you're asking *me* to stop your boyfriend from doing something that worries you? Great relationship you've got there, babe."

More silence.

"Tori?"

"Please, Sam." The little squeak in her voice made his own throat ache. "If Julian gets hurt, it will be my fault. That's why I'm begging you not to—"

"I've already agreed to ski with him tomorrow," Sam said wearily. "But I'll take good care of him, Tori, I promise."

Suddenly her anger returned, full strength. "If anything happens to him, Sam, I'll never forgive you." Her bitter words slashed at Sam's heart like a razor. "Do you hear me? Never!"

He opened his mouth to reply, but the line clicked and she was gone.

Chapter Eleven

J ust after sunrise, Sam looked out his window and groaned at the cloudless sky. He'd been hoping for weather bad enough to ground the helis, but this was going to be a perfect day for skiing.

And he would have to spend it with Julian.

They met for an early breakfast, then Sam dropped Julian off for a mandatory orientation and safety briefing. Sam was always dead serious about his clients' safety, and not only was Julian a client, he was somebody Victoria Talcott didn't want coming home all banged up. So although Sam allowed himself to fantasize briefly about shoving the professor off a tall, pointy mountain, he fervently hoped that Helga, the guide who was conducting the two-hour briefing and avalanche-rescue drill, would put a good healthy scare into the guy.

Julian was going to be tied up for a while, so when Sam found the twins checking weather bulletins at the front desk, he decided to head out with them to burn off some energy and frustration. Two hours later he caught a lift on a heli making a refueling trip and returned to the lodge, where he met up with Rafe Gunderson. Together he and Sam collected a sober-looking Julian and stuffed him into a heli.

Rafe was a gruff, sixty-year-old athletic wonder with thinning salt-and-pepper hair which he wore in a ponytail. The guide took nothing on faith and since Julian's skills were unproven, Rafe chose a gentle, treeless slope for the first run.

Their pilot found a level spot and set down, and the passengers climbed out into knee-deep snow. They unloaded their gear, then huddled together in the swirling whiteout as the whine of the rotors increased in pitch and the heli lifted off, leaving the three men alone on the mountain. They strapped on their backpacks, snapped into their ski bindings and conferred briefly. Then Rafe dropped in, followed by Julian.

Sam held back, watching with grudging approval as Julian carved out some very nice short-radius turns. By the time Sam pushed off, he was thinking it might not be such a horrible day after all.

He was wrong about that. Things started going sour after the second run, when Julian became unbearably smug. Recognizing his behavior as the chest-beating it was, Sam remained fairly calm, although he couldn't help wondering why *winning* Tori was so important to Julian. The whole world was waiting for him back in Chicago; what was he doing in Canada?

After they'd climbed in and out of the helicopter several times, Julian picked up on the fact that every time Rafe pointed to a nice run, Sam was shaking him off and suggesting something less challenging.

"I was skiing the expert slopes when I was fifteen years

old," Julian said in a tone that made Sam long to pop him one. "Could we please get serious now?"

Rafe was all for it. "Want to try some hucking?" he asked Julian, leaning past Sam to point out a beautiful glade Sam had skied with the twins two days earlier. "Lots of nice little cliffs down there."

"I'm not up for that," Sam said before Julian could answer. Rafe's jaw dropped and Sam regretted not having a private chat with the guide earlier, but who knew old Julian would turn out to be an expert skier?

Rafe tipped his head to one side and gawked as if Sam had just suggested they all go sit by the fireplace and knit socks. "You feelin' all right, Sam?"

"I'm great." Sam pointed to a long, shallow slope with no trees. "That looks fun," he said brightly.

Julian cocked a skeptical eyebrow but said nothing. After flashing Sam another concerned look, Rafe gave instructions to their pilot.

The sky was a dazzling blue and the powder sublime, but aside from that time in the Swiss Alps when Sam's friends had dug his unconscious body out from under six feet of snow, this was the worst day he had ever spent on skis. He watched like a nervous grandmother as Julian took one unnecessary risk after another and by late afternoon he had reached the end of his endurance. When he spotted a pretty little granite cliff that on any other day he'd have hucked over even with Reid watching, his heart leaped into his throat. Had Julian seen it?

Yes, he had.

"Please don't, please don't," Sam chanted under his breath, but of course Julian did.

His approach was flawless and he looked fine as he sailed off the top. But the professor didn't exactly nail his landing, not unless he *meant* to do that clumsy cartwheel and scatter his gear all over the slope before coming to a stop in the dead-bug position, on his back with his arms and legs pointing at the sky.

At least he was moving. That was a fairly good indication he hadn't broken his dumb neck. Sam sighed and went down to collect Julian's things.

Rafe had reached the bottom of the slope and was looking up at them. Sam signaled that Julian was physically, if not mentally okay, then he tugged the dazed professor's hat back onto his head.

Just in time, Sam remembered Rafe's penchant for tweaking skiers about their more spectacular wipeouts. Rafe would have to restrain himself today, Sam decided, because if Julian Knowles possessed a sense of humor, he sure hadn't brought it with him to Canada and Sam didn't need any more trouble.

He skied straight toward the guide and at the last possible moment, twisted his hips and turned his skis perpendicular to the slope, making a perfect hockey stop that showered Rafe with snow. "Wipe that smirk off your face," he commanded in a low voice. "Julian's doing great. Understand?"

Rafe pushed his goggles up to his forehead and blinked at Sam like a snowman with living eyes. He was clearly baffled, but he worked for tips and Sam always made sure he got good ones.

"Hey, you're doing great," Rafe said loudly as Julian glided toward them. "Anybody could have missed that landing."

As Julian came to a shaky stop, Sam forced a smile. "I couldn't believe it when I saw you heading for that cliff." And wasn't *that* the truth?

Julian's chest expanded visibly.

"Our ride's on his way," Rafe said as he tucked his two-way radio back into his pack. "You're doing great, Julian, but you're still adjusting to this altitude and it's not smart to push it on your first day. What do you say we go one last time?"

Sam shook his head. "Sorry, guys. I'm done."

Rafe's mouth dropped open. Sam ignored him.

"Come on, McGarry," Julian urged. "One last run."

That was exactly what Sam was afraid of—that it would be Julian's last run. And Sam had promised he'd keep Tori's professor safe. "Sorry," he repeated, clapping a hand on the guide's shoulder. "I'm ready for the hot tub."

"If you're tapped out, we'd better not push you," Julian said in a superior tone. "That's how accidents happen."

Sam had as much pride as any other man, but he was desperate to get Julian safely back to the lodge, so he swallowed it. But Rafe still looked shocked, so when he opened his mouth to speak, Sam leaned heavily on his shoulder and helped him say the right thing.

"Never thought I'd see anybody run Sam McGarry into the ground," Rafe said as obediently as a ventriloquist's dummy.

Julian's mouth worked as he tried to conceal his satisfaction. "I guess we're finished here."

"Good." Sam was so relieved, he spoke without thinking. "Let's get you back to the lodge so you can call Tori and tell her you're not hurt."

Julian's eyes narrowed. "Why would I be hurt?"

Sam realized his mistake. "Don't get me wrong," he said quickly. "She's a sweet woman. But how do you stand the way she worries about every little thing?"

"I'm used to it." Julian appeared to relax. "But maybe we'd better keep all this right here in the mountains."

"Hey, no problem," Sam said airily. "I don't ski and tell." From the corner of his eye, he caught the sudden lightening of Rafe's face as comprehension dawned. He fired the guide a keep-your-mouth-shut look.

Julian unbuckled his backpack and shrugged out of it. "This has been great, but I'm having second thoughts about taking this time off. I might just head back to Chicago." He dropped his pack on the ground and as he turned to watch the helicopter land a short distance away, Sam saw his lips curl into a slow smile.

The ride to the lodge was interminable. Julian's smug expression and Rafe's speculative looks had shortened Sam's fuse to the extent that he didn't dare speak to either of the men. But when the heli landed and Julian walked away with a new spring in his step, Rafe's hand came down hard on Sam's shoulder, holding him back for a private word.

"You wasted a perfect skiing day to babysit that guy for some *woman*," the guide accused.

Sam opened his mouth but just couldn't tell another lie.

Rafe studied him for a moment and then his weathered face split into a grin. He shook his head, half amused and half sympathetic. "You poor, dumb kid."

Sam shrugged off the guide's heavy hand and stalked toward the lodge.

"You going home tomorrow?" Rafe called.

"No," Sam snapped. "I came up here to ski."

"It was just so unlike you, Julian, running off on an impulse." Tori stuck a bookmark in the novel she'd been reading and pressed the phone tighter against her ear, straining to hear Julian's words over the ambient noise of the airport's baggage-claim area.

"I won't go up there again, Tori. You have my word." His voice deepened. "I'm sorry for making you worry."

She closed her eyes, remembering the card in her desk at work. *Im sorry for makeing you worry.* "Will Sam be up there much longer, do you know?"

"A few more days, he said. If the weather holds out."

Why, *why* had she asked? It was hard enough, knowing the crazy man was out there somewhere risking his neck. She didn't want to know where or how.

"I know you see him as larger than life," Julian said. "But men like that are never satisfied for long. They're always chasing the next big thrill." His voice softened. "He would never have given that up, Tori. Not even for you."

She swallowed. "Could we please talk about something else?"

"Good idea," Julian said briskly. "How about dinner tomorrow night?"

"Thanks, but I can't. I'm going to Corinne's after work."

"Mind if I tag along? It's been a while since I've seen her and the triplets."

Tori had meant what she'd said about his being as dear to her as ever, but right now she needed a little space. "Some other time, Julian."

He sighed into the phone, which was strange, because Julian wasn't a man who sighed.

Neither was he man who went heli-skiing on a dare, Tori reminded herself. Yet he had done exactly that, and for what? To prove he could be as exciting as Sam.

She had to make him understand she was never going to change her mind. "Julian, I—"

"Excuse me," he said. "My ski bag just came up on the carousel."

While she waited, Tori indulged in a sigh of her own and wondered what she had said or done that had caused him to hope again.

"All set," Julian said. "I'm heading home now."

"Be careful driving," Tori said automatically. They needed to have a serious talk, but she wasn't up to it tonight.

She ended the call, then began her bedtime preparations. For some reason she deviated from her usual routine and switched off the living room lights first and then the one in the kitchen. She had just stuck her toothbrush into her mouth when she realized she hadn't checked the front door since she'd come in tonight.

Staring into the mirror at her own wide eyes, she recalled Sam's mischievous grin as he'd stood beside her spice rack. *I'm going to shake up your system,* he'd teased.

He had done that and more. Sam had wrecked her whole life. But at least he had cured her of one very troublesome habit.

Even though the heli pilots flew lunches out to the skiers each day, Sam was usually ravenous when it came time to head back to the lodge. But today he hadn't bothered with lunch and he was equally uninterested in dinner. He'd barely touched his breakfast, come to think of it, because he'd awakened with an odd pain in his belly. It might be a pulled muscle, but given his lack of appetite, it was more likely he was coming down with something, so he apologized to the twins and knocked off early.

Back in his room at the lodge, he stood by the window watching the sky fill with clumpy gray clouds. The storm that hadn't been expected until well after dinnertime appeared to be pushing in ahead of schedule. Soon the pilots would be scrambling to pluck their skiers off the mountains before bad weather grounded the helis.

The phone rang and Sam turned too quickly, throwing his gut into a spasm of pain that unleashed a wave of dizziness and caused him to break into a cold sweat. His world was looking a little blurry around the edges as he picked up the desk phone and grunted a greeting.

"Sam?" Gray's voice sharpened with concern. "Is that you?"

Sam pressed his free hand against his lower abdomen and winced at the pain. He'd never had a stomach virus hit him this hard and fast. "Gray, I—"

The phone slipped from his grasp and bounced on the nubby carpet. As he bent to retrieve it, the room darkened suddenly and Sam realized with disgust that he was going to pass out.

Chapter Twelve

Tori slid her arms into her coat and gave her watch another worried glance. She was late getting away from the office and before heading up to Corinne's she needed to stop by her apartment to pick up the pink-frosted sugar cookies she'd made last night for the babies. As she hustled out to her car, she phoned Corinne and explained the delay so her sister wouldn't worry.

When she pulled into the residents' parking lot at her apartment building, she saw Reid leaning under the hood of his SUV. As she nosed her car into her reserved space, his head swung in her direction. He raised one hand in a silent greeting, but his expression was stony and he immediately turned back to his engine.

Tori approached him warily. "Are you having some kind of trouble?"

"No." His lean jaw twitched. "Just routine maintenance."

It was already dark, so although Reid was parked directly under a security light, Tori wondered if he could see well enough for whatever he was doing. "I'll get you a flashlight," she offered.

"I'm fine," he said shortly. "Thank you."

Clearly, Reid wasn't going to forgive her for hurting his brother. Sorrow settled so heavily on Tori that her head and shoulders bowed under the weight as she turned away.

She changed into jeans and a sweater, then hurried to the kitchen to get the cookies. Just then her phone rang and when Tori answered she was startled to hear an unusually deep, oddly familiar masculine voice.

"Victoria? I have some—" The caller paused. "I'm sorry. This is Grayson Traynor. And I have some upsetting news about Sam."

Tori's knees buckled and she caught the edge of the countertop for support. *Not dead, Lord. Please, not that. Please don't make me live in a world where there's no Sam.*

"How badly is he hurt?" she squeaked out, still desperately praying that he *was* only hurt and not—

"I don't know. I was just talking to him on the phone and something happened. I sent people to his room to check on him and they found him unconscious."

In his room? Tori's heart was slamming so hard against her ribs that she could barely breathe. "It wasn't…a skiing accident?"

"Hold on," her caller said abruptly.

They'd found Sam in his room. Not under tons of snow. In his room. But what was wrong with him? Tori's thoughts spun in sickening circles.

"They're getting ready to transport him now," Grayson Traynor said. "He's bleeding from some kind of head injury."

A head injury. Tori shut her eyes, squeezing out hot tears as she absorbed those awful words. A head injury.

Just like Bill.

"The hospital's forty minutes away," Grayson Traynor said distractedly. Tori could hear a woman speaking in the background and he seemed to be relaying snatches of information to Tori as he received them. "They've got a whole fleet of helicopters at that lodge, but they're all hustling to pick up skiers right now because a storm's moving in. Even if they could spare a helicopter, they couldn't fly to the hospital because the weather's coming from that direction." He drew a shaky breath. "Victoria, do you have any idea where Reid might be? He's not answering his cell phone."

Before he finished speaking, Tori was heading for her front door. She hit the sidewalk at a dead run, shouting Reid's name. His head jerked in her direction and he watched in openmouthed concern as she skidded to a stop in front of him.

"It's Grayson Traynor," she panted out, thrusting the phone at him. "Sam's hurt!"

Reid's face blanched as he hurriedly wiped his hands on the rag he held, then dropped it and snatched the phone.

He spoke with his cousin for a minute, barking out questions, but Tori was unable to follow the one-sided conversation. Finally he pressed the phone against his chest and looked at her. "Gray's going to fly me there in his private jet. He wants to know if you're coming."

Yes. Tori nodded violently, too worried about Sam to give any consideration to her fear of flying.

Reid's eyes narrowed. "What about your boyfriend?"

They didn't have time for stupid arguments. Tori

grabbed his arm and tried to shake some sense into him. "You have to take me with you. *Please*."

"She's coming," he told his cousin. Handing the phone back to Tori, he gave her a hard look. "I'm leaving in ten minutes. I won't wait for you."

He didn't have to wait. She was ready before he was.

Tori had flown only once before and it had been a horrible experience—a turbulent ride through a thunderstorm. She'd ended up buying a bus ticket for the trip home. She had the idea that a private jet was even more dangerous than a big airliner, so the drive to the airport passed in a blur of apprehension interspersed with silent, desperate prayers for Sam.

Her grim-faced companion didn't speak to her, not even when he shouldered his bag and grabbed Tori's small suitcase in one hand and her arm in the other and hustled her across a windy tarmac.

Tori cringed at the earsplitting whine of jet engines as she battled tearing gusts of wind to reach Grayson Traynor's private plane. On the steps she was greeted by a very tall middle-aged man with dark eyebrows and neat silver hair.

"I wanted to meet you, but not like this," Grayson Traynor shouted over the whine of the engines. Ignoring the hand Tori held out to him, he pulled her into a brief but oddly comforting embrace. Then he let her go and ducked through the door opening, gesturing for Tori and Reid to move past him.

Both men had to stoop under the low ceiling, which couldn't have been more than six-feet high. Tori wasn't normally claustrophobic, but the confined space, luxurious as it was with its camel-colored leather, ratcheted up her anxiety.

On one side of the cramped cabin were two captain's chairs with a small table between them. On the other was a sculpted sofa with seat belts. There were two more seats further back. Tori wasn't sure where she was supposed to sit, but the point became moot when her legs quit on her and she sank onto the sofa. Grayson Traynor, now speaking urgently into a cell phone, folded his long body and sat next to her.

Reid stowed the bags and then took a seat across the aisle. "This is the smallest of Gray's jets," he explained as he shrugged out of his jacket. "But it's the fastest."

A man came out of the cockpit and closed the plane's door with a muffled thump. The aircraft rocked sickeningly and Tori was on the verge of a full-fledged panic when she realized what Reid had just told her: this was the fastest way to get to Sam. She held on to that thought as she fumbled with the buttons of her coat.

When she rose slightly and slipped out of the garment, Reid took it and tossed it onto an empty seat. Murmuring her thanks, Tori avoided his eyes by buckling and adjusting her seat belt. After Reid's harsh judgment of her, she couldn't have borne his knowing just how close to hysteria she was right now.

"Mr. T-Traynor?" she croaked when the man beside her ended his phone call.

"Gray," he corrected.

"Gray." Tori swallowed. "Do they know anything yet?"

He glanced at Reid. "Sam just arrived at the hospital. They're saying the head injury is minor—just a lot of blood.

They think he must have hit the corner of a table when he fainted."

"That doesn't tell us *why* he fainted," Reid pointed out. "What's wrong with him?"

The billionaire hesitated. "He may have a perforated or ruptured appendix."

Tori's hand flew to her mouth. A ruptured appendix could result in peritonitis and...*death*. Was that really what was wrong with Sam? And if it was, could the doctors move quickly enough to save him? Hadn't it been an awfully long time since Sam had collapsed in his room?

She looked at Reid and saw her own desperate questions reflected in his hazel eyes. His mouth tightened and he turned his face to the window, his hands curling into fists on his knees.

"Mr. Traynor?" Tori flinched as a man's drawling voice came out of a speaker somewhere behind her. "If y'all don't mind puttin' up your seats and trays and so forth, we just got clearance from the tower."

"Excuse me." Gray reached a long arm across Tori and pressed a button on the burled wood panel set in the sofa's armrest. "Thank you, Miles," he said into the intercom. "Get us up there."

As the jet began to roll forward, Tori shut her eyes and sat very still, her palms flat on her thighs, as if that might help stabilize the aircraft.

"You don't like flying?" Gray asked.

"No," she squeaked, not opening her eyes. "But I'm okay."

She felt a warm hand cover hers. "My wife had the same problem, but she got over it. There's nothing to this, sugar. Just keep reminding yourself that a man in my position can afford planes with reliable engines and pilots who didn't buy their licenses off the Internet."

Tori tried to smile at his joke, but couldn't quite manage it. The jet pivoted, making her stomach spin, and seconds later the whine of the engines increased in pitch and volume. Then they were thundering down the runway.

It helped that Gray held her hand and kept talking, mostly about his late wife and how she had learned to love flying and had eventually earned a pilot's license. Tori focused on the soothing timbre of his deep voice, not really following his words until she caught Sam's name. Then she opened her eyes, all attention.

"A few years ago he saved my son's life," Gray said. "We've been close ever since, but I never realized until now just how much I..." He trailed off.

"I know," Tori said, gently pulling her hand out from under his to signal she was all right now. "Everybody loves Sam."

From across the aisle, Reid gave her a long, freezing look, then jerked the buckle on his seat belt. "I'm going up to see Miles."

Gray's mouth hung open as he watched his cousin stalk toward the cockpit. "What's going on?" he asked Tori.

"He thinks there's another man in the picture." Tori stared out a small window framing a patch of featureless dark sky. "He's wrong about that, but he's right that I don't belong here."

Gray laid his arm along the back of the sofa, behind Tori. "I'm not following you."

"Sam and I aren't right for each other," she said miserably. "But that doesn't mean we don't—" She stopped herself just in time.

"You don't, what? Love each other?"

Tori couldn't bring herself to meet his eyes.

Gray let out a long breath. "Sam's told me a lot about you. And, no, he's never used that word you're dancing around, but I believe he's been thinking it."

Tori shook her head. "We're too different. Sam realizes that, but Reid doesn't understand."

"I don't understand, either. But Reid's going to treat you like the lady you are, or I'll have something to say to him."

Tori did her best to smile. "You're a nice man."

He lifted one dark eyebrow in pretended disdain. "Clearly, you don't read the tabloids."

"I called Sam the other night," she confessed, emboldened by Gray's kindness. "I said something really awful and then I hung up on him."

Gray uttered an amused grunt. "Oh, sugar, don't worry about that. Sam doesn't hold grudges."

"But I told him if he allowed my friend to get hurt skiing, I would never forgive him." How could she have said such an ugly thing to Sam, of all people?

Gray's smile was almost unbearably tender. "He knows you didn't mean it."

That was probably true, but it didn't erase Tori's guilt.

And Reid was right. After rejecting Sam, it was hardly Tori's place to go running to him now. Not unless she had changed her mind—and she hadn't.

"I was married for fifteen years," Gray said. "We had some rocky times, but we loved each other, so we just held on tight." He smiled gently. "What I'm saying is that real love forgives. Every single time, it forgives. So don't you worry about Sam holding anything against you. Trust me, he won't."

He unbuckled his seat belt and stood, hunching his shoulders under the low ceiling. "Would you like something to drink?"

When Tori shook her head, he opened a small refrigerator at the other end of the sofa and retrieved a bottle of fruit juice. "Help yourself if you want something later. There are snacks in here, too." He twisted off the cap and took a long pull from the bottle, then pointed its neck at the console beside Tori. "And if you need to make any calls, use that phone. I'm going to the cockpit for a minute." He paused. "Will you be all right alone?"

Tori gave him a nervous smile. "As long as you're back in time to hold my hand for the landing." She had read that was the most dangerous part of any flight.

Gray winked at her. "I'll look forward to that."

When he had gone, Tori reached for the phone. She had turned her cell phone off even before boarding the jet, afraid that it might interfere with some crucial electronic device. But Gray wouldn't have invited her to use this phone if it wasn't safe, so she entered Corinne's number. She was surprised when her father answered.

"Daddy?"

"Where *are* you?" he demanded. "Couldn't you pull over and answer your cell phone?"

Something was horribly wrong. Tori pressed a hand to her throat. "Daddy, what's going on?"

"It's Bill." Her father sounded dazed. "Baby, he—"

"Rinny?" Tori would have leaped to her feet, but her seat belt held her back.

"She's fine," her father said quickly. "Bill wasn't here. He was in the psych hospital when he got hold of an electrical cord and—" Her father's voice broke. "They don't think it was an accident." He paused before adding, "Baby, he's dead."

"No," Tori moaned, covering her face with one hand. They had known Bill would never get better, but this was still a horrible shock.

"How soon will you be here?" her father asked.

"Daddy, I'm not coming." The high, tight voice coming out of her mouth sounded like a stranger's.

"Corinne says you should have been here by now. Where *are* you?"

"I don't know, exactly." Scalding tears rolled down her cheeks. "I'm calling from an airplane."

She felt a touch on her shoulder and looked up to find Gray standing over her, deep lines of concern etched between his eyebrows. "Can I help?"

Tori stared at him and tried to form an answer, but her overloaded brain just couldn't process any more. Bill was dead. Corinne needed her, but she wasn't there. Sam might be dying, and she wasn't *there*. Somewhere over Wisconsin or maybe Minnesota, sick with fear and grief and separated from all the people she loved, Tori reached her breaking point. She thrust the phone at Gray and slumped forward, covering her head with her arms as she pressed her face against her knees and began to sob.

She was vaguely aware that Gray had resumed his seat beside her and was explaining to her father about Sam. When he ended the call, he placed his hand on the back of Tori's neck and gave her an encouraging squeeze.

"Your parents are taking good care of your sister and I

just promised your father I'd look after you. We'll get you through this, sugar."

Rubbing her eyes and hiccupping, Tori sat up. "Thank you, Gray." She drew a steadying breath. "I'm s-sorry about—"

"Don't you apologize," he said tenderly, smoothing back some wisps of hair that had stuck to her wet face. "You're having about the worst day a person could have." From somewhere he produced a soft linen handkerchief and pressed it into her hands. "If it helps to cry, then you just go ahead and cry good and hard and loud."

She gave him a trembling, sheepish smile. "I think I just did." One corner of her mind was amazed that she was sitting in a luxurious private jet, blowing her nose into a billionaire's handkerchief, but mostly she was heartsick for Corinne and terrified that Sam was going to— No, she wouldn't even *think* that word.

"How long before we get there?" she asked.

Gray looked at his watch. "Less than four hours. If the weather clears up, we'll be able to take a helicopter to the hospital."

Tori's mind stumbled over that. If it wasn't safe to fly a helicopter out of whatever airport they were heading to, how could it be safe for this plane to *land* there?

"But even if we have to drive," Gray was saying, "we'll be there soon."

Four hours didn't seem very soon to Tori. And what if it wasn't soon *enough?* She leaned her head back against the sofa and closed her eyes.

"That's right," Gray said approvingly. "You try to rest.

I'll get you a pillow and blanket and you can stretch out right here."

Tori appreciated his kindness, but she wasn't planning to sleep. She had too much to pray about.

Chapter Thirteen

"Sam?"

He tried hard, but even when he managed to lift his heavy eyelids, he couldn't hold them open. Which was a real shame, because there was someone very much worth looking at standing right beside his bed. He pushed her name out of his dry throat.

Tori laid a cool hand against his forehead and smoothed his hair back. "Praise God, you're okay."

"You didn't have to come." His words came out raspy.

"Yes, I did. I was worried about you."

He finally got his eyes mostly open and lifted his hand. She grasped it in both of hers and all Sam could think was, *soft*. Not just her hands, but her brown-velvet eyes. Her sweet, wobbly smile. And her voice, pitched a little higher than normal but still reminding him of the way a summer breeze sighed through the treetops of a lush forest.

"I prayed and prayed for you." She squeezed his hand, then lifted it and pressed the back of it hard against her mouth.

"You didn't have to come," he said again. "I'm all right."

"Well, we didn't know that," Reid said from somewhere nearby. His tone was edged with an exasperation that told Sam *he'd* done a bit of worrying, too. "If you were determined to pop your appendix and scare us all to death, couldn't you have done it closer to home?"

"Sorry," Sam mumbled, coming more awake as he looked into Tori's enormous, shadowed eyes. He'd put that worry there and it broke his heart. "I'm all right," he repeated, wishing he knew how to make her believe it. "Just a little druggy, that's all."

Her full bottom lip trembled as she stared at a spot just above his left eye. Something up there felt a little bulky, so Sam lifted his free hand. His probing fingers encountered a thick gauze pad taped just above his eyebrow.

"You hit your head when you fell in your room at the lodge," Reid explained.

"We've all seen you looking better." That was Gray's voice. Sam didn't see him until he moved next to Tori and slipped his arm around her shoulders. "But at least you're still with us." Gray looked down at Tori. "We'd better be going, sugar. He needs to rest."

"I'd rest a whole lot better if you'd keep your hands off my girl," Sam grumbled.

His girl? He must be drugged half out of his mind to have allowed *that* to slip out.

"Hey, I brought her to you, didn't I? How about a little gratitude?"

Sam hated it that Tori had been worried about him, but she was here and that felt good. He wasn't going to act like it didn't. "Thanks," he said to Gray. "Now get lost." He looked again at Tori and dragged his hand—to which both of hers had very pleasantly fused—to his chest. "You stay."

"Nobody stays." A large, round woman in a white uniform shook her head at Gray. "You're not even supposed to be in here."

"We'll be just down the hall," Tori said in a cracked little voice. Letting go of Sam's hand, she watched him with wide, moist eyes that told him everything her stubborn mouth was never going to. As Gray gently tugged her toward the door, her gaze clung to Sam until she was eclipsed by the massive nurse.

"I shouldn't have let them in," the woman said good-naturedly as she adjusted Sam's IV drip. "But they were threatening to tear this hospital apart if they couldn't see for themselves that you were all right. That's some fan club you've got there, Mr. McGarry."

Sam turned his head on the pillow. "Thank you," he sighed, partly to the nurse but mostly to God. And then he went back to sleep.

Standing before the window in Sam's private hospital room, Tori slid her hands into the pockets of her jeans and watched the last pink bands of a spectacular sunset fade in the darkening sky.

She had been here for several days. Gray and Reid had flown home as soon as the doctors managed to convince them Sam was out of danger, but they'd pressed Tori to stay. Gray had insisted Sam would make a faster recovery with Tori nearby; Reid wanted somebody other than strangers watching over his brother. Both extracted promises of daily phone updates from her.

She hadn't required much persuading to stay. Only now was she beginning to recover from the shock of seeing vital, adventurous, fun-loving Sam lying still, helpless and pale, in that stark white bed.

They had almost lost him, but Sam's excellent physical condition had given him the edge he'd needed to battle the massive infections. Tori was grateful that he slept constantly; that meant his body was devoting all of its resources to getting well.

In two days he'd be flown home in one of Gray's jets. A private nurse had already been hired to accompany him. Sam wasn't wild about that plan, but it would ensure Gray's peace of mind, so he had acquiesced.

He didn't yet know that Tori meant to leave sometime before that on a commercial airliner. She felt that would make a cleaner break than riding home with him and saying goodbye in Chicago. And goodbye it had to be, because nothing had changed. Sam would make a full recovery and return to his adventuring ways, a life Tori could never share.

Rubbing her arms to ward off a sudden chill, she stared at her reflection in the window. At least her fear of flying was no longer an issue. The hours she'd spent begging God to spare Sam's life had put that irrational terror into perspective. But where she was going to find the will to leave Sam, she didn't know. At the end of each day she walked to a hotel two blocks from the hospital, where she made her nightly phone calls to her family and then read her Bible for a while before crawling into the strange bed. Emotionally exhausted, she scrupulously avoided thinking about any future beyond the next morning, when she would see Sam again.

Gray hadn't allowed her to pay for the hotel. He had even pressed some cash on her for meals. She had tried to protest, but he wouldn't listen to any argument. "This is about Sam," he'd said, glancing at Reid and getting a firm nod of agreement. "He'll do better with you here and we don't want him worrying about whether you can afford to *be* here."

Hearing a rustling behind her, Tori turned from the window and found Sam struggling to sit up. He was always thirsty when he awakened, so she reached for his water pitcher.

"I like how you fuss over me," he said, watching her fill a glass. His emerald eyes had lost their sparkle and instead of his usual engaging grin he offered a wan, close-mouthed smile. "I've decided to take my time getting well."

It wasn't much of a joke, but Tori rewarded his effort with a chuckle.

He swallowed some water, then briefly shut his eyes as though gathering strength to speak. "Did you talk to Corinne after the service?"

"Yes." Tori's throat tightened at the reminder of her sister's grief. Today Corinne had buried her husband.

"You should have been there," Sam reproved gently.

So Tori's father maintained, to the point of having made her spill tears of guilt and frustration when they'd talked earlier today. But rushing home to comfort Corinne would have meant leaving Sam before knowing he was out of danger.

Corinne understood and had urged Tori to stay in Canada. "I have Mom and Dad," she'd said. "And Tori, this isn't that much harder than what I've had to face every day since Bill's accident."

At the memory of her sister's brave words, Tori's heart swelled with love and admiration. "Corinne will be fine," she said confidently. "She's amazing."

"No more amazing than you." Sam drank the rest of his water and set the glass on his bedside table. He watched Tori for a moment, his expression unreadable, then said, "Julian can't be too thrilled about your being here."

It was the first time he'd mentioned Julian. Unsure how to respond, Tori busied herself with refolding the newspaper she'd left scattered across the bottom of Sam's bed. "I make my own decisions," she said finally.

"Have you made the big one yet?"

Not understanding, she straightened and just looked at him.

"Are you going to marry him, Tori?" The question was barely audible.

She turned away, busying her hands with more tidying-up. "I'm not in love with Julian."

"That's not what I asked. I know you're not in love with Julian. You're in love with—"

"Don't!" she cried, rounding on him. "It isn't right, Sam, and you know it. We're too different."

He studied her face for several heartbeats before breaking the awful stillness. "Different can be good, Tori."

"Not this kind of different. It would never work."

"We could make it work. We just have to find some middle ground." He extended his hand. "Come on. I know we can do it, Tori. Let's take a leap of faith."

"That's just like you," she said bitterly. "Risk everything." She flung her arms wide, then dropped them, her hands smacking her denim-covered thighs. "Take a leap of faith!" she shrilled. "That's *you*, Sam. But it isn't *me*."

He looked stricken, but made no response.

"I need everything safe and predictable," she said more gently. "That's not something I can change."

He folded his arms across his chest and she bit her tongue to keep from reminding him to be careful of the IV attached to his left hand. "Then explain to me why you're here right now," he challenged. "Tell me why you're here with me instead back in Chicago with your safe, predictable professor."

Tori dropped her head and stared hard at the chipped corner of a floor tile, willing herself not to cry.

"Gray told me you were terrified of flying. But you got on his plane, didn't you?" Sam's voice turned almost harsh. "You got on his plane because whatever it took, you had to be here with *me*."

He had some nerve, saying that; dragging the truth out into the open and pressuring her to acknowledge it. Tori looked him in the eye. "I'm not going to marry Julian," she said crisply. "But I do want a family, so I *will* get married, just as soon as I find a nice man who—"

"Oh, come on," Sam scoffed. "That's just plain stupid."

Tori felt her eyes bulge as outrage sizzled through her. "You think marriage is stupid?"

"No, Victoria," he said with exaggerated patience. "What's stupid is your plan to marry a man you think you can live with." He paused, tipping his head forward and looking at her from under raised eyebrows. "Instead of the man you can't live *without*."

She huffed out a breath. "I can live without you, Sam."

"I don't think so, brown eyes."

She was almost grateful to him for aggravating her because it made this easier. "I'm leaving tomorrow," she announced, gathering up her coat and purse. "I can't afford to stick around here any longer. Corinne needs me and work's piling up at the office and—"

"What's wrong with Julian?"

She blinked. "What?"

He pushed against the mattress to sit up straighter. His arms trembled and his face paled with the effort, but there was a belligerent light in his eyes. "You're looking for a nice guy to marry," he reminded her. "So I was just wondering what's wrong with good old Julian."

"I can't marry Julian," she said impatiently.

"I know." Sam nodded with smug satisfaction. "You've been friends forever and your family's crazy about him, but that's not enough, is it? And if the professor isn't enough, Tori, what man ever *could* be?"

She stared at him, dumbfounded. Until this moment she hadn't realized that her feelings for Sam had shipwrecked her entire future. But she refused to acknowledge that fact while he sat there congratulating himself on his cleverness. "I have to go," she said, backing toward the door.

His smug expression vanished. "Stay," he said urgently.

She hardened her heart. "Sam, I can't."

"Don't run away from this," he pleaded. "We'll work it out."

If he thought that were possible, he was kidding himself. Looking at the floor again, Tori shook her head in a wordless apology, then she turned and walked out of his life.

Chapter Fourteen

Tori had been home for three weeks. She knew she ought to feel relieved that Sam had made no attempt to contact her, but she was hurt. Had she been so easy to forget?

She had spent Thanksgiving with her family and Julian's, as usual, and was now preparing for Christmas. But she was finding little pleasure in it because her favorite dream had been shattered.

There would be no Christmas wedding for her, no church decorated with holly and red roses, not next year or any other year. How could she in good conscience ask any man to be satisfied with less than her whole heart?

For her family's sake, she hid her sorrow and carefully observed all of the traditions, doing her best to bring comfort and some quiet joy to Corinne, in particular. But she wondered if she would ever again look forward to this season.

One night as she filled tins with homemade cookies to give to friends, she decided to pack one for Reid, whom she hadn't seen since Canada. He wasn't home, so she placed her gift in a festive bag and hung it on his doorknob with a note that said, "Wishing you a blessed Christmas. Tori."

She heard him enter his apartment an hour later, but she waited in vain for a friendly knock on her door.

Late the next morning as she sat in her office twiddling a ballpoint pen between her fingers and wondering if she should just leave her prickly neighbor alone, her phone rang. She tossed the pen aside and answered the call.

"Hello, Victoria."

Sam. Relief exploded in Tori, pushing the breath out of her lungs.

"I just wanted to thank you for the cookies," he said.

"Cookies?" She shook her head in confusion.

"Oh." His voice had gone flat. "I guess you intended them for Reid."

Tori's bewilderment quickly morphed into anger. Once again, Reid had interfered and made a mess of things. "Oh, Sam, I'm so very—"

"It's not important," he said briskly. "I apologize for bothering you at work."

Just that, and he was gone.

Tori stared at the dead phone in her hand. It wasn't important, he had said, meaning his phone call had been nothing more than a perfunctory thank-you. Sam had already moved on.

For the rest of the workday Tori stayed busy enough to crowd Sam out of her thoughts. Even on the drive home, she refused to think about him. But her roiling emotions demanded an outlet and they found one in her anger at Reid.

At her apartment, she kept one eye on the front walk as

she worked next to the windows, stringing lights on the fragrant Scotch pine tree she'd dragged home. When at last she spotted Reid, she ran to her door and flung it open.

"Why did you do it?" she cried. "You had no right to—"

"Don't trouble yourself," he said, raising both hands in a gesture of surrender. "Sam already let me have it."

"Good," Tori said viciously.

"He's been a bear since he got home," Reid complained. "I've been trying to get him to call you, but…" He shook his head, defeated. "I'm sorry. I was just trying to help."

Tori's anger subsided and depression rushed in to fill the space it had left. "There's nothing you can do, Reid."

"Then why don't *you* do something?"

"I can't," she said wearily. "I can't change who I am any more than he can change who *he* is."

"Can't?" Reid asked sharply. "Or won't?"

Tori didn't bother to reply. Reid had never understood.

He gave her a long, measuring look, then made a disgusted noise in his throat and turned to unlock his door.

Tori went back inside and sat on the floor next to her unfinished Christmas tree. She drew her knees to her chest and hugged them hard.

Her mother had fallen in love with a police officer, and every day when Blake went to work, Regina had worried. But that unhappiness had been mitigated by the knowledge that Blake was protecting their community. And at the end of every day, he had come home to his family.

It would be even more difficult for the woman who married Sam. *She* would have to watch the man she loved go off for days, perhaps even weeks at a time to risk his neck in some obscure corner of the world, not out of duty to his country or to God but simply for the adrenaline rush.

Sam was wrong. There was no middle ground. Either a person could accept that kind of life or she couldn't.

"I can't," Tori whispered, staring at the string of gaily colored lights that snaked across the floor. When her tears blurred the lights' brilliant hues into a smudgy rainbow, she closed her eyes. "I just *can't.*"

Tori hadn't forgotten Senator Danvers's mysterious letter, she'd simply been too busy to pursue the matter. Now, however, the secret project was a welcome distraction from her troubles, so she spent every spare moment scouring old newspaper and gossip columns for clues. Beginning with the letter's postmark date, she worked backward, searching for any mention of a close personal or professional relationship between the senator and a woman whose first name or nickname began with a K.

Just a few days before Christmas, she found something. At the memorial service after the death of Benjamin Burns, a high-level official in the senator's party, the senator had been photographed with his arm around a young, pretty blonde woman. They stood together on the steps of a downtown Chicago church, his head bent close to hers in the way of friends sharing grief.

According to the photo's caption, the woman's first name began with a K. But it was her *last* name that made Tori gasp. She was looking at a photograph of Kathy Traynor.

Traynor wasn't that common a name, and considering the rich-and-powerful company this woman was keeping, she had to be Sam's cousin, Kath. Gray's sister.

G. knows, and is supporting me.

Had Kathy Traynor written those words to the senator? This picture proved they were together in Chicago just three months before the letter had been mailed, but that was hardly conclusive. Tori scanned the short column next to the photo, hoping to learn more. A moment later she sat back in her chair, stunned. Apparently, there were *two* women named Kathy Traynor.

The woman with the senator wasn't Gray's sister. She was the deceased man's daughter, Kathy Burns Traynor.

Gray's *wife*.

Pulling in a deep, steadying breath, Tori reviewed her facts as deliberately as a child dropping pennies into a coin bank. Singly, they were worth little. The time, the place and the initials didn't mean anything until they were added to Sam's bizarre reaction to hearing about the letter.

He was protecting a family secret, no question. It must have deeply offended his innate honesty to look into Tori's eyes and pretend he didn't know exactly what she was seeking.

Regret saturated every cell of Tori's body, but now that she'd glimpsed part of the truth she needed to know the rest. She performed a quick Internet search and learned that Gray's wife had died eight years ago. Tori checked her birth date and calculated that at the time of her father's funeral, Kathy had been twenty-nine. Far too young for the senator, who had turned sixty-four that year. And yet…

How old, exactly, was Austin Traynor? Another trip to the search engine and a few clicks later, Tori learned that on the date the letter was mailed to the senator, Kathy Burns Traynor had been roughly three months pregnant with Austin.

Overwhelmed by her discovery, Tori dropped her face into her hands.

Real love forgives, Gray had said on the plane. *Every single time, it forgives.* And Gray was in a position to know. He had forgiven his wife's infidelity and accepted the senator's child as his own.

Tori raised her head. Why had the Lord answered her prayers about finding Elmira's grandchild? Why hadn't He just slammed this door in her face? Weren't some secrets better left undisturbed?

Chewing a fingernail, she winced as she imagined a tabloid headline: *Billionaire Raising Love Child of Dead Wife and Senator Danvers: "He's Not My Son!" Grayson Traynor Admits*

Resting her elbow on the desk, Tori leaned her forehead against one cupped hand. She had realized Elmira's grandchild might not know the truth—or might know it and not want it made public. But she had hoped, for the college's sake and for her own selfish reasons, that it would be otherwise; that Elmira's only living descendant, now an adult, would eagerly step forward and acknowledge the relationship. Tori had imagined all kinds of scenarios, but never one in which the senator's baby had been claimed by a wronged husband who happened to be a famous billionaire.

Unable to imagine what God's purpose might have been in allowing her to make this discovery, Tori closed her eyes and asked what she was supposed to do now.

Ten minutes later she had a clear answer. "I'm going out for a while," she told Francine as she shoved her arms into her coat and tucked the letter into a pocket. "Personal business," she added, pulling on her leather gloves.

Heavy snow had begun falling by the time she eased her car into a parking space almost a block away from the Extreme Adventures offices. She pushed some coins into a meter and hurried down the slick sidewalk, past several opening and closing jingle-belled shop doors. Christmas music and the aroma of gingerbread swirled around her with the snowflakes; behind her, she heard a child's delighted laugh.

And every bit of it hurt. For the first time in her life, Tori wished Christmas would just hurry up and be over.

When she reached her destination, she paused in front of the big window filled with travel posters and sports equipment. Knowing this was the right thing to do wasn't going to make doing it any easier.

Just then the door opened and Sam strolled out. Spotting Tori, he startled and one heel skidded on the snowy walk. His arms flailed, uncharacteristically graceless, but he managed to regain his balance. He looked cautiously pleased as he stood in front of Tori and waited for her to speak.

"This isn't about you and me," she said quickly, before he got the wrong idea. "It's something else."

His face fell. "I was just on my way to meet someone, but she won't mind waiting."

"She?" The question was involuntary, and as the plaintive syllable hung in the thick air between them, Tori silently berated herself. Of course Sam had female clients. And friends. Maybe even—

"You think I have a *date*?" he asked, looking amazed.

Humiliation burned Tori's cheeks. "I'm sorry," she muttered. "It's not my business."

"You think I have a date," he repeated incredulously. "You actually think—" He stopped and shook his head at the sky. "Well, I don't know how to break this to you, brown eyes, but I happen to be in lo—"

"Don't!" Tori cried, afraid that if he finished that sentence, the words would haunt her for the rest of her life. "Please don't," she said, more gently. "Sam, there's something I need to—"

"No," he interrupted, panic flashing across his face. He raised both hands, palms out. "If you're about to tell me that you and Julian—" He stopped and his Adam's apple moved convulsively as he let his hands fall. "I don't want to hear it," he said in a defeated tone. "Don't try to explain it to me, Tori, because I'm not capable of understanding. Just turn around and walk away."

"That's not why I'm here." Dangerously moved by the desolation in his eyes, she dropped her gaze. Maybe he did love her, but it wasn't enough. "I have something I'd like you to deliver to Gray," she said, watching snow collect on the toes of her boots. She hesitated, then made herself look up. "It's a private matter."

Sam blinked away a snowflake that had landed on his eyelash. "Kathy's letter to the senator," he said tonelessly.

"You knew all along." Tori pulled the envelope from her coat pocket and held it out to him.

He made no move to take it. "Yes. I'm sorry."

Tori ached to rip off her gloves and smooth the two deep lines that had formed between his eyebrows, but she cleared her throat, instead. "I don't blame you for keeping it from me, Sam. It wasn't your story to tell."

He opened his mouth, then closed it and shook his head.

"I was so careful," Tori said. "In the beginning I told myself there might be secrets involved, but I never realized what a huge hornet's nest I was poking at."

Compassion widened his eyes. "I know you didn't."

"Nobody knows about this, Sam. Just you and me." She offered the envelope again, but he leaned away from it.

She understood and admired his reluctance. "The senator didn't leave us all of his personal papers, Sam. Just the ones that mentioned his mother. And this doesn't, so he couldn't have meant for us to have it."

Sam gazed at the envelope with naked longing. "Accident or not, it belongs to the college now."

She was trying hard not to love him, but how could she help herself when he stood there being so noble? "It's my job to appraise the materials we receive and determine whether they should be accessioned into our archives," she said primly. "And I say this item is not relevant to our collection."

Hope lightened Sam's expression. "You don't have to keep it? You can just—" he waved a hand "—get rid of it?"

"That's correct." Tori pushed back the hair a gust of wind had whipped against her face. "Archivists commonly sell, trade or donate materials they can't use to other libraries, but in this case, I'd have some serious ethical concerns about doing any of those things."

"Tori." His voice deepened. "Are you sure?"

"I'm the archivist," she said, adopting an air of injured dignity in order to convince him. "This is entirely my call."

"You're amazing." Admiration shone from Sam's emerald eyes as he plucked the letter from Tori's gloved hand and stuffed it inside his coat. "I knew that the first time I saw you."

The wind caught her hair again and this time it was Sam who smoothed it away from her face. His bare hand was cold and rough against her cheek, but it felt frighteningly good. Tori longed to shut her eyes and lean into his palm, but somehow she resisted that temptation.

"Ah, Tori," he breathed, dipping his head and swaying toward her.

She jerked away just in time to avoid his mouth.

Anger flashed in his eyes. "You won't give an inch, will you? I could understand if you weren't able to meet me halfway, but what I *don't* understand is why you won't even try."

A hot protest sprung to her lips, but she bit it back. This could only end in an argument and Tori bursting into tears right here on the sidewalk. "I'm sorry," she mumbled, turning away.

"You're acting like a coward," Sam called after her. "And I know you aren't one!"

Two women coming out of a shop looked at Sam and then stared at Tori, but she hurried past them, uncaring. She couldn't change the way she was made. If Sam thought it was such an easy thing to do, why didn't *he* change?

There were only two possible answers to that question: either he couldn't change or he didn't love her enough to try. The truth hardly mattered because either way, Tori was left with a broken heart.

* * *

"Did you read it?" Gray asked that evening as he and Sam stood together before the marble fireplace in his study.

Surprised, Sam shook his head. "It wasn't addressed to me."

"Or me." Gray turned the envelope over and over in his long hands, then he stepped closer to the fireplace and unceremoniously dropped it on top of a glowing, half-burned log. The paper crinkled and blackened and disappeared.

"He was more than twice her age," Gray said, stirring the fire with an iron poker to make sure no trace of the letter remained. "A close friend of her father's. She was hurting and I was working too many hours. I wasn't there for her."

"You don't have to tell me this," Sam said.

Gray stared into the fire, speaking as though to himself. "I hate it that she had an affair. But I wasn't able to give her the baby she wanted, so it was hard to see the pregnancy as a disaster. From the first time I felt Austin kick inside her belly, that boy was *mine*."

Emotion had tightened Sam's throat, so he just nodded.

Gray put the poker back in its stand and gazed up at the portrait of his wife that hung over the mantel. "I wish I hadn't burdened you with this, Sam."

Four years ago, Sam had saved Austin's life, jump-starting this friendship with Gray. Shortly after that, Gray had shared his secret, expressing his fear that an inherited medical condition might one day require Austin to know about his biological father. Sam was meant to be the safeguard. If Gray was gone and Austin ever needed to know the truth about his genes, Sam could explain.

Gray's revelation had been accidentally overheard by his sister, so Kath had been drawn into the secret. She and Sam had lobbied Gray to tell Austin the truth, but Gray had steadfastly clung to the promise he'd made to his wife.

"What will Victoria do now?" Gray asked.

"Nothing." Restless, Sam shifted his weight from one foot to the other and back again. "Nobody knew what she was working on, and she had the authority to dispose of the letter as she saw fit. So it's like none of this ever happened."

"She's an exceptional woman, Sam."

No kidding. Sam thrust his hands into his pockets and stared into the flames that had consumed the troublesome letter. "Why did God allow it to fall into her hands?" he wondered aloud. "There had to be a reason for all of this."

Gray was again looking at Kathy's portrait. "If she could see this mess, I know she'd release me from my promise. Austin's old enough to understand." Gray folded his arms and looked over his shoulder at Sam. "And generous enough, I think, to forgive."

Sam laid a hand on his cousin's shoulder, silently reaffirming his support as they stood together and stared into the dying fire.

"Do you ever think that maybe Mom has wasted a big chunk of her life?" Corinne asked on Christmas Eve as she pulled a perfectly browned turkey out of her mother's oven.

Tori's gaze jerked up from the pot of gravy she'd taken over stirring while her mother carried a platter of hors d'oeuvres to the guests in the living room. "What do you mean?"

"I'm talking about her worrying." Corinne settled the hot roasting pan on top of several thick potholders. "What did worrying ever do for her?"

What did it do for any of them, apart from making them miserable? Tori stared at the glossy surface of the gravy as she put her wooden spoon back to work. "Worry is the glue that holds this family together," she quipped.

Corinne ignored the feeble joke. "I was just thinking about all those years Mom wasted worrying about Dad."

Tori was in no mood for this conversation, but if Corinne insisted on having it, they were going to keep the facts straight. "Rinny, she had reason to worry. He ended up getting shot, remember?"

"But he lived through it. She kept expecting him to be killed in the line of duty, but he wasn't." Corinne leaned back against the counter and folded her arms. Because she looked a smidgen too nonchalant, Tori wasn't blindsided by what came next. "So maybe you should stop worrying about Sam. For all you know, he's going to die in bed when he's ninety-two."

"That's possible." With an effort, Tori held on to her patience. "But it's far more likely he'll die young."

Corinne pinched off a piece of turkey skin and popped it into her mouth. "But what if he *doesn't*?"

Tori closed her eyes briefly and reminded herself that Corinne had just lost the man she loved. If her way of coping with that was focusing on Tori's heartache instead of her own, Tori would just have to deal with it. "I love Sam," she admitted, and then she nearly choked up because she had never said the words out loud. "But our lifestyles aren't compatible."

Corinne shrugged. "Then find a lifestyle you can share."

"Neither of us can change that much, Rinny."

"Mom and Dad did it."

"Did they?" Tori wasn't convinced. "Mom was always worried sick and Dad was always drowning in guilt. Yes, they love each other, Rinny, but would they do it all over again?"

"I'd marry Bill again," Corinne said. "A lot of women never have anything half as good as what I had for those first three years." She made a fist and swiped at her moist eyes with her knuckles. "So in spite of everything, I still feel blessed."

"But you and Bill wanted the same things out of life," Tori argued, holding back tears of her own. "Before the accident, you were perfect together."

"Tori, all I'm saying is that real love is worth the risk. So if you love Sam, find a way to make a life with him. You'll never be sorry."

As Tori stared unseeing at the gravy swirling around her spoon, Sam's words echoed in her mind. *I know we can do it, Tori. Let's take a leap of faith.*

"Maybe you'll get fifty years," Corinne said. "But even *three* years would be worth fighting for. Trust me on that."

"What's worth fighting for?" Julian asked pleasantly as he strolled into the kitchen. He had evidently picked up Corinne's last few words, but not their serious tone.

"Mom's gravy," Corinne answered without missing a beat. She reached for a cloth and made herself busy polishing the already spotless countertop.

Julian moved behind Tori and placed his hands on her shoulders. It was a friendly touch, nothing more. He had finally accepted that although what Tori felt for him was deep and true, it was the affection of a sister for a brother. "It smells delicious," he said.

Tori dipped a teaspoon into the gravy and held it to his mouth. He tasted it and gave an exaggerated moan of pleasure.

Corinne beamed at him. "Nobody makes better gravy than our Mom."

Julian patted Tori's shoulder and moved away to inspect a pecan pie. "Don't tell *my* mother, but I happen to agree."

Corinne snitched a pecan half from the top of the pie and popped it into Julian's willing mouth. "We're spoiled," she said. "We've tasted the real thing and now nothing less will ever satisfy." She looked over her shoulder. "Right, Tori?"

Tori grasped the long-handled spoon and resumed her stirring, acutely aware that Corinne wasn't talking about gravy at all.

Chapter Fifteen

Sam smiled as his mother again offered the plate of cookies. He didn't want her thinking her hospitality was unappreciated, so he took another one, afraid she might not remember he'd already eaten four. He shot a pleading look in Reid's direction, but his brother was still standing by the windows watching snow fall, even though common decency demanded he get over here and take a turn eating Christmas cookies.

"Your tree is nice," Sam said around a mouthful of cookie. He knew she wouldn't remember that he and Willa had helped her decorate it just last week.

"Oh!" she exclaimed, setting the plate of cookies on the coffee table and clasping her hands like a delighted child. "Will it be Christmas soon?"

"It's Christmas right now," he said. "Christmas Eve."

Her pleasure quickly faded to concern. "You boys must have a family waiting for you," she scolded sweetly. "You should be with *them* tonight."

Sam took one of his mother's fragile hands in both of

his. "We're *your* family," he said gently. "Don't you remember us?"

It was always a risky question, but tonight it didn't appear to distress her. She studied Sam's face intently.

Just once, he begged silently, even though he didn't really believe it could happen. *Just this once, Lord, let her remember.*

"Green eyes," she said finally. "You have the clearest green eyes, Sammy, just like your father." She smiled at Reid, who was still gazing out the window. "And your brother got mine."

Reid turned in slow motion, his eyes wide with wonder. "Mom?" he croaked.

Sam held his breath and waited for more.

It never came. As Sam watched her face, her moment of clarity faded and she resumed her pleasant, vague expression. Heartsick, he released her hand and stared hopelessly at the sparkly gold star on top of the Christmas tree.

"You boys are sweet to visit me," she said a few minutes later. "But you don't belong here on Christmas Eve. Go home to your family."

A heavy snow was falling in damp clumps, muffling the city traffic noises as Sam and Reid trudged without speaking to Reid's SUV. When they climbed inside, Reid put his key in the ignition and then sat back in his seat, looking at Sam. "Did you hear what she said?"

"She knew us," Sam said dully. Their mother's fog of forgetfulness had lifted for only a moment, so he was having trouble being grateful.

"I'm not talking about that. I'm talking about the way she kept telling us to go home."

Sam had an inkling what his brother was driving at, and he just wasn't up to that tonight, so he put his brain to work thinking up excuses.

"She told us to go home," Reid repeated. "The house is sold, Dad's with the Lord and Mom's here. But we still have a home, don't we? Let's go there."

Sam shook his head. "Not tonight, Reid. I'm tired."

"It won't take long," Reid said mildly.

Sam glanced down at his jeans and the "Ski Starwood" sweatshirt he wore under his open coat. "I'm not dressed for church."

"Like that matters?"

"It's too late, anyway." Sam pointed at the digital clock just above Reid's CD player. "The service started ten minutes ago and it would take another fifteen to get there."

"So we'll be late. The old ladies will shake their heads and mutter about those incorrigible McGarry boys. It'll be just like old times." Reid started the engine and switched on the windshield wipers to push away the accumulated snowflakes. "If you want to make a paper airplane out of the bulletin and toss it at Mrs. Whetstone's big hair, I'll look the other way."

Another time, Sam would have grinned at the memory of nine-year-old Reid loudly apologizing for his little brother's transgression, but tonight he was too depressed. He'd tried and failed to whip up even a modicum of Christmas spirit. Crushed by grief, all he could think about was how much he missed his father's wisdom, his mother's kindness, Rich's camaraderie…and Tori. Of all Sam's losses in the past four years, that one was the hardest to bear.

"The Christmas Eve service never starts on time," Reid

remarked as he looked over his shoulder and backed out of the parking space.

The last thing Sam needed right now was to go to church and get slapped on the back by deacons and hugged by overly perfumed old ladies while he tried to pretend it didn't bother him to see another man standing behind his father's pulpit.

"Just drop me at my apartment," he said to his brother.

"I will," Reid said. "Right after church."

Three weeks after handing over Kathy Traynor's letter, Tori remained confident that she'd done the right thing. Clearly, God hadn't meant for her to use the letter to attract publicity for the college. He had simply wanted her to deliver it to Gray.

Maybe this whole thing had been a lesson in letting go. Maybe Wheldon College's time was over and God was telling Tori to move on.

The rumor mill said staff cuts were imminent, so Tori wasn't surprised on Thursday afternoon when she was summoned to the president's office. She reported to the vice president of academics, not directly to Dr. Goodman, but she supposed it didn't matter which of them told her to clean out her desk. When she arrived at Dr. Goodman's offices, his assistant escorted her to the doorway of an oppressive, dark-paneled room that smelled strongly of cherry pipe-tobacco.

"Ms. Talcott." Standing behind his desk, the bald, portly Dr. Goodman gestured to a red leather chair. "Please."

Tori sat and mentally braced herself. How much notice would she get? Would she have time to finish the centennial exhibit? She'd been praying that God would allow her that closure.

Dr. Goodman cleared his throat. "I have received a letter that will interest you." He pushed his wire-rim glasses up on top of his bald head and picked up a single sheet of paper from his desk. "Permit me to read two brief excerpts."

Puzzled, Tori inclined her head respectfully.

"It has come to my attention that your fine college has reached the brink of financial disaster," Dr. Goodman began. "Hearing of your plight from someone who is acquainted with Ms. Victoria Talcott, your archivist, I was interested enough to look into your financial situation."

Dr. Goodman glanced up as though to gauge Tori's reaction, but she was too baffled to have one. Why had her name been mentioned?

"I'll skip to the closing paragraph," Dr. Goodman said, and began reading again. "I wish to offer a substantial endowment that will enable Wheldon College to provide serious students with a quality liberal arts education for many years to come. Please contact my personal assistant to set up a meeting during which we may discuss this in person." Holding the paper by one corner, Dr. Goodman raised it level with his face and turned it so Tori could see it. "This was signed by Grayson Traynor."

Gray was going to save the college! Tori clutched the padded arms of her chair, desperately trying to remember how to work her lungs.

Dr. Goodman smiled. "You might want to close your mouth, Ms. Talcott."

Her lips made a small popping sound as she snapped

them together. Was Gray rewarding her for keeping Kathy's secret? No, that wasn't his style. After a moment Tori's brain settled comfortably on the fact that Gray was a remarkably unselfish man. He might desire to keep the circumstances of Austin's birth from the public, but he'd found a way to privately acknowledge his son's biological heritage. It was a beautiful gesture.

Tori blinked back tears of gratitude. So *this* was why Kathy's letter had fallen into her hands. God had been planning this all along.

Dr. Goodman slid his glasses back down and peered at Tori through them. "What exactly is your connection to Mr. Traynor?"

"I dated his cousin," she said carefully. "For a very short time. I don't see him anymore."

Dr. Goodman gave her a long, appraising look. "So you never actually met Mr. Traynor."

"Oh, I met him." Tori wondered what Dr. Goodman would think if he knew she'd held hands with Grayson Traynor and cried into his handkerchief and even let him pay for her hotel room. "But we never discussed the college. The circumstances of our meeting weren't conducive to..." She trailed off. "We never discussed the college," she repeated, deciding to stick with the simplest truth. "And I don't expect to meet him again."

Dr. Goodman's leather chair creaked as he leaned back in it. "Be that as it may, it appears he's going to save your job." He glanced down at the letter and added in an undertone, "And mine."

Honesty compelled Tori to disabuse him of any notion that

she had talked Gray into this. "Believe me, Dr. Goodman, I'm as surprised as you are. I never lobbied Mr. Traynor to—"

He stopped her by waving a hand. "Since your name is mentioned, I can only conclude that in Mr. Traynor's mind, at least, you had something to do with this."

Tori shifted uncomfortably as he continued to study her with a piercing gaze. She couldn't explain without provoking some very awkward questions, so she said nothing. If he thought she was stupid or stubborn, that couldn't be helped.

"Very well." He got to his feet, signaling the discussion was at an end. "I'm sure you realize the confidential nature of this letter."

"Of course," Tori murmured, rising.

"One more thing," he said. "I believe you did undergraduate work in history and hold a master's degree in library science?"

"Yes." She squared her shoulders. "And last year I was accredited by the Society of American Archivists. I'm eager to begin pursuing my doctoral studies, but I've been uncertain about my future here at Wheldon."

He gave her a long, considering look. "You will understand that, at present, I'm unable to offer you any assurances. But if matters proceed in the direction I'm beginning to hope, Ms. Talcott, I would strongly urge you to get to work on that doctorate."

Tori left his office in a happy daze and made her way to the frozen pond, that special place where her career at Wheldon had begun. She brushed snow off the wrought-iron bench and sat for a long while watching the willow branches sway in a light breeze.

She was too grateful for words. Not just because of Gray's letter, but because she had finally learned an important lesson: If God wanted her here at Wheldon, He would make it possible for her to stay. And if she got edged out, that would mean He wanted her somewhere else. What was the point in worrying?

Her excitement dissipated as she remembered she could never share any of this with Sam. Within moments, a fierce loneliness swallowed up her joy. She trudged back to her office, put off Francine's questions, gathered up her things and headed home, as low as she had ever been in her life.

When she approached her door and saw Reid come out of his apartment carrying a bulging plastic trash bag, she wanted to groan in dismay. The very last thing she needed right now was a run-in with Mr. Sunshine.

"Hi," he said, pleasantly enough. "How are you?"

She started to say she was fine, but Reid wasn't a man who tolerated polite lies. "I've had better days," she admitted.

Reid nodded sympathetically. "He misses you, Tori."

"Don't do this," she begged.

He put his trash bag down. "You two have something special. Don't throw it away because of some unreasonable fear."

"My fear is not unreasonable," she said evenly. "What Sam does is dangerous."

"There's some risk involved," he conceded. "But I think what you've built up in your mind is a whole lot scarier than the reality."

"Are you saying he'll never get hurt?" she challenged.

Reid folded his arms. "No. But you could marry a nice,

careful guy like Julian and see him get hit by a bus a month later." He gave her a couple of seconds to think about that, then his voice softened. "Life is uncertain, Tori. Just ask your sister how uncertain it is."

Tori shut her eyes and heard Corinne's voice in her mind: *In spite of everything, I still feel blessed.*

"You think you're in control," Reid continued. "But ultimately, it all comes down to what God allows and what He doesn't. So maybe it's stupid to run from Sam just because he takes physical risks."

"But the risks he takes aren't necessary."

"Maybe they are to him."

Tori ignored that. "So what's he up to this week?" she asked bitterly. "Dangling off the side of some mountain by a strand of dental floss?"

"No." There was something smug in Reid's expression as he peered at his watch. "Right now he should be arriving home from Palm Springs, where he's been playing golf with Gray."

Golf? She almost laughed. "Since when does Sam play golf?"

Reid nailed her with one of the aggressive stares he excelled at. "Since he stopped doing dangerous sports."

Tori's breath caught in her throat. *"What?"*

"He couldn't stand it that you worried so much, so he quit. Everything. No risks."

Dazed, she shook her head. Just a minute ago, she'd been seething with resentment because Sam didn't love her enough to stop taking risks. But hearing that he'd done exactly that didn't please her, either.

Reid's eyes glittered. "Isn't that what you wanted?"

She had thought so, but she'd been horribly wrong. Sam didn't have a death wish; he wanted to *live*. And that was exactly what he did, at full throttle. Sam embraced life with a wild enthusiasm that was uniquely his own.

"He can't quit," Tori said. "Not for me."

Reid looked exasperated. "Well he *has*. Because he's crazy in love, just like you. Why are you being so stupid about it?"

The verbal punch knocked Tori's breath out. For a long moment she just stared at Reid, her brain scrambling to form words. "He hasn't even called," she said weakly.

"He's been busy reorganizing his life," Reid said. "And maybe he's giving you some breathing space. I don't know. What I do know is that he bought an engagement ring the day after Christmas and he's been carrying it in his pocket ever since." Reid picked up his trash bag. "He's going to kill me for telling you that, but I'm afraid if I don't give you a little push, you're never going to get off your backside and work this out."

"We're too different." The old argument had sprung to her lips before she realized it might not be true anymore. Maybe it never *had* been true. Maybe Sam was right; maybe some differences could be good.

"You almost died," Reid reminded her, his harsh words tempered by a softening in his eyes. "*He* almost died. Life is uncertain, Tori. Shouldn't you grab it with both hands and enjoy whatever time you might have together?"

"Take a leap of faith," she murmured, remembering Sam's words.

"That's right. That's what Sam's doing."

The truth hit her hard. She'd been running from love because she was afraid something awful would happen to

Sam. But now she understood what Corinne had been trying to tell her. Real love was worth the risk.

"He's been going to church," Reid offered. "He finally got past all that bitterness about Dad being gone."

Gratitude flooded Tori's eyes with hot tears.

"There's something else you ought to know," Reid continued, watching her closely. "To hear Sam tell it, his trips are all about having a good time. But you wouldn't believe how many men he's led to the Lord while pulling off his ski boots at some backcountry lodge. He never goes anywhere without his Bible and somehow he talks those guys into studying it with him after dinner instead of heading for the bar."

"But…Sam can barely read."

"True. But he has a fantastic memory, so he hands his Bible to some guy and asks him to read such and such a chapter out loud. And then they discuss it."

Tori was dumbfounded. "He never told me that."

"He wouldn't. He's never accepted that he has a gift for evangelism. Our dad went to seminary and learned Hebrew and Greek and read all the great Christian thinkers, but Sam hasn't done any of that."

"But those things aren't what makes an evangelist," Tori protested.

"I agree."

"Are you saying God *called* him to his lifestyle?"

Reid shrugged. "All I know is that a lot of those guys who have never been inside a church will listen to Sam because he's earned their respect. Sam says he's not doing anything out of the ordinary. I happen to believe otherwise."

Tori stared at the narrow brick wall between her door

and Reid's, thinking hard. How could she allow Sam to give up a lifestyle God might have called him to?

"He's on his way home from California right now," Reid said. "We're having a late dinner with clients tonight, but he'll be in the office tomorrow morning at nine." Reid's mouth tilted into a sly smile. "I mention this on the off chance that you might want to stop by and get engaged. Mind if I take my trash out now?"

It all took a minute to sink in, but finally Tori gave a strangled cry and flung her arms around Reid's neck. The trash bag smacked against the sidewalk as Reid's arms wrapped around her in a brotherly hug.

"For such an educated woman, you can be awfully dumb," he remarked.

"I know." She grinned up at him. "And for such a sweet guy, you can be awfully nasty."

A minute later Tori entered her apartment in a blur of happiness. Sam loved her so much that he had actually changed for her. He'd have to change right back, of course; she wasn't going to let him stop being Sam. And if he was telling others about God, that certainly wasn't anything she wanted to get in the way of. But it thrilled her to know he'd been willing to bend so far in order to make her happy.

She could bend, too. She could stop second-guessing and double-checking and being so ridiculously careful about everything. She could worry less and trust God more, starting right now.

She dropped her keys and her purse onto a chair, then shrugged out of her coat and dumped it on top of them. Something inside her had just shifted and she felt eager, excited. Moving to the middle of her living room, she lifted her arms like a ballet dancer and allowed her head to fall back. Then she closed her eyes and imagined herself letting go, falling forward.

Taking her very first leap of faith.

Chapter Sixteen

The fully-loaded airliner was on its final approach to O'Hare as Sam arched against his seat to remove a small velvet box from the pocket of his jeans. He opened it and positioned it under the beam of his overhead light so he could watch the emerald-cut diamond throw colorful sparks.

He cupped his hands around the box, concealing his treasure as well as he could from casual observers. He shouldn't have taken it out on a crowded plane, but he liked looking at it while he imagined sliding it onto Tori's finger.

He'd shown it to his mother four times. She might not recognize her son, but she knew an engagement ring when she saw one and Sam got a huge kick out of watching her admire Tori's diamond.

"Now there's a pretty thing." The bulky Irish priest wedged into the seat next to Sam nodded pleasantly at the ring. "And when will ye be askin' her?"

Sam snapped the box shut and returned it to his pocket. "Just as soon as she realizes God means for us to be together."

"Ah. So you're a man of faith."

Sam nodded. "I tried to push her once, but I won't make that mistake again. I've learned I can wait."

"Patience is a grand thing," the priest said approvingly.

"I've never been known for it," Sam admitted.

The priest laughed, showing two rows of large, crooked teeth. "Not many of us are known for it, boyo. So God's been giving you lessons, has He?"

Sam nodded and left it at that. But when Reid had dragged him to church on Christmas Eve, something had shifted in Sam's heart. That night a stranger's sermon had made him hunger to know the Lord in a new and deeper way and Sam had finally let go of his crippling grief. It no longer hurt to walk into the church his father had pastored for so many years; now it felt right.

Another thing that felt right was his love for Tori. Sam wanted to make her happy more than he had ever wanted to ski and skydive, so he'd given up those things. With God's help, he was carving out a new life; one that Tori could be comfortable sharing with him.

The airplane's tires hit the runway hard, jerking Sam forward in his seat, and he felt a rush of gratitude. He didn't expect to see Tori anytime soon, but it felt good to be back in the same city as her.

As the plane pulled up to its gate, Sam turned on his cell phone and checked his missed calls. One in particular caught his interest, and he hit the callback button.

"Hey, Sam," Austin Traynor said a couple of rings later. "You back in town yet?"

"Yep. Just arrived at the terminal."

"Heard you played a little golf this morning. What did you shoot?"

"None of your business," Sam said amiably.

"Ninety-four," Austin hooted. "I just got off the phone with Dad. I don't think golf is your game, Sammy-boy."

"Hey. It's not like I've ever played before." He'd been surprised to learn golf was actually a fun game. There was all that walking, for one thing, and all those trees and green, grassy hills to appreciate. And hitting those little balls where you wanted them to go wasn't anywhere near as easy as it looked. "I'll get the hang of it," he assured Austin.

A bell sounded in the cabin and Sam heard a chorus of metallic clicks as a couple of hundred people unbuckled their seat belts. He remained in his window seat as everyone around him tried to crowd into the aisle. In the past, he'd always been the first to spring up from his seat, but he was feeling downright laid-back these days.

"I have some news," Austin said. "But first, you know Dad told me about the senator, right?"

"He mentioned it." Sam hesitated. "Are you okay with all that?"

"Oh, yeah," Austin replied breezily. "I don't know what everybody was so worked up about. I mean, it was always obvious that Mom loved Dad. And even good people get offtrack sometimes, right? Besides, it's not what's in my blood that makes me who I am. I'm Gray Traynor's son, not the senator's."

Emotion tightened Sam's throat, making a reply impossible.

"But back to my news," Austin said. "Wheldon College's library is going to be restored and upgraded, et cetera. And it's getting a new name. The Austin G. Traynor Library. What do you think?"

Sam was amazed at the rightness of it. Tori would be thrilled half out of her mind when she heard that Elmira's library was going to be restored to its former glory and would carry her grandson's name. "I think that's extremely cool, Aus."

"Yeah. Dad says this is my secret to keep or tell, although he's not recommending I mouth off about it anytime soon, because of the media. He thinks it won't be all that sensational a story by the time I'm out of college."

"That's probably true."

"I'm not very interested in the senator," Austin said. "Not at the moment, anyway. My dad's always been enough for me."

Sam's throat swelled again. "Your dad's great."

"Yeah." After a brief pause, Austin said, "Hey, I've gotta go meet some friends. I'll talk to you later."

"Austin?" Sam said urgently. "If you're driving, you be careful."

Austin snorted. "Didn't I just finish saying one dad is enough for me? Later, Sam."

Sam flipped his phone closed, surprised by the way that *be careful* had slipped out of his mouth. Next he'd be saying, *call me when you get home.*

As the cabin door was opened and the river of people beside him surged forward, Sam leaned back in his seat and closed his eyes, silently laughing at himself.

At precisely nine o'clock the next morning, Tori gave her name to the receptionist at Extreme Adventures and asked to see Sam.

The young woman nearly choked on the chewing gum

she'd been snapping. "It's *you*! I can't believe you're finally here!"

Startled, Tori backed up a step.

"I'm Willa Traynor." The receptionist gave Tori a broad wink. "Soon to be your cousin-in-law?"

A movement caught Tori's eye and she turned in time to see Reid, wearing a smug grin, disappear around a corner.

Willa pointed at the narrow, carpeted hallway beyond her desk. "Second door on the right. Hey, can I be in your wedding?"

Tori chuckled. She had never felt so lighthearted in all her life. "Let me get engaged first, then we'll talk."

She found Sam's office and looked through the open doorway. He was just ending a phone call and happened to glance up. Surprise and pleasure flickered across his face, but they were quickly followed by doubt. Hanging up the phone, he sucked his bottom lip into his mouth and eyed Tori nervously as he pushed back his chair and stood.

"Hello, Sam." She strove for a brisk tone. "I'm here on business."

His tawny eyebrows drew together. "Business."

"That's right." Tori kept her expression carefully blank. "May I come in?"

He stared for another moment, then moved his head in a jerky nod.

The dramatic blue walls of Sam's office were hung with several huge, back lighted photographs. In one, a deranged man dangled from a rope next to the granite face of an impossibly tall cliff. In another, some nut on a bicycle hung suspended in clear blue sky, the rocky ground a good ten feet beneath him. Tori swallowed hard.

Sam indicated one of the strappy leather chairs in front of his desk. Tori eased into it as Sam resumed his seat behind the desk.

"I want an adventure," Tori said, crossing her legs and tugging self-consciously at her skirt.

Sam dragged his gaze from her calves up to her face. "An adventure," he repeated.

"A big one," she said airily. "I was thinking of—" She stopped, distracted by the photograph behind Sam, in which a lunatic on skis had just sailed off a rocky cliff on a snow-covered mountain and appeared to be doing a backflip. The skier wore goggles and a knit cap pulled low, but his head was thrown back, showing the profile of a nose and chin Tori had no trouble recognizing. Sam's mouth was wide open and for a moment Tori's imagination played a trick on her and she heard his whoop of delight.

"Tori?"

She jerked her gaze back to him. "I was thinking of marriage."

"Marriage." There was no mistaking the satisfaction that lighted his emerald eyes for just an instant before his expression settled into one of cool interest. "I've never arranged anything like that, but it shouldn't be too difficult to put something together for you." He leaned forward, resting his elbows on the desk as he steepled his fingers together. "You do realize," he continued, watching her intently, "that while most of the adventures I arrange for my clients last anywhere from a few days to several weeks, this one would require a lifetime commitment from you."

"I understand that." Tori's fingers curled nervously around the shoulder strap of her handbag.

His mouth quirked as he picked up a ballpoint pen and toyed with it. How long could he keep this up? Tori was about to crack and throw herself at him.

He twirled the pen around his fingers like a miniature baton. "It would also involve a certain amount of risk. Are you sure that wouldn't be a problem for you?"

Tori sat up straighter. "I happen to be a woman who enjoys a certain amount of risk."

He snorted. "Since when?"

"Well, to tell you the truth, I didn't know that about myself until last night."

The pen stopped moving and Sam's expression darkened.

"I've changed," she insisted. "It still scares me, what you do, but what good is my safe little world when you're not in it? I can be strong, Sam, you were right about that. I know I can face my fears about your adventuring."

"You won't have to," he said, flipping the pen onto his desk. "I've quit that stuff."

"That's what I hear," she said crisply. Did he actually think she would stand for this? "But you're just going to have to start back up again. I won't let you make that sacrifice for me."

"And you think I'm going to let you sit at home and worry yourself sick about me?" He leaned back in his chair and folded his arms. "Think again, sweetheart."

She was almost annoyed with him. "I'm *changing*, Sam. This is what I want." When he opened his mouth, she raised a hand, forestalling his protest. "We'll hammer this out later," she said firmly. "Maybe it's something we'll have to work on every day for the rest of our lives. But we're going to *do* this, Sam. I'm going to stop running like a scared rabbit and you're going to stop making heroic gestures and we're going to do this."

He swiveled back and forth in his chair, a smile tugging at his handsome mouth as he watched her. "You are really something else, brown eyes."

"So you'll set up this adventure?" she asked. "And...accompany me?"

"I'll accompany you," he said slowly. "But we'd still need a guide."

"I realize that." Emotion added a little quaver to her voice.

"We'd have to put our complete trust in Him," Sam continued. "We'd have to follow His directions always."

Tori's heart burned with love and hope. "That's exactly the kind of adventure I want." She hesitated. "Is it a deal, then?"

"It's a deal." He rose and walked around the desk, extending his right hand. Tori stood and took it, thinking he meant to shake with her and prolong the game. But he yanked her into his arms and before she could catch another breath, Sam's mouth was on hers, warm and sweet.

"I love you," he said after a minute. "So if my life isn't a comfortable fit for you, then I'll just get a new life. We'll work it out, Tori. With God's help, we'll work it out."

"We will," she agreed, leaning her forehead against his chin. It might never be easy, but what choice did they have?

"I've been going to church, Tori." Sam's mouth tickled her hair as he spoke.

"Reid told me. I'm so glad."

He lifted her face with gentle hands and kissed the tip of her nose. "I'll switch to your church if that's important to you."

"We'll talk about that," she promised.

"Something's happened to me, Tori. God's been work-ing in my heart and I feel closer to Him than I've ever been in my life."

She stroked his smooth cheek with her fingertips.

"As much as I missed you, I knew it was right to wait," he said. "We both had some things to work out on our own, didn't we?"

She nodded. God had been nudging her in this direc-tion all along, and now that she had finally moved, every-thing made perfect sense.

"Oh, and another thing." Sam leaned back a little to look at her. "Since I've had all this free time, I've been going to one of those adult learning centers. My instructor's not as pretty as you, but that's good because she doesn't distract me the way you did."

Tori grinned at that, then remembered something im-portant. "Sam, about your ministry…"

"Ministry," he repeated, frowning. "You *have* been talk-ing to Reid."

"He says your daredevil friends listen to you because you're one of them." With a fingertip, Tori smoothed the two deep lines between Sam's eyebrows until they disap-peared. "What if you were wrong to quit?" she asked boldly. "What if that was where God wanted you?"

He seemed to hesitate. "I've been sure for a while now that God's pleased about the feelings I have for you and the promises I want to make to you. But Tori, I'm not sure about anything else."

"Okay," she said slowly, considering that. "Maybe we're supposed to think about this for a while. Maybe your taking some time off is a good thing. Maybe God wants you to scale back on some of the riskier things you do." She gazed into his eyes, so overcome with love and pride she could barely get the next batch of words out. "But I don't want you trying to be somebody you're not. I want *you*, Sam."

He looked away from her, shaking his head, still uncertain.

"We'll figure it out," Tori said when those wild green eyes met hers again. "Let's trust God to show us what He wants from us both."

Unable to tear his gaze from Tori's, Sam turned just his head toward the open office door. "Willa! Hold my calls and reschedule my appointments. I'm getting engaged and then I'm taking the day off."

As Tori giggled at the squeal of delight emitted by her future cousin-in-law, Sam backed up a little and dug the tiny velvet box out of his pants pocket. "Victoria," he began in a husky voice. "I love you and I would be deeply honored—"

"Reid!" Willa shrieked from the doorway. "Angie! Come on, you're *missing* it!"

Sam let go of Tori and strode to the doorway. He pressed his palm against Willa's forehead, pushing her back so he could firmly close the door with his other hand.

He returned to Tori and started over. "Victoria, I love you and I would be deeply—"

"Yes!" she cried, throwing her arms around his neck. "Oh, Sam, *yes*!"

She was strangling him, but he was too thrilled to care. Somehow he got the little box open and held it under her nose.

She gasped, then moved back, offering her left hand and allowing him to push the sparkly symbol of his love onto her finger. She said it was beautiful and then she slid her arms around his neck again and pulled his face down to hers.

"Kids," Sam murmured between kisses, remembering her desire for a real family. Lord willing, he would give her that and everything else she wanted. "Lots of kids."

"You want kids?" she asked breathlessly.

Oh, did he ever. With *her*? "Yes, please." He kissed the tip of her nose. "As many as you want, as soon as you want. Feel free to have triplets."

"Oh, thank you," she said dryly.

"I'll be a good dad," he promised. "I won't let them do anything that worries you." He'd make them wear their raincoats and he'd never let them eat too much sugar and when they grew up, they'd call their mother every single night when they got home. He'd see to it.

But Tori was shaking her head. "I don't want our children to grow up the way I did, worrying about everything. I want them to run out and embrace life."

"As long as they don't get carried away," he said sternly. "I'm not going to let them terrify you."

She laughed. "Oh, Sam. *All* kids terrify their parents."

A frisson of pure happiness shot through him. "I can't believe you're really mine."

She sobered instantly and her warm brown gaze made his breath hitch. "I think in a way, I've always been yours, Sam. Since that very first day."

He leaned his forehead against hers. "I felt it, too. When you fainted in my arms. I know it sounds crazy and I'm not saying I believe in love at first sight. I mean, real love isn't just a feeling, it's a commitment, and how could any sane person hand over his heart just like that? But the interest was there. Just a little spark at first, but it kept growing."

Tori gave him a dreamy smile. "You know, there's an old Chinese proverb that if you save someone's life, you're responsible for it from that day on."

Sam swallowed the mighty burst of laughter that rose in his throat. "Is that right?" he said, doing his best to look interested.

Tori nodded. "I think the idea is that after you've snatched that individual from the clutches of death, he or she belongs to you. Of course, we Christians don't think that way. I know it was God who saved my life. But He used you to do it, so ever since that day, I've felt a connection to you. Like you said, it was just a little spark at first. But I felt it."

"Well, forget those little sparks." Sam brushed his thumb over her lush bottom lip. "I'll show you some real fireworks," he promised, and then he lowered his mouth to hers.

Epilogue

Tori was worried about Sam. In the four months leading up to their wedding, he had become almost as neurotic as her mother. So maybe she shouldn't have been surprised that today, when the time had come for them to take this irrevocable step, his increasingly cold feet had turned into solid blocks of ice.

From behind her, his hands gripped her shoulders as he spoke in her ear. "Tori, let's give this some more thought."

"Stop worrying," she said, half amused and half annoyed at his last-ditch effort to get her to call this off. "People do this every day and live through it. We're going to be fine."

"I just don't see why you're in such a rush," he grumbled. "I'm willing to do this if you're sure it's what you want, but we don't have to do it today."

She turned her head and gave him a stern look to cover her fear that if they didn't do this today, *right now*, they might never do it. Then she faced forward again and steeled her nerves, silently praying that all would be well.

Sam tugged on her arm. "Honey, there's no shame in admitting we're just not ready to—"

"Get a grip, McGarry." She had indulged his jitters long enough. Tori hauled in a breath and took a bold step forward.

Clipped at four points to the back of the harness she wore, Sam had no choice but to scuffle after her as she edged closer to the gaping doorway of the airplane. Three veteran jumpers and another tandem student with an instructor clipped to his back had just disappeared through the opening in rapid succession, so Tori was worried. If she and Sam didn't hurry, they might miss their drop zone.

She reached for the steel bar above the doorway. When she had a good grip on it, she looked down.

Oh.

She would have clapped a hand over her mouth, but she didn't dare loosen one from the bar. Feeling sick, she squeezed her eyes shut. Yeah, okay, this was a bad idea, and just as soon as she was able to speak again, she was going to tell Sam that he was right, they didn't have to do this, *she* didn't have to do this, she must have been insane to think she could *ever* do this, and—

"I've got you!" he yelled over the roaring wind and the Twin Otter's engine noise. He pried her frozen fingers off the bar. "Hands on your shoulders, like we practiced."

Tori crossed her forearms like an Egyptian mummy, trusting Sam not to let her fall out of the plane while she struggled to find the words to tell him she'd changed her mind.

"Ready?" he shouted. Something in his voice told her that although he was still holding onto the plane, he'd just let go of his reservations. He sounded eager now. Excited.

He was going to get them both killed.

"Here we go!" he yelled, and then he pushed her.

Tori was pretty sure she screamed, but either her voice wasn't working properly or the sound was snatched away by the wild wind that rushed up at them. Her eyes remained tightly shut, but after the first couple of seconds there was really no sensation of falling, just the hurricane-force wind slamming against her body.

She kept her arms crossed over her chest, out of Sam's way so he could deploy the drogue chute that would slow their rate of descent to what he called a "sedate" hundred and twenty miles per hour. When he tapped her shoulder, Tori obeyed the command by extending her arms and arching her back, assuming the free-fall position they'd practiced on the ground.

Deciding it might be less scary if she could see what was happening, Tori opened her eyes. She wasn't quite gutsy enough to look down, so she fixed her eyes on the hazy horizon—not that any image actually registered in her shocked brain.

Sam had explained that the wind screaming past them would make it impossible to communicate except by hand signals. Now he put his left hand in front of her face and gave her a thumbs-up. *So far so good*, the gesture said, But Tori was only marginally reassured. They would spend about sixty seconds in free fall, he'd told her when he'd clipped on to the back of her harness and snugged the straps, pulling her tightly against his body. But it already seemed like sixty *minutes* had passed since the lunatic behind her had shoved her out of that perfectly good airplane.

If they lived through this, she was going to kill him.

She turned her head to the right and there he was, grinning at her, his clear green eyes dancing behind a pair of goggles, the crazy man she was crazy about.

Tori sighed into the wind. She was so hopelessly in love that last Saturday night she had actually become Mrs. Sam McGarry. No, theirs hadn't been a Christmas wedding—it was barely the middle of May. Tori had given up her girlish dream when she'd realized a Christmas wedding would mean waiting almost a year to get started on her life with Sam. Even four months had seemed like an interminable wait, but at last their wedding day had arrived.

Now Tori was praying that they'd survive their honeymoon.

Once again, Sam thrust his hand in front of her face—five fingers this time, meaning they were now at five thousand feet and he was about to hit the brakes. Tori's stomach lurched as she recalled Austin Traynor's exceedingly unfunny joke that Sam would save their lives by pulling the ripcord when they were "roughly twenty-five seconds from *splat.*"

Before she could even send up another prayer, she heard or felt something flap in the wind and then she felt a jerk and sank down into her harness. And there was no more blasting wind.

"We're floating," she whispered to herself, lost in the wonder of it.

"Look up," Sam said in a normal voice. "Always check your canopy, first thing. If anything's wrong up there, you need to know it right away so you can deal with it."

When she'd asked about safeguards, Sam had shown her the reserve chute he carried. If the main canopy failed to open properly, they'd have to release themselves, go back into free fall and then deploy the reserve. So it was with no minor trepidation that Tori tipped her head back and looked up.

A hysterical laugh gurgled out of her throat when she saw the bulging rectangle of blue and green stripes.

"Isn't this amazing?" Sam asked as he passed her the steering toggles.

Tori grasped one in each hand. When Sam told her to practice a couple of turns, she tugged gently on the right side and was delighted when she and Sam rotated slowly in that direction. Thrilled by the idea that she could actually *fly* this thing, she pulled again, too hard, and threw them into a dizzying spin.

She emitted a horrified squeal, but Sam just chuckled. "You might want to ease up on that before you lose your lunch."

"*You* drive," she said, eagerly surrendering control of the lines. Seconds later Sam executed a gentle turn, bringing the golden, low-hanging sun into view.

"Beautiful," Tori breathed.

She would probably never do this again, but she'd had to do it once, to prove to Sam that she accepted his need for these thrills. He'd been appalled when she insisted on spending part of their honeymoon at the airfield, and right up until the moment they'd exited the plane, he had tried to talk her out of this.

Of course she had been nervous, but every time she'd looked into Sam's eyes and seen her own worries reflected there, her resolve had been strengthened. She'd lived long enough with her own crippling fears to know that was no kind of life for Sam. Now her heart hummed with gratitude because God had granted her the courage she'd needed to make this leap of faith.

Sam would understand now that she didn't want him to give up the sports he enjoyed. She had married an adventurer and she didn't want to change him. She just needed him to remember she was counting on him to always use good judgment and not take any stupid risks.

That would be enough. For the rest, she was learning to trust God.

Sam had said they'd float under the canopy for about five minutes, and suddenly that didn't seem like a long enough ride. Tori hadn't liked the first part at all, but *this* was beautiful. Scissoring her legs like a kid on a swing, she accidentally kicked Sam. "Look at me," she said as he chuckled and made another slow turn. "I'm walking on air!"

"That's because you're in love." Bending his head to hers, he dropped a kiss on her ear and then his voice turned husky. "Tori, except for my relationship with the Lord, loving you is the greatest thrill I've ever known."

He couldn't have said anything more perfect. Tori knew she'd remember those words for the rest of her life.

She couldn't know what happiness and sorrow the coming years would bring, but God had given her this beautiful day and she was determined to live, really *live* every moment of it. Joy bubbled up in her throat and she released it in a shout: *"Woo-hoo!"*

Sam laughed and then added a whoop of his own.

As the sun spilled its golden light in the western sky,

Tori leaned her head against her adventurer's shoulder, completely unafraid as they drifted back to God's green earth, together.

* * * * *

Dear Reader,

The inspiration for this "opposites attract" story came from a line in the Drew Barrymore movie, *Ever After*: "A fish may love a bird, but where would they live?" In *A Season of Forgiveness*, Tori believes she and Sam are too different to build a future together—but then she remembers that with God, all things are possible.

Are you a worrier? If so, I hope this story has served as a gentle reminder that God has a plan for your life; He's just waiting for you to leave your fears in His capable hands and take that leap of faith. When you do that, He will lead you on some wonderful adventures.

If you'd like to know more about me and my writing, please visit my online home, www.BrendaCoulter.com. I answer all e-mail personally, so if you'd like to tell me what you thought about this book, address me at ASOF@BrendaCoulter.com. You can also write to me in care of Steeple Hill Books, 233 Broadway, Suite 1001, New York, NY 10279.

Trusting Him,

QUESTIONS FOR DISCUSSION

1. At what point do you think being careful can prevent us from living life to its fullest?

2. While Sam admits to a certain degree of recklessness, he believes God gave him his thirst for adventure. Where would you draw the line between acceptable risk and foolish behavior? How do you think Tori, Reid and Sam would answer that question?

3. What was your favorite scene in this story and why?

4. Why was Reid so hard on Tori when he clearly believed she was the right woman for Sam?

5. How well does the Bible verse in the front of this book fit the story? Would you have chosen a different one?

6. In A SEASON OF FORGIVENESS, Tori discovers that Grayson Traynor forgave his wife's infidelity. How many other examples of forgiveness can you cite in this story?

7. Although she had given serious thought to the qualities she was looking for in a husband, Tori fell hard for Sam, who wasn't remotely "safe" or predictable. What was it about Sam that captivated her?

8. Why did Sam allow Julian to win the duel on skis?

9. Did it seem believable to you that Sam and Tori were so determined to meet in the middle that Sam began to worry and Tori participated in a dangerous sport? At the story's end, did you believe the couple would find the right balance for their life together?

10. Many people report that reading inspirational romance novels challenges them to examine their own relationships with the Lord. Did reading A SEASON OF FORGIVENESS prompt you to do that? If so, have you resolved to make any changes in your actions or attitudes?

Love Inspired®

Celebrate Love Inspired's 10th anniversary
with top authors and great stories all year long!

Look for

Shepherds Abiding in Dry Creek

by Janet Tronstad

*Dry Creek: The small
Montana town with
a heart as big as heaven.*

Lonely after her husband's
death, Marla Gossett moved
to Dry Creek, Montana, for a
fresh start. Yet when an unusual
Yuletide theft cast suspicion on
her young brood, the assistance
of the handsome Dry Creek
deputy sheriff proved more
welcome than Marla anticipated.

Steeple
Hill®

www.SteepleHill.com

*Available November
wherever you buy books.*

LI87457

REQUEST YOUR FREE BOOKS!

2 FREE INSPIRATIONAL NOVELS
PLUS 2
FREE
MYSTERY GIFTS

Love Inspired®

YES! Please send me 2 FREE Love Inspired® novels and my 2 FREE mystery gifts. After receiving them, if I don't wish to receive any more books, I can return the shipping statement marked "cancel." If I don't cancel, I will receive 4 brand-new novels every month and be billed just $3.99 per book in the U.S., or $4.74 per book in Canada, plus 25¢ shipping and handling per book and applicable taxes, if any*. That's a savings of 20% off the cover price! I understand that accepting the 2 free books and gifts places me under no obligation to buy anything. I can always return a shipment and cancel at any time. Even if I never buy another book from Steeple Hill, the two free books and gifts are mine to keep forever.

113 IDN EF26   313 IDN EF27

Name _____ (PLEASE PRINT)

Address _____ Apt. #

City _____ State/Prov. _____ Zip/Postal Code

Signature (if under 18, a parent or guardian must sign)

Order online at www.LoveInspiredBooks.com

Or mail to Steeple Hill Reader Service™:

IN U.S.A.: P.O. Box 1867, Buffalo, NY 14240-1867
IN CANADA: P.O. Box 609, Fort Erie, Ontario L2A 5X3

Not valid to current Love Inspired subscribers.

Want to try two free books from another series?
Call 1-800-873-8635 or visit www.morefreebooks.com

* Terms and prices subject to change without notice. NY residents add applicable sales tax. Canadian residents will be charged applicable provincial taxes and GST. This offer is limited to one order per household. All orders subject to approval. Credit or debit balances in a customer's account(s) may be offset by any other outstanding balance owed by or to the customer. Please allow 4 to 6 weeks for delivery.

Your Privacy: Steeple Hill is committed to protecting your privacy. Our Privacy Policy is available online at www.eHarlequin.com or upon request from the Reader Service. From time to time we make our lists of customers available to reputable firms who may have a product or service of interest to you. If you would prefer we not share your name and address, please check here. ☐

LIREG07

Love Inspired

SUSPENSE
RIVETING INSPIRATIONAL ROMANCE

STRANGER IN THE SHADOWS

by Shirlee McCoy

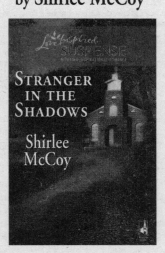

After a heartbreaking tragedy, Chloe Davidson relocated to sleepy Lakeview, Virginia, where handsome minister Ben Avery welcomed her. Yet Chloe kept seeing a stranger lurking in the shadows. Was it just her fragile imagination, or was a sinister somebody much closer than she ever expected?

Available November wherever you buy books.

Steeple
Hill®

www.SteepleHill.com

LIS44266

TITLES AVAILABLE NEXT MONTH

Don't miss these four stories in November

FROM THIS DAY FORWARD by Irene Hannon
Heartland Homecomings

After a frightening attack, Cara Martin needed a safe haven. So she accepted her estranged husband's offer to share his home. The man who'd broken her heart had become a different person—no longer a workaholic surgeon but now a general doc who cared about people. Could their relationship be healed?

GIVING THANKS FOR BABY by Terri Reed
A Tiny Blessings Tale

Trista Van Zant came to Chestnut Grove to start over with her infant son. Still healing from a painful divorce, she found comfort with local pastor Scott Crosby. But when her ex came to town demanding custody, could Trista see beyond her present trials to trust God for her future?

SHEPHERDS ABIDING IN DRY CREEK by Janet Tronstad
Dry Creek

Dry Creek, Montana, looked like the perfect place for Marla Gossett to raise her children. But an unusual theft cast suspicion on her family and brought deputy sheriff Les Wilkerson into her life. Now she'd have to depend on this big-hearted lawman to save her family.

YULETIDE HOMECOMING by Carolyne Aarsen

Sarah Westerveld's father summoned her home after years of estrangement, but a stroke delayed their long-awaited talk. Sarah desired to be forgiven for the past. Yet that past—and the future she dreamed of—included darkly handsome Logan Carleton, son of her father's sworn enemy.